PERKY

JULIA KENT

سلیم
احمد

PERKY

by Julia Kent

One hundred years ago, when I was young and impulsive (Okay, it was five, all right? *Five* years ago), I let my boyfriend take, let's just say... *compromising* pictures of me.

Shut up. It made sense at the time.

Surprise! The sleazy, backstabbing jerk posted them on a website and, well, you can guess what happened. That's right.

I'm a meme. A really gross one.

You've seen the photos. And if you haven't, don't ask. And don't look!

As face recognition software improves, I get tagged on social media whenever anyone shares my pictures. You try getting a thousand notifications a day, all of them pictures of your tatas.

So. I'm done.

It's time for revenge. Let *him* see how it feels! But how do you get embarrassingly intimate photos of your jerkface ex who double-crossed you five years ago?

Especially when he's a member of the U.S. House of Representatives now?

Getting sweet between the sheets with a congressman is

pretty much every political groupie's dream, right? I'm one in a crowd.

Except... to this day, he swears he didn't do it. Pursued me for months after I dumped him five years ago. Begged me to take him back.

And I almost did it. Almost. I was weak and stupid and in love a hundred years ago.

Okay. Fine. *Five*.

But I still have the upper hand. Second-chance romance has all the emotional feels, doesn't it?

I can't wait to punch him in the feels.

All I need to do is sleep with him once, take some hot-and-sweaty pics of him in... *delicate* positions, and bring him down. That's it. Nothing more.

Pictures first. Revenge after. And then I win.

At least, that's how it was supposed to happen. But then I did something worse than all that.

I fell in love with him. *Again*.

Cover designer: Hang Le

Editor: Elisa Reed

Author website: http://www.jkentauthor.com

I am kissing my ex-boyfriend, Parker Campbell–yes, *Congressman* Parker Campbell–and I have no idea how the hell this is happening.

But I really *like* that this is happening.

Yet I hate Parker for what he did to me five years ago. He's my ex.

And his tongue is unbelievable.

One of his hands sinks into my hair, fingers threading through it, tugging just hard enough to make all the blood in my body rush between my legs, a tidal wave of–

No! No! I *can't* let this happen!

I break the kiss. Parker's eyes are still closed. Most guys would look stupidly awkward with that face, but not him, with blond hair cut fashionably close, enough wave to the bangs to make him, um…

Bangable.

His close shave makes his cheek so soft, but his jaw is strong and hard, the scent of aftershave and his natural musk making me weaker than I should be.

He's kissable and hot and one thousand images of his naked body mashed against my naked body run through my mind until they suddenly stop, like a slot machine going *Ping! Ping! Ping!*

And the final *ping!* is a picture of me, naked on a bed, with my boobs on display.

And two dogs humping on the pillow above my head.

I'm not making this up. You've seen the damn meme.

What would you do to the guy who posted that picture on the web? The one who ruined your life by turning you into an object of worldwide mockery?

I do what any sane woman would do.

I punch Parker in the gut.

That's right. And you'd do it, too.

He *whoofs* slightly, but I'm the one who makes a louder sound. Pain radiates through my knuckles because this man has abs of steel underneath that fine, bespoke wool suit, the charcoal gray perfectly offset by a red and navy tie at the neck of his white Brooks Brothers Oxford. Is there a spandex S underneath my pained knuckles?

I look at his face to double check he's not Henry Cavill.

Nope.

Parker grabs my wrist before I can actually make contact with his cheek as I go for a good old-fashioned, outraged slap, even as my knuckles scream *Uncle.*

His eyes are wide open, amused, the color of opals mixed with whiskey.

"Predictable *and* impulsive. I always loved that about you, Persephone." When one corner of his mouth goes up, I swear I can taste his lips again. I press my fingers against my mouth as if creating a barrier between us, a wall, a way to stop myself from letting him kiss me again.

Because I'm weakening.

"Don't call me Persephone."

"Okay. Sweetheart."

"Definitely don't call me that."

"What should I call you?"

"An Uber. I'm out of here." I turn to leave, but he grips my wrist. Not hard enough to hurt.

Just enough pressure to make me halt.

And my pulse race.

"You just assaulted an elected federal official," he informs me with all the sincerity of a frat boy, lips twitching. Sure, he's right. He's a thirty-one-year-old member of the United States House of Representatives now, but that's not why he says it.

"I also assaulted an asshole who ruined my life five years ago."

"One of those could come with jail time."

My *heart* has spent plenty of time in prison.

I don't actually say that to the rat bastard, because then I'd be admitting feelings for him, and being vulnerable to Parker Campbell comes with consequences.

Life-crushing ones.

"Go ahead. Call the cops." I get right in his face, the taste of his kiss still on my lips. I lick them, welcoming his eyes as they track my tongue. Tracing slowly, I watch to see if he's watching me.

He is.

While laughing.

And still holding my wrist.

"Let go of me."

"Promise not to hit me again?"

"No."

His thumb slides against the soft skin of my wrist, slow, like a lover's touch. I shiver. I can't help it. The shiver is an entirely autonomous response that has nothing to do with the fact that my panties are wet and I'm throbbing for him between my legs like the opening bass lines to "Uptown Funk" and holy bejeezus, is Parker about to kiss me again?

Not that I want him to.

Really.

Damn it.

That wicked grin makes it clear he thinks he owns my reaction to him, like he knows he's making it happen in real time as our eyes lock and I try to kill him with a death glare that I can't hold because behind my eyes, inside my brain, a series of memories is being triggered by his touch.

Five-year-old memories.

Five years of *not* being touched like this.

How the hell have I lived for five whole years without being touched like this by Parker Campbell?

The whimper crouches in the back of my throat, coming out like an escaping butterfly fleeing a fairy, so light, so sweet, it's like it didn't happen.

Except Parker heard it.

And his smile fades, eyes serious. For a moment, I have reason to believe those same five years have taken their toll on *his* heart, too. He's so focused on me, it's like no one else exists.

Until my best friend Mallory clears her throat.

"Um, Perky, you okay?" Her words are soft, but the meaning behind them is titanium. I look at her, hating to turn away from being the center of Parker's attention.

I realize, though, that she and Will are a wall between us and the rest of the restaurant, all of the patrons streaming into the larger outside room in twos and threes, no one noticing us.

Yet.

Parker and I absolutely, positively should *not* be the focus of attention here. We're gathered in a small room off the main dining room of this farm-to-table restaurant for Will and Mallory's pre-wedding dinner, an eye-rollingly cheesy event that is all about them. Ten of us–the bride and groom and eight of the members of the bridal party–are gathered to "get to know one another," according to Mallory, though most of us have known each other forever–long before the wedding itself.

I'm making a spectacle. Mallory doesn't need her best friend to suck all of the oxygen out of the room. I need to get a handle on my reaction to seeing the man who betrayed me in the worst possible way. I need to rise above it all in a display of maturity and focus on my friend's happiness.

But Parker totally deserved that punch.

Will is giving Parker a deeply troubled look. I should know. He normally only looks at *me* that way.

"Skip? What's going on?" His eyes go to Parker's fingers, wrapped around my wrist, his touch gentle but a clear claim.

"*Skip*?" I wrench my wrist out of his grasp, hating the cold of my skin without his touch.

"*Perky*?" The tone he uses makes it clear he doesn't like my nickname, the one I started just after he screwed me over.

His opinion does not matter. "Like *Skip* is any better? *You're* Skip?" I demand.

"Long story." Parker doesn't look at Will. He doesn't blink as he gazes at me, either.

"I don't care." My words are a lie, of course, but I have to say them. Five years ago, his betrayal was so enormous. When someone hurts you that much, you can never be vulnerable with them again.

Not even about a stupid nickname.

"Can we keep this quiet?" Will asks, jaw tight, eyes jumping between me and Parker. "This is *our* wedding party event. Whatever past you two have needs to stay there for the next three hours, if you don't mind."

"'Whatever past'?" Mallory gasps. "'Whatever *past*'?" Accusing eyes stab Parker like she's got knives in her irises. Shoulders tense, lips curled back in a snarl, my goody-two-shoes, always-friendly BFF is turning into a street fighter, ready to unleash whoopass on Parker.

Will takes her in like she's shedding her human skin and turning into a demon before his eyes.

Attention suddenly on Parker, she opens her mouth and hisses, "You show up here and waltz in and think you can–"

"Hold on," Will says, contradicting her, or maybe just cutting her off so he can regroup. "Skip's *invited*. My cousin Fred was going to be a groomsman, but then he got a chance to join some dog sled team for a freelance article he's writing and bagged out of the wedding. I asked Skip yesterday, and he flew up here from–"

"Texas," I say flatly. I know all about Parker and his life

down there. *Back* there. After we broke up, I moved back home. He got a job as an aide with Representative O'Rollins' office, and then he saved the guy's life, performing CPR on national television after the congressman collapsed giving a press conference. O'Rollins told his wife he wanted Parker to run for the seat, then lived for five days.

At that point, no one expected him to die, of course. But he did.

My ex was suddenly the young, anointed heir. One special election and a write-in campaign now famed on the internet for the millennial turnout and *bam*–the guy who ruined my life became a sitting member of Congress.

And I just assaulted him.

In public.

"WILL!" Mallory hisses through clenched teeth. "How could you do this?"

Will isn't looking at her. He's looking at me, then Parker. "Me? You're blaming *me*? What the hell is going on between you two?"

It occurs to me that *really,* he doesn't know. Has no idea at all.

How can he *not* know?

"Oh. My. God." Mallory's fists relax. She reaches for Will's arm, stands on tiptoe and whispers in his ear. "You *really* don't know who Parker is?" Clutching his biceps, Mallory's leaning in to her fiancé, brain running a mile a minute, trying to assemble all the parts of this completely unanticipated moment.

"You mean Mr. Hotshot Congressman here? We met at Oxford. Then he worked as a DA in Texas and joined Congressman O'Rollins' staff and got lucky when he died."

No sense of competition in *that* line.

"'Luck' isn't the word I'd use," Parker protests mildly, voice low and smooth, emotions utterly in check.

"This isn't about you!" I practically scream.

"No, Will. Not the congressman part. I mean Parker–

Skip–is Mr. Meme!" Mallory insists, pert nose turned down, mouth tight.

"Mr. Meme–oh, *hell*." Now Will's glaring at Parker like he's ready to take him back into the alley and beat the crap out of him, which makes me suddenly love Will like a brother. He isn't like most men.

Bet *he* would never snap a nude pic of Mallory and post it all over the internet.

Parker's tongue rolls in his mouth and he leans toward Will. "Can we keep this discreet?"

"You're Mr. Meme? *You*?" He's agog. Guys like Will don't rattle easily. I should know.

Because Parker is one of them.

"Mallory told me the whole story, but she never mentioned your *name*." Will's baring his teeth now.

"How did she manage that?"

"She used quite the string of profanities as substitutes. Smegmaface, Asshat, and my personal favorite, Twatwaffle."

Parker looks at Mallory like he's impressed.

"You came here knowing Perky was in the wedding party, man? You *used* me?" Anger goes up a notch in Will. There's nothing worse than being played for a sucker by someone you trust.

I should know.

"It's not like that," Parker insists.

I snort.

"It's *not*. You called my office and got my assistant," Parker says calmly. Will's face is turning an impressive shade of rage red.

"I did. And she called back and said you'd accepted, but were too busy to talk."

"That's right. She scheduled this. I had no idea your fiancée was connected to Persephone."

"PERKY!" Mallory and I shout.

Parker's eyes drop to my breasts. I swat him. Even that tiny bit of contact arouses me.

My wiring is *so* messed up.

"I think you should go, Skip. Parker. Smegmaface. Twat-waffle," Mallory spews.

"Douchenozzle," I add.

Will frowns. "I don't even want to think about what that means."

Parker clears his throat. "Look, everyone, I–"

"Whatever your name is," Will demands, the stare hardening as he inserts himself between me and Parker, "you need to leave. Now."

As people walk past us into the main dining room, glancing curiously, it occurs to me that this has turned into A Scene. Mallory hates scenes. Her older sister, Hasty, is the queen of creating A Scene. I have no desire to wear that crown. *Miserable* doesn't wear well on my best friend's face, so I need to make this stop.

Make this all stop for her sake.

Blood pumps so hard against the surface of my skin. Will is a few deep, angry breaths away from making an even bigger scene at his own event, and suddenly, I feel guilty.

That's a new emotion for me. Ouch.

"No," I say, stepping between them, giving Will a deeply grateful look as I splay my palm over my heart. "No. Please. Not because of me."

"I know what Mr. Meme did to you, Perky, and it's disgusting. He nearly ruined your life. My twelve-year-old cousin uses that picture all the time to make new memes and post on Snapchat. You're an object of public ridicule. No way am I letting Skip stay when he did that to you."

Will's words trigger a mixed bag of reactions in me.

"I never did that to her!" Parker's voice is on the rise. "That's the whole point!" To my surprise, he doesn't look around to make sure he isn't hurting his political image. Emotion got the better of him.

"Is that why you're here? Why you're using me?" The space between Will and Parker narrows, Will's hands curling into fists.

"Will. No, man. I'm not. I swear." Palms up, Parker's beautiful, multi-colored eyes widen, muted pastels and brown blending into a reflection of sincerity and perception. He's not afraid. I know he's not, because he doesn't take a step backwards.

Parker was never one to avoid conflict. He was always good with confrontation. Great, even. This is the guy who mediated every friend dispute and somehow made it right.

A perfect character trait in a congressman.

"But you knew Perky was Mallory's best friend." Will's in Parker's face, defending me.

"I didn't when I said yes. But I realized it about ten minutes ago."

"You should have said something right away."

"Yes." Disarmingly forthright, Parker's admission makes us all stop breathing for a second or two.

"So you *are* using me," Will finally says with a long, disgusted sigh.

"I wanted to help you out when Fred dropped out of the wedding. And when I saw Persephone here, I also wanted to talk to her. So forgive me for not turning around and leaving the second I put it all together. My assistant, Omaia, wasn't there the day you called, and my staffers had no idea there might be a conflict of –"

"See her on your own time. Not at my wedding rehearsal rehearsal dinner." Will ignores the dignified apology. Parker's going to have to dig out all his considerable charm to get out of this mess.

He has lots of shovels in his tool shed, though.

"Persephone refuses to see me." Eyes cutting to me, Parker's attention feels like a dare.

Dare me to *what*?

"Then figure that out for yourself. Don't violate rules of consent because your dick got curious," Will snaps, arms akimbo, a wall between me and my nemesis.

My *hot* nemesis.

I really adore Will right now.

"Yeah!" I pipe up, using Will's body as a shield. "Listen to your friend!"

"And you!" Mallory says, turning on me. "You don't go around punching people at my wedding rehearsal rehearsal!"

"Why do you and Will keep saying the word rehearsal twice?"

"Because we're rehearsing the rehearsal."

"That makes no sense."

"We want people to get to know each other before the rehearsal."

"But we already know each other! Even more than you'd think, apparently." I glare in Parker's direction. "You're bordering on bridezilla territory here, Mal."

"It's my day. My wedding. Promise me no punching."

"I can't promise that if Parker's in the wedding party."

"Then he's out," Will says flatly.

In my family, people don't talk like this. Will is making declarations on the spot, sweeping decisions that open doors and close them. Mostly close them. My parents would convene a family therapy appointment, complete with two different therapists to help facilitate, and we'd talk and talk and *talk* until unstable consensus was achieved, complete with guided meditation, the right crystals, and a little past-life regression thrown in to determine motivation for anyone not in one hundred percent agreement with the majority's decision.

Will is just... acting. Deciding. Proceeding.

Unilaterally.

Without hesitation.

"Let's talk in private," Parker says to him, jaw going tight in that way I know so well.

Not know. Knew.

I *knew* so well, five years ago, before I had any idea that someone you adore could betray you so spectacularly.

Mallory looks around the room nervously. A part of me feels bad, because this is supposed to be her day. Her time. Her *turn*. No, this isn't the wedding. It's not even the wedding rehearsal. The idea of a rehearsal-rehearsal is so twee, I want to find a kitten sling and put it on her, stick a hedgehog in it, and give her a string of Christmas lights made of mason jars.

And yet... punching Parker wasn't exactly fair.

Will's phone buzzes just as he and Parker start to move out of the room. He checks it and looks at Mal. "Sorry. Jim and Kevin are stuck in traffic on Route 1. Bad accident. Detours are clogged. They're trying to get here."

She nods quickly, urging him to go with Parker with a clear chin thrust.

"I'm sorry," I say to her, earnest and meaning it, even as I hate the words. "I can behave."

"*You're* sorry? Parker's the one who should be apologizing!" She frowns. "And I'm not even touching that 'behave' comment."

"I know. But I should, too."

Mal's eyes flit to the door. The taste of Parker is still on my lips, the feel of his abs on my bruised knuckles. They throb, the skin hotter than the rest of the back of my hand. The room we're in is small. It's only ten of us, and four are already here.

"Drink," Mal says, handing me her blood orange martini. Without arguing, I do as I'm told, the sweet juice making me gulp, the boozy afterkick welcome. I don't drink often. If ever there was a time, though, it's now.

And five minutes ago, when he kissed me.

"Can someone make me three more of these? That was good," I say, tongue poking out to lick a drop from the corner of my mouth. What I'd rather have is a cigarette, but if I'm turning to a vice to tamp down my emotions, alcohol will do.

"One more and then you're cut off, Perky. I can't have you drunk *and* punching people at my rehearsal rehearsal. Pick one."

"Apparently, I already did," I mutter.

"Where are Fiona and Raye?" Mallory mutters, not quite under her breath. "I need reinforcements."

I jiggle my now-empty glass. "This makes a good reinforcement."

"Alcohol is not going to solve the Parker problem."

"No, but it makes me care less, and that's close enough."

Mallory's sister, Hasty, comes rushing in. She's a blur of perfectly cut blonde hair and resting bitch face so strong, it has its own reserved parking spot in San Francisco, where she lives.

"What's *she* doing here?" I gasp.

"She's my sister. Mom made me ask her to be a bridesmaid. Will's sister is one, so..."

"I know all that. I thought Hasty wasn't coming to this?"

"Mom guilted her. Plus, she hates Will's sister, so when she found out Veronica wasn't going to be here for the rehearsal rehearsal dinner, she decided it was a chance to shine."

I snort. "You'll have to do better."

Mallory lets out an aggrieved sound. "Hasty realized she could schmooze up some of Will's rich friends to help with her work."

"That's more like it. Hasty Monahan: Why do something nice for no reason when you can use your sister to gain monetary benefit? Oh, God. I shouldn't have chugged your drink!"

"Why not?"

"Because you really need it more than me now. First Parker, then Hasty? Is Mercury in retrograde?"

A whimper of acknowledgment comes out of Mallory before she squares her shoulders and faces her sister, who comes in for the fakest of fake kisses and hugs.

Hastings—Hasty for short, though we don't dare call her that to her face—is the opposite of Mallory. If you took my best friend and systematically described her reverse self, it would be her own sister. The answer to how two people can start from the same DNA soup of two parents and come out so radically different is going to make someone a Nobel Prize winner someday.

"You're right," I hear Parker say, his voice loud, the sigh

after the words an aggrieved but not angry sound. "I was wrong."

"Say that again," Will insists.

"I was wrong."

"And?"

"I was an asshole."

My whole body turns toward them. Instinct is powerful. I can't help but eavesdrop.

"You could have told me right away that you knew her," Will adds.

"I should have. And I swear I wasn't using you. Not like that. I thought she'd be more..."

"Adult?" I don't appreciate the laugh they share after Will says that word.

"Discreet." Parker clears his throat. "I thought staying would be a win-win."

"For who?"

"A win for you because I'd fill in for your cousin. A win for me because I'd finally get Persephone alone and have a chance to really talk to her."

"After what you did to her?"

"I told you. I didn't *do* it."

Always a low baritone, Parker's voice drops into the determined territory of the wrongly accused. People do that when they get defensive. Voices change. Mannerisms shift. Work in a coffee shop long enough, like I do, you see it. All the permutations of conflict in the world are on display in your average coffee shop if you stay there long enough.

And Parker's voice, right now, is one I know well.

A rush of adrenaline makes my ears ring.

He's *serious*.

Five years after he blew up my life, he's still claiming innocence.

What kind of jerk does that?

One I'm still in love with.

Damn it.

2

"Perky!" Hasty says to me, hands out for the fake hug that matches her fake interest in me. I'm her kid sister's best friend from kindergarten, the annoying little girl who teamed up with Mallory to pick on Hasty all those years ago. No matter what, whether we're twenty-nine and thirty-three or six and ten, to Hasty, I'm the abomination who destroyed her new pair of jellies with Barbie nail polish while she was taking her piano lesson.

My parents paid her back for them, so I don't understand the lingering anger, but whatever.

Fake hugs exchanged, we stand with fake air between us, fake smiles faker than the fake eyelashes she's wearing, the ones that look like Australian spiders were glued onto her eyelids.

Hasty works in the Bay Area for a financial start-up. She's married to Burke, one of those hipster guys who runs ultra-marathons for fun and raises money on Facebook on his birthday every year for diabetes research for dogs. He's tall, has six-percent body fat, and laughs like he can't quite believe anything out of your mouth is serious. When he makes eye contact with you, steel blue eyes widen as you speak, narrowing when he does.

His eyes are narrow a *lot*.

If a computer program hand picked someone for Hastings Monahan to marry, it would be Burke Oonaj.

Competitive yoga is Hasty's thing. I know, right? Yoga shouldn't be competitive.

Yet Hasty's found a way.

"Who all is coming to this rehearsal rehearsal *rehearsal* dinner?" she titters. "I just deplaned in Bedford, so I'm a bit undercommunicated."

Hasty's also fluent in Jargon.

"Bedford?"

I fell into a trap, her smug smile making it clear she dangled a worm in front of me and I bit. "Private jet share right off the old military base."

I throw her a bone. "Private jet?"

"Yes," she coos, looking around, hoping for an audience. "I've just been onboarded with a venture capital firm. It's a perk of the job. Best invention since sliced bread."

One sweep of her manicured hand behind her long, perfectly straight blonde hair and she completes the condescending affect of a corporate chaser who knows exactly where she stands in her internalized hierarchy of the room.

We're all just the tops of heads to her.

"Sliced bread really isn't that profound."

"Neither are you, Two Dogs Humping."

And there it is.

"Ha ha. Why be original when you can be Hasty?"

"It's Hastings."

"Sure, Hasty."

"You are so juvenile."

"Hey!" Mallory says, inserting herself between us. "I see you two are catching up!"

"More like revisiting old territory," I say with a brittle grin meant to parody Hasty.

"Nostalgia?"

"No, torture."

Hasty's attention is drawn away from us, like old times. The second anything better comes along, Hasty bolts.

"Is that Parker Campbell? *The* Parker?"

"The asshole who ruined my life five years ago? Yes."

"No, no. I mean the new congressman from Texas." Her eyebrows go up. "Wait. Parker. *Your* Parker? *He's* the dog-humper-picture-taker?"

"Say that five times fast with a mouth full of marbles."

"Why would I put marbles in my mouth?"

"Think of them as tiny balls without pubic hair. Should be easy for you, given your husband."

She ignores me.

"If I weren't married," Hasty says, eyeing Parker like he's a side of grass-fed organic beef and she's Michael Pollan, "I'd tap that." She elbows me. "Why'd you let him get away? You could be on your way to the White House."

Before I can answer, she looks me over, top to bottom. Her expression morphs as she takes in my long, honey-brown hair, my fancy jeans studded with tiny pearls, V-neck camisole under a light silk kimono top. My four-inch strappy heels. Her lips curl in tighter and tighter contortions that remind me of a Venus flytrap with an unsuspecting fly landing in it.

"Huh. Never mind. Maybe Parker's lucky he did such a stupid thing to you."

"HASTY!" Mallory explodes, cheeks turning red, the flame of her hair against flushed skin beautiful yet painful to behold.

"Don't call me that," Hasty says, cutting her off. "You know I'm Hastings."

"I know you're a bitch," I say straight out.

She grins. "I always liked you. You may look like you dress yourself out of a clothing donation bin in Las Vegas, but you're direct."

"Screw you, too, Hasty." I pluck at the hem of my flow-ered kimono jacket. It follows my curves. It's festive and pretty. Isn't that appropriate for the occasion?

I look at her and realize there's no comparison. Her

clothing is all tailored and shaded, subtle color palettes, a fashion plate. Modern urban chic.

She may have style, but I have a soul.

"Proving yet again that Parker dodged a bullet," she whispers as I nudge her, the dirty vodka martini she's mainlining spilling over her pinkie finger.

Mallory lets out a long breath as Hasty walks toward Parker, who suddenly heads for the bar. Hasty halts, pulls out a compact and touches up her lipstick, one eye on my ex, one on her reflection.

"Mom owes me big. *So* big. I didn't want her in my wedding," Mal grouses.

"She's your only sister. It's kind of required."

"Why couldn't *you* be my sister?"

"Because I didn't come out of your mom's vagina."

"Great. Now I'm thinking about my mom's vagina! Perky!"

"Did I hear the word vagina? Are we talking about the honeymoon already?" Will asks smoothly, arm wrapping around Mallory's waist, his other hand holding a fresh blood orange martini, which he hands to her with the perfect grace of a man serving his woman whatever she needs to be happy.

Despair rises up in me.

Despair that requires alcohol.

Today started out with great promise, I think to myself as I storm off to the bar, ready to double fist some drinks to get through this dinner. At no point was Parker Campbell on my mind this morning.

Okay. That's not quite true. He's always on my mind.

But earlier today, he wasn't so... *here*.

Rayelyn Boyle, one of Mallory's geeky friends from high school, pokes her head into the room and flashes a grin at me. An anemic smile is all I can muster before I'm rudely interrupted.

"Persephone," Parker says. I turn around to find him standing before me, arm extended with my favorite beer in it. "For you."

Despair turns into a fluttery panic in my belly. I can handle a defensive Parker. I can handle an angry Parker. I can even handle a besotted Parker.

But a grown-up bringing me a drink like a man who wants to make a woman happy?

I don't know where to fit that in around five years of righteous anger.

"Thanks. Will didn't kick you out?" I peer at his face while sucking down some of the beer, ignoring my rapid heartbeat and how my skin feels like it's been removed from my body and dipped in a novocaine bath. "No bruises. No black eye."

In my peripheral vision, I see Raye and Mallory hug. Raye knows how to be a supportive, no-drama friend. She's nothing but attentive, touching Mallory's bracelet with an admiring gesture that makes me feel like a heel.

A pang of confused emotion gongs through me. I'm ruining Mal's first big moment on the road to matrimony.

Wait a minute.

I'm not.

Parker is.

He laughs. "I smoothed it over with Will. We didn't take it out behind the kitchen and turn to fists."

I pout. I drink. I openly size him up. Parker is sun-kissed blond and Texas sharp. No accent unless you listen hard, but that's up here in Boston. In Texas, where I met him and where we lived together for nine glorious months, he can twang and hang like the local he is. Tall, cool, and slick as hell, the man knows what he wants and is going for it, step by step, leap by leap.

Assistant DA.

Congressional staff member.

Congressman.

Senator.

White House.

Maybe the timeline won't be quite what he planned, but

that doesn't matter. Eyes on the prize, Parker has one quality that stands out among all the others.

No. Not his tongue.

Wait.

Hmmm.

What was I saying? Because now all I can think about is his tongue.

"Persephone? You're blushing. Thinking about me?" One step closer and he's in my space, crossing a line I didn't know I had, a line some part of me is begging him to transgress.

But I have other parts. Parts that silently size him up.

Parts that are starting to feel like someone poured a Costco-sized bottle of warming gel on them.

Finally, I have to ask. I shouldn't.

But I do.

"Why would you lie to your friend to crash an event like this?"

"I didn't lie. My staffer scheduled this for me, so I had no idea Mallory was Will's fiancée. I just didn't tell the whole truth the second it revealed itself."

"You really *are* on a path to the White House," I marvel, taking a longer sip of this delicious pale ale.

Pure mirth pours out of him. "I'm not sure whether to be insulted or flattered."

"I never, ever shined you on, Parker. You know that."

"Ah. Right. Insult it is."

"The only words I'll ever send your way."

"Ever? Forever's a long time."

You were supposed to be with me forever.

The thought slams into me full force, rocketed into my frontal lobe by spontaneous combustion and five years of furious mourning for a man I should not be suffering over. We all have the one who got away, but he's not supposed to *also* be the one who cruelly exposed my most vulnerable moment to seven billion people.

For *fun*.

"Forever, Parker. You made that choice. Don't try to turn it around and make it my burden."

"Persephone, I–"

"Well, well, *well*. Who do we have here?" Hasty interrupts, voice smoothed over with alcohol, resting bitch face tucked away behind the black curtain that surrounds her soul to protect it from sunlight. "Parker Campbell? Congressman Campbell? I haven't seen you in–"

"Never, Hasty. You've *never* seen him," I say through gritted teeth.

"Hastings," she says reflexively, offering Parker her hand. "Hastings Monahan. I'm with Keating Xin Luis." It's clear she expects Parker to know what that is. Spoken aloud, it sounds like a wine, but it's a giant venture capital firm. I only know what it is because my parents are into all that and Hasty used them as a connection to get an interview there. And now, apparently, a job.

Hasty *loves* to namedrop. If you watch her face carefully, she twitches slightly on the last syllable, as if a teeny orgasm slips out.

"You're doing great work with cryptocurrencies in China," Parker notes, face neutral, taking her in.

Chin up, Hasty takes him in with an impressed look. "You know your finance."

"I'm learning on the job." He pauses. "Monahan? You're Mallory's sister?"

"Yes."

"I don't remember you from my visits here–" His eyes dart to mine. "Before."

"I was long gone by then. I have my own life in California."

"I see."

"Too bad, though. I had no idea my sister moved in the same circles as a future congressman."

"I had no idea I'd end up in Washington, five years ago," he says with a shrug.

"Bull," I say under my breath.

"Excuse me?"

"Your mother practically got induced so she could give birth to you on the steps of the Lincoln Memorial, Parker. She planned your political career since your umbilical cord was cut."

"I'm not in DC because of my mother," he bristles.

"Of course not," Hasty jumps in, smelling blood. "You're there because you are effective."

"And because O'Rollins died and you're photogenic," Will adds, appearing at my elbow. "Never underestimate the power of political man candy." A tight smile gets flashed at Parker, a dare. His eyes meet mine.

They say, *We'll talk later.*

Mallory's next to him, grinning at me, eyebrows up. Her expression mirrors Will's.

Lots of talking.

Later.

But apparently, for now, Parker stays.

"My looks aren't what got me the seat," Parker shoots back, but he's jocular. That private conversation they had seems to have cleared the air.

"They certainly don't hurt," Hasty murmurs.

I point to her left hand. "Love that wedding-ring set, Hasty. How *is* Burke doing?"

Behind Will, Mallory holds her hand up like a cat's claw and mouths, *Meow.*

"My husband, Burke Oonaj," she says pointedly to Parker, like she wants to spell it out, "is great. He just closed a nine-figure deal for some Japanese investors and is being considered for the board of two different Fortune 500 companies. He might run for office in California," she says to Parker, nudging him in a friendly way. "Mind if I connect you two?"

"What's he considering? Local or national?"

"Attorney general, then maybe a House seat."

"Nice. Good luck to him." Parker pulls out his card and hands it to her. "Give him this."

She holds it like Dobby palming a sock from his master.

My spine starts to tingle. Dread pours through me. It comes out of nowhere, completely distinct from the conversation in front of me.

But I know exactly why.

And then:

"I swear to God, it's her," whispers a man's voice from a cluster of people behind us. We're at the edge of the small, private area where our group of ten will be sitting. I turn around to find a round table with four guys my age all sitting there in suits, various half-empty cocktail glasses in front of them.

One looks at me and winks, then points to his phone.

I groan. Hasty frowns at me, annoyed that I'm ruining her perfect political ass-kissing moment.

"What's wrong?" Parker asks as I assess the situation second by second. This dinner means a lot to Mallory. Seeing Parker isn't my idea of bliss, but ghosting on my best friend at her wedding rehearsal rehearsal dinner–as stupid as that name is–would hurt her.

"Nothing." Snickers continue behind me as I turn away.

"Persephone." It's the way he says my name that makes me yield.

"That guy. Behind us. He recognized me."

"You know him?"

"No."

"Then how–*oh*." Parker hasn't spent the last five years having his boobs and face recognized by tweens, teens, and twenty-somethings with meme fetishes.

I have.

But he gets it, instantly.

"Damn it," he mutters.

"Right."

"Want me to say something to him?"

"Like what? You think you can ride in on your white horse now, Parker? Save my honor? What the hell?"

"That's not what I–" Pivoting, he shears us away from the others, pulling me aside.

"This has been my life ever since you posted that picture online, you asshole," I say through gritted teeth. "People recognize me. They're always guys, by the way. *Always*. Guys who looked for free porn or sex memes online and got the thrill of a lifetime five years ago when my naked boobs were flashed everywhere with your mom's dogs humping each other on the pillow above my head." I yank my arm out of his grasp.

His jaw clenches, face going tight with something that damn well better be shame.

But I'm just getting started.

"You wanted to see me? You kept a secret from Will for the right to stay here? Well, Parker, now you've got me. In fact, you get a front-row seat at the Perky Tsongas Humiliation Show. Every week some dudebro realizes who I am, and I get the snicker. The come on. The friend nudge. The look that says my eyes relocated to my nipples. Whatever you want to call it, I get to be the object of mockery. My parents did their best to scrub the internet of that picture, but as you can see, you left me with one hell of a legacy."

"I want to talk to you. To talk about what happened. You've never given me a chance, Persephone–"

"And quit calling me by my full name! Everyone calls me Perky now!" I shout.

"Damn straight you are," one of the guys says, loud enough for me–and Parker–to hear.

"What's going on?" Will approaches us just as I decide I'm done.

So done.

I run out the back door, Mallory calling my name, as Parker and Will walk toward the round table, a determined set to their shoulders. From behind, they could be twins.

Good.

Let Parker deal with the mess he's made.

3

This happens all the time. Being recognized.

It's part of daily life.

But it's not part of daily life with *Parker* in the room.

People live inside their phones. Or if you're older, it's your laptop. You spend hours online, needing that dopamine hit.

Pow pow pow it comes, scroll by scroll, like by like, share by share.

A funny meme picks up steam like an asymptote, as Mallory says. The rise is meteoric.

A meme that gets recaptioned over and over is even worse.

Welcome to my world.

Because guys who live inside their phones use that same technology to connect. To brag. To preen. That random dude in the restaurant recognized me. Pattern-matched and reached inside his brain–aka phone–and used that picture to reinforce being part of the "in" group.

By making me "other."

The air outside is crisp. Fall in New England has its own taste. I want a different taste in my mouth, one that doesn't include Parker's tongue, which still lingers. Alcohol, coffee, chocolate–they would all taste better. My blood is begging for a nicotine fix, because a cigarette right now would solve everything, right?

But no. I know what would taste even better.

Revenge.

It's *bad* when a failed nicotine addict can think of something she wants more than her fix.

There's an edge to me, a rising fury that is building. No way to stop it now–the momentum is kicking in and I have to give in to it. Mallory is the epitome of calm, cool, collected, if a bit naïve and a homebody. Fiona is all soft edges and sweetness with a kickass urban fantasy hero buried deep inside.

Me? I'm energy. Call it whatever you want, but as my organs start to synchronize, my heart, brain, and memory uniting, I reach up with my fingers and wipe Parker away. The smear of the taste of him in the corner of my lips is like nothing more than a stray bit of whipped cream.

He's extra. A crumb. A bit of detritus.

Something you leave behind.

"Persephone!"

And he's right behind me. Now.

"You would think that a congressman, of all people, could read social cues. Leave me alone."

"No. I came to apologize."

"Finally! Then you admit it? You sent the picture?"

"Not for that. For upsetting you now."

"That's not how apologies work. You have to say you're sorry for the soul-sucking chest wound you caused five years ago before you're allowed to apologize for being a creepy wedding rehearsal rehearsal dinner stalker."

"I didn't know there was an apology protocol. Duly noted."

My fists curl, chest rising and falling with a rapidity I despise. I don't want to move in front of him. Breathe before him. Every movement holds the potential to reveal my emotions. I'm a sitting duck here, under a microscope, Parker's gaze so direct with expectation.

Now? Why *now*?

"You cannot seriously think you'll get away with this, Parker."

"Get away with talking to an old friend?"

"Get away with being an elected official who stalks his old flame. One social media comment and you're toast."

"I'd imagine you're an expert at being on the receiving end of that."

"Because of *you*! How dare you make a joke like that?" All the air in my lungs is flattened by his fading grin.

"It wasn't a joke."

"Then why did you smile?"

"It was a smile of empathy, Persephone." He steps closer to me. My fists tighten again. "What happened to you was awful."

"And your fault!"

"No. No, it wasn't." The slow shake of his head, adult and mature, reasoned and contemplative, makes me seethe.

"STOP IT!" I scream, able to handle his surprise appearance, able to handle some jerk in there recognizing me, but wholly unable to have Parker Campbell, the love of my life, treating me like I'm some sad woman deserving of pity for not believing he *didn't* ruin my life.

Finally, *finally*, Parker looks around, clearly concerned for the first time in his crazy pursuit of me that someone will see the scene we're making.

And for whatever reason, it's his look around that makes me *really* lose my temper.

"Do you understand? I've spent five years hating you! Five years building this identity inside me around how I've been destroyed by you! How you hated me so much–no, worse than hate! How you had so little respect for me that you would post that picture online and not care that it ruined me." I thrust my fingers into the hair along my brow and pull up, as if that will somehow clear my head.

It doesn't.

"You haven't lived through what I've lived through, Parker. You didn't have to hire attorneys and sit in a room with five associates staring at a picture of your bare breasts, day in and day out, analyzing all of the legal strategies while my nipples said 'Hello!' with *your* mom's dogs going at it in the picture."

So help me God, if he laughs, I'll kill him.

He doesn't.

"Thousands of notifications every day. Being tagged over and over. Made fun of online, shamed, turned into an international joke. I had to cut my hair, dye it different colors, hide out at my mom and dad's house, come crawling back home with my tail between my legs because you..." the sob starts, deep in my throat, "...because *you* released a picture that guys like that," I thumb toward the restaurant, "guys like that think is *hilarious*."

"Persephone, I–"

"And you're a lawyer!" I continue, as if he hasn't said a word. "Have you ever thought about what it was like to copyright my own picture as a legal maneuver to get these websites to stop using it? It was taken on my phone and sent to you, so the lawyers determined I held copyright. You and I made a split-second, impulsive post-sex decision together, and then I had to sit there for months–years!–and go over it with achingly shameful precision. We were dissected. Hell, one eager summer intern at the law firm spent days using Photoshop to determine examine the dog's penis for some legal reason I still don't understand!"

He grimaces and rubs his eyes, blocking out the visual.

The weight of my words drags down the air between us, as if our pain invented gravity itself. Inside that restaurant, my dear friends are entertaining their guests, who are showing up for this ritualistic dinner that celebrates the joining of two wonderful people.

Meanwhile, Parker and I are mourning the death of the very same connection we once had.

He forces me to look him in the eye, bending just enough at the knee for his thighs to pop against the fabric of his dress pants, the clear outlines of thick muscle distracting me for a split second.

Until he speaks.

"How do you think *I've* felt all these years, trying to get you to believe me? You ghosted. *Poof.* Disappeared on me. Stopped answering calls, blocked me online, turned me into a monster I never was. Do you know how that felt?" Outrage and lust light up his eyes. This was a hallmark of any given conversation with this man. Reality.

We were so real together. No need for pretense or games. I could be me and he could be himself.

No sugarcoating.

No b.s.

I guess we still have that.

So here we go.

"I cannot believe that you *didn't* do this to me, Parker. I can't. I can't believe you never released that picture."

"Can't, or won't?"

"Won't."

He lets out a huff of frustration.

I move in, getting right up close, trying to ignore the sudden heat trapped between us.

"Hey! HEY! *I'm* the victim here, you asshole. You don't get to be dismissive of *my* experience! And besides, buddy, you passed the difference between *can't* and *won't* a long, long time ago. You don't get to judge me."

"But it's *true*, Persephone! I never released that photo." His hand goes to my wrist. Knowing his blood beats inside skin touching mine makes me even blunter.

And hotter.

And maybe... weaker.

So I yell.

"Don't call me that!"

"Don't call you by your name?"

"You're summoning a ghost from the past. The woman I

28

was. You're the only man I've ever loved who's called me Persephone."

I can't tell him he's the only man I've ever loved, *period*.

Jaw dropping slightly, he breathes through parted lips, his clean-shaven chin making me want to kiss it, to inhale his aftershave, to feel the warm, smooth skin against my neck, to be so close to him.

"So you *did* love me?" The words come out like crema on top of a perfectly pulled shot of espresso, so unexpectedly beautiful.

"Of course I did. Of course I *do*." I am no longer in control of my mouth. I lost control of my heart so, so long ago. "God, Parker, I can't believe I'm letting you do this to me."

"Do? As in present tense? What am I doing?" He moves closer, knowing damn well what I'm feeling, but forcing me to say it.

"Making me hope."

"Hope for what?"

"For you. For *you*, Parker. There. I said it. Happy?"

"No. I won't be happy until you let me kiss you again."

The slap isn't planned, any more than the punch was earlier. He takes it, eyes on mine until they aren't, my hand burning, my hips rotated in from force, so much that I fall forward into his arms.

"If slaps and punches are what it takes to get you into my arms, I'll take it," he murmurs in my ear. "Anything to get you to listen to me. Please listen, Persephone. *Please.* "

"Who says I'm *listening* to you?"

"GET YOUR HANDS OFF HER!" Will roars as the back door to the restaurant bursts open like the bulls being let loose at a bullfight, the thick metal door ricocheting off the brick wall, almost chopping someone in half. Mallory teeters through on her high heels, followed by Fiona, who looks like the bastard child of Stevie Nicks and Khaleesi, flowing dress and long, wavy hair a platinum hippie-punkass weapon for my side.

"What the hell, Will?" Parker shouts as the man charges, moving with sure foot and livid glare.

To his credit, Parker holds his space, spine straight, body loose but primed.

"She just slapped you, man. That means you back *off.*" Will's palms go flat against Parker's chest but he holds, wrists capable of the pure strength it takes to shove a two-hundred-pound, six-three man built like Parker Campbell, former nationally ranked wrestler.

"Will, stop!" Mallory cries out, grabbing his elbow. "He's a congressman! I think it's a form of treason to hurt him. Perky's already done it. I can't have my best friend *and* my fiancé in jail at the same time!"

"Nah," Parker says, staring Will right in the eye, daring him. "It's just a bad idea. Assault is assault, whether your target is bought and paid for by lobbyists or not."

The edges of Will's lips twitch.

Damn it. There goes Parker.

Pulling out the charm.

"Thank you, Will," I say, inserting myself between them as Mal peels one of Will's arms off Parker, using as much precision as a vehicle owner with a new registration sticker to add to a license plate. "I appreciate the help."

He tenses. "So he *was* bothering you?"

"Not the way you think." I tap his shoulder. Deeply protective eyes meet mine. I know Will's not just playing a role. We've become friends in the year or so since he and Mallory started dating. I also know that a part of him is protecting Mallory, really.

Parker's appearance is upsetting the order of things with this pre-wedding ritual, and probably messing up the feng shui or flower essence or whatever the hell Mallory's into now when it comes to holding space and using design to build a Perfect Life.

"I would never hurt her," Parker says, offended without blustering.

"You're stalking her!" Mallory argues. "Crashing our wedding rehearsal rehearsal!"

"I'm here under slightly exaggerated pretenses."

"FALSE," Will barks at him, crossing his arms over his chest in a bid to hold off from hitting Parker.

"Fine. False pretenses. But only after I arrived here, and even then, I made a split-second decision. I wanted Persephone's friends to surround her when I first saw her, and this was a perfect chance."

Will just glares.

"Besides, Will–you know how your father and my mother are working on that literacy program together? There's a funding opportunity coming up. I wanted to talk to him about it."

"You're dangling my father's pet project in front of my face in an effort to get me to forgive you?" Will asks. Mallory's face turns pink in outrage.

"Yes," Parker says, brazen and bold.

Direct.

"He's in Florida right now," Will grumbles, but the gesture softens him.

"Please play nice?" Mallory says to everyone and no one at the same time, as if she's simply letting an intention out into the universe, hoping it will magically manifest.

Shaking his head, Will gives a reluctant half grin. Oh, no. Parker's doing it again.

"Don't let him get away with it!" I shout.

"Get away with what?" Fiona asks, clearly just rubbernecking.

"He's making Will smile!"

"And that's... bad?" Her face screws up in confusion.

"It means Parker is smoothing everything over!"

"Why shouldn't he?"

"Because I still love him," I hiss through the corner of my mouth.

"We know," she and Mallory whisper in unison.

"And I don't want to love him! When he finds a way to make conflicts okay, it makes me fall deeper for him!"

"IS THERE A DOCTOR OR A NURSE IN THE RESTAURANT?" someone shouts from inside, the sound followed by a very harried-looking chef bursting through the door, white hat askew. "Are any of you nurses or doctors?" he demands of us.

I mentally check and no–not a single one of us is.

"No, sorry!" we all answer, befuddled.

The guy retreats, but we all look at each other, attention now diverted.

"But I don't understand–" Mallory starts to say before screams inside the restaurant make Will and Parker look at each other, then sprint through the open door, Mallory, Fiona, and I on their heels.

"HELP!" a woman shrieks. "PARKER! WILL! COME HELP! HE'S DYING!"

4

It's a short run. The small room where our party of ten was to be seated is empty, one of the dudebros at the table where I was recognized is now bellowing for help, and Hasty is next to him shouting for Will and Parker, her phone in her hand.

"Ambulance on the way!" Hasty hollers as restaurant staff race through the place, calling out for nurses and doctors. Fellow diners are watching the choking man in horror, hands on phones, hesitation and fear rippling through the crowd. Everyone wants to do something, but no one's trained.

"He's choking! I tried the Heimlich!" Dudebro points to his friend, who is slumped over the table. One of the other men is pounding furiously on his back, but all he's accomplishing is to shove the poor choking man's face into the tablecloth.

Parker jumps forward and grabs the guy, fists positioned just so under his diaphragm.

"I TRIED THAT!" his friend booms, but Parker ignores him, Will at his side, shoving his fingers in the guy's mouth in a sweeping motion.

"Nothing," Will says. Parker nods once and, as if they choreographed it, Will steps back, Parker holding the man from behind. He's gone rag-doll limp, his face an unnatural purple, eyes wild.

Like Chris Hemsworth playing a superhero, Parker lifts the guy a few feet off the ground and bends back, then pulls his arms up, one thumb joint curling in as he heaves-ho, and out comes a hockey puck from the poor guy's mouth. It flies across the room and nails poor Mallory right between the eyes before plunking into her blood orange martini, which sloshes up in an impressive, artistic splash, a demented melting orchid on a canvas.

Did I mention she's wearing a white dress?

A whoop of painful air, like a pressure hose being used in a tunnel, fills the space. Collective breath from witnesses holding theirs is let out, the effect like a concert where all the musicians are using lungs as instruments.

Uniformed paramedics rush in.

Fiona begins blotting Mallory's breasts with her cocktail napkin.

"I'm sure some club soda will fix that," she says unconvincingly, while Mallory's eyes bug out of *her* head.

Phones, some with flashes engaged, continue filming Parker, Will, and the poor man, who is taking in ragged, pain-filled breaths.

"Holy shit!" Will hisses to Parker. "You did it, man."

"*We* did it."

"Congressman Campbell!" A woman in a tight, red dress scooches through the crowd, her phone held out like a microphone. "I'm Saoirse Cannon, from the–" As she names a local newspaper, a big one, then a cable news channel, too, my body flushes.

Saoirse Cannon.

No way. That *can't* be Parker's ex-girlfriend, can it? The one he dated right before me? The one who dumped him when he decided to become an assistant district attorney instead of working for Big Law and going for the bucks and fame?

The one with the name no one can pronounce? SAIR-sha?

Then again, my name is Persephone. Most of Fiona's preschool class (and half of my high school enemies) call me Purple Stephanie, so people who live in glass houses and all that.

The smile on her face is intimate. *Knowing.*

And makes me want to peel it off and turn it into a Halloween mask.

Then shred it with some shattered glass.

"Congressman Campbell, you've just engaged in an incredible act of heroism. Could you comment on–"

Parker holds up a palm and says, with a charming smile, "Ms. Cannon, good to see you again."

I narrow my eyes at her. Again?

She really *is* his old college girlfriend. What's she doing here? Last time I saw her, she worked for a Texas affiliate doing man-in-the-street interviews about town festivals and construction detours.

And now she's here in Boston? Working for the biggest newspaper and cable news channel in town?

"But no comment right now. The priority is him." He points to the gasping man, who currently has a clear oxygen mask being held over his face, the paramedics doing their job. "Not me."

"But after what you did for Congressman O'Rollins last year, it seems you have a penchant for rescuing people."

The look she gives him makes it clear she'd like to be rescued. Mouth-to-mouth. Hands on her chest.

In bed.

"Just doing what any other decent fellow human being would do in a crisis." Parker grabs Will in a bro-hug, pulling him into the pictures all the patrons are now taking. "My good friend, Will Lotham, jumped right in with me to help."

Fiona appears, her cold fingers on my upper arm making *me* jump. "Here." She hands me a fresh blood orange martini, reminding me of poor Mallory.

I look down into the drink. "No chunk of steak as garnish?"

She snickers, collecting glares of disapproval from spectators. "Mal is changing into a new dress. Raye is helping her with her hair."

"She brought a spare?"

"Of course she did. You know Mallory. Always prepared."

"I thought that was the Boy Scout motto. And besides, Mallory lets her phone battery die all the time. How can you call someone like that 'always prepared'?"

"We're allowed to have one weakness, Perk."

I point to Parker. "Not him."

"That was incredible."

"Yep. *He's* incredible."

"You still love him."

"As if I ever stopped."

Hasty appears, wedging herself between Parker and Will, grinning like a Victoria's Secret model on a runway. "Saoirse writes articles that read like they wrote themselves," she says loudly as Will's right eyebrow cranks up, held in place by a heaping dose of skepticism for his future sister-in-law.

Will peels himself away, giving Hasty exactly what she wants:

Unfettered access to power.

Parker Campbell is power. I've known it for years. He's alluring in an undefined way, in a space you don't know is wide open, where trying to explain why you're drawn to him is as foolish as trying to define what makes a kiss so special. It's intuitive, felt before it's understood.

I get why Hasty can't leave him alone.

And I hate him for it.

That's right. *Him*. Not her.

Because Parker can't help himself. This is who he is. Nothing in the way he looks at people with his whole, entire self is about artifice. No wrinkle of his brow in empathy or nodding in understanding as someone tells him a story is fake. Parker was built like this, his double strand of DNA encoded with some unique residue that makes him seem so casual, so connected, so deeply invested in you when he speaks that you feel uplifted.

And if a single conversation with the man can have that impact, can you imagine what making love with him was like?

Not just sex–*lovemaking*. The kind that comes from having another person give over their whole self to you, and demand that you do the same.

Being loved like that by Parker was an impossible dream.

Which makes his betrayal so much harder to accept.

Heat blasts through me, a mixture of lust and disgust. I chug the entire martini in one burning swallow, as if that will teach Parker some kind of lesson.

"Pace yourself," Fi murmurs.

"Since when do I do that? Ever?"

"Can you try? Just for tonight? I think we've all had enough drama. And you're not a drinker."

"I'm not the one choking to death."

"No, but you look like you want to put your hands around Parker's neck and squeeze."

"More like my thighs," I say before I can stop myself.

Turns out I said that a wee bit loud.

Will clears his throat. I don't look up. "Where's Mallory?" he asks.

"Changing her dress." Fiona points to the hallway of the women's restroom just as Mallory emerges, wearing a gorgeous green peplum frock, Raye behind her, chatting on her phone.

Deep concern flits across Will's face, emotion he's not afraid to show as he gathers Mal in his arms, his head dipped down as they murmur. Most of their words are punctuated by glances at me and Parker, to the point of eyeball ping-pong.

"This isn't going as Mallory planned," Fi says dryly, looking around.

"Nothing ever does." I stare at the bar. "Think I can get another drink before the rehearsal rehearsal dinner starts?"

"No."

"Why not? The bar doesn't seem too busy, and the crowd is settling down now that the ambulance has taken that guy away. It's just down to the world *ooohing* and *ahhhing* over Parker."

"Because you can't improve this situation by getting drunk."

"I can't? Watch me."

"I won't let you."

"Who put you in charge of me?"

"Mallory."

"That was a rhetorical question."

"My answer was not rhetorical."

"Mallory assigned you to babysit me?" I peer at her. "Before or after Parker appeared?"

"I plead the Fifth."

"This isn't a trial!"

"You've definitely turned it into one."

"Excuse me," Parker interrupts, nodding at Fiona with a gesture that says *hello* and also *we know each other.*

The look she gives back says, *I hope your dick gets caught in a door hinge while you scratch yourself to death from scabies.*

"There is no excuse for you," Fiona says with a sniff that reminds me a wee bit of Parker's mother, Jennifer.

"I would like a moment alone with Persephone."

Fiona holds out her flat, empty palm. "Then give me your phone."

Recoiling, Parker stares at her like she's an exotic insect that just crept out of his jacket pocket. "My what?"

"Your phone. You long ago lost the privilege of being alone with Perky while possessing any device with a camera."

Instantly, his phone is in her palm.

And his hand is on my waist, steering me away. "Where are you taking me?" I ask, but I don't resist. Something about the way he's touching my body tells me I need to wait until we're away from the crowd. Charged with an energy I don't understand, that simple point of contact carries more meaning than I expect.

We find a small alcove near the bathrooms, where I realize his grip is tight on my hip, his hand bones rigid, muscles tense.

His face is the same.

"Parker?" I whisper, compassion in my tone. Worry floods me, because I've never seen him so serious, so drawn.

So somber.

His spare hand reaches up to his face, the palm making a brushing sound against his chin as he rubs it, eyes closing, shoulders dropping. "Persephone," he says, his voice low, almost choked.

I touch him, sure and bold, because it's dawning on me that he's not trying to corner me to be a stalking asshole.

He's pulled me aside because he *needs* me.

"Are you okay, Parker?"

"I just–what if he'd died? Back there?" Panicked eyes meet mine, pale irises with flashes of pastels and browns, pupils the size of quarters. Cool and calm in a crisis, Parker falls apart afterwards. Always did.

Apparently still does.

"He didn't," I assure him, completely flummoxed by the emotional change between us. How did *I* become his source of comfort?

And why do I get such a thrill out of being in this role?

"He could have. O'Rollins did."

"He–but you saved him."

"I gave him five extra days of life." The sound he makes after that flat statement is one of self-directed loathing.

"Five days his wife and kids will appreciate forever." I grasp his shoulders, the feel of expensive wool against my fingertips one that makes me greedy for more. I remember tying his tie for him before a high-stakes trial. Picking up his dry cleaning when he worked long hours on a big case.

Unwrapping his taut, tanned body as that suit became a discarded mess on the floor, found later over takeout Chinese in the afterglow of hurried sex, the food our intermission between acts.

All that is conjured by the sweep of my fingers against his broad shoulders.

How much memory do we pack into our skin?

More than I realized.

He leans into me, one hand moving up to my waist, the other cupping my jaw. "You always knew how to make me feel better. Always said just the right words."

"I'm not saying this to make you feel better. I'm speaking the truth. I'm not doing anything special."

"That's just it, Persephone. Telling the truth *is* special."

"That's because you're in politics."

"No. That's because you have a unique ability to see me for who I really am."

"Who are you, Parker?"

"Right now, I'm a man who just held another man's life in my hands. My brain and my body haven't quite gotten over the sheer terror of that kind of responsibility."

"You're an elected official. You have plenty of responsibility."

"Not in the form of a heart inside a chest I had to compress. Or an airway I had to clear."

"And now you've done it twice. Saved two men during their near-fatal moments. It's becoming a hobby for you, Parker. Or maybe a vocation."

Light laughter comes out of him, almost profane. "Only you could make a joke after something like that." He thumbs down the hall toward the dining room. "And make me feel better."

"No. Plenty of people make sick jokes after a crisis." I let the *feel better* comment slide.

"But none of them look as beautiful doing it as you."

Under my touch, his shoulders lose some of their tension.

"And only you would hit on me while I'm giving you a pep talk after you saved a guy's life."

"Plenty of men would do the same."

Daring doesn't come easily when I'm staring into the eyes of the rat bastard who took my soul and shredded it into a thousand pieces five years ago. The world doesn't move forward in a straight line, though.

And emotions have their own drunken-line algorithm.

"Parker. It's okay to fall apart. You just went through something intense. Remember when you first saw me?"

"In the back of a paddy wagon with your wrists zip tied in front of you?" His mouth goes up, dimples showing, in a tight but wistful smile. Blinking rapidly, he stares over my shoulder, retrieving the visual of that.

"Yeah."

"You were screaming at the top of your lungs. Something about the dual indignity of the maquiladoras factories making women produce sex toys made of carcinogenic materials."

"I believe I was screaming, 'Their orgasms give us cancer!'"

"I was being tactful."

"You never have to be tactful with me."

"Why did you bring up how we met?"

"Because it was what happened after that. It was how I started trembling."

He nods. "I happened to be at the police station that day, when they hauled all of you in from the protest. A wave of educated, extremely articulate, really pissed-off women. It was exciting and exhausting at the same time. You were my very first case."

You were my first and only love, I want to say, but don't.

"You broke protocol. You came over to us and our eyes just..."

"Yes, Persephone. I remember."

"You melted me."

"No. We... we melded. It was–"

"Indescribable." My pulse quickens.

"Yes."

"You sat down next to me. Asked me my name."

"You told me it was Pinky Thunderpissflaps."

"I've had people bungle my name in worse ways."

"And then I asked you to spell it."

I brighten at the memory. "I spelled it F-U-C-K-Y-O-U-W-I-T-H-A-G-A-R-D-E-N-G-N-O-M-E."

"And I actually put that on the paperwork. You have any idea how much crap I took for that from my boss?"

I shrug.

"Every single woman in that protest group gave us fake names." He laughs. "It was trial by fire for me. First case. My boss laughed her ass off watching me fumble."

"You were kind."

"I was?"

"I wasn't expecting *kind*, Parker. I went there to take on the system, fight the man, and instead, I got you."

"And now *you're* being kind. To me."

"A man almost died in your arms. That would make anyone feel traumatized."

He stiffens. "I'm fine."

"That's the thing, though. You don't have to be." I let go of his shoulder, feeling like I'm on the edge of a huge canyon, ready to tip in.

"I never had to be fine with you. You always let me be real."

"Yes." I close my eyes, the room a bit wobbly from the alcohol. I haven't had too much, but just enough to be dangerous. This Parker isn't the unbearable being who lives in my mind, the one who is evil and cruel, the man I loved who cackles insanely at my destruction by the topless meme.

He's standing before me, stressed and hurting.

And... this is all I can offer.

One step closer and I'm all in.

And while I have weathered being betrayed by him, I cannot betray myself.

"After this, can we please go somewhere and talk?" he asks.

"No."

"Really?" The word comes out of him with so much

emotion, it stops me in my tracks, my own feelings running amok, my body drawn to him. My refusal is because I know how dangerous it is to be so close to him. The man has already invaded my world in a big misunderstanding, kissed me, saved the life of a man from a group of leering meme-bots who ogled my boobs like they're a public utility, and now he's asking to go somewhere and talk?

When he knows we won't just *talk*?

"Really. No."

"You don't want," he says, voice husky and fading at the end of the word *want*, "to be with me? At all? Even to talk?"

The backs of my knees turn to quivering tingles, any shaky resolve left in me fleeing. Our eyes lock across five years of absence and what I see in him makes my next breath so hard to take.

My tongue presses hard against the roof of my mouth and I dig my fingernails into my thigh, all to ground me, all to stop me, all to hold myself back because I know it's useless, but I have to try.

Right?

I have to try not to grab him as he reaches for me and pulls me in, this kiss clinching the deal, one that isn't taking me by surprise but instead is taking me by storm. I'm all in, my hands so grateful to touch him again, my breasts so happy to rub against his suit jacket, my lips so joyfully engaged with his. Every part of me is thankful to be wanted right back, at the same time that I hate him so fiercely for what he did.

I'm one big contradiction.

I am hypocrisy personified.

I am betraying my own dignity as his hands cup my ass but by God, this feels amazing.

And worth it.

When you fall for someone as hard as I fell for Parker Campbell nearly six years ago, and you experience that kind of love, you can't ever let go of how it made you feel.

Of who it made you *into*.

"We wouldn't just talk, Parker," I whisper, looking up

43

into eyes that acknowledge every word from my lips, lips that want nothing more than to taste him again. "You know that."

"Do I?"

"Yes."

"Then why hold back?"

"Because you hurt me!"

"Let's talk, Persephone. Please." His breath warms the tops of my breasts, cleavage enjoying the rhythmic heat. As he begins to breathe faster and harder, I find myself matching him, inhaling and exhaling as if we are one person.

Until suddenly, we are.

Parker's grasp as we kiss is masterful, his hips pivoting until we're in a tiny closet, the door shutting behind us, our bodies surrounded by coats. At any second, someone could walk in, find us, interrupt and embarrass us, but I don't care as my fingers grasp his thick, hard chest. He doesn't care as his hand slides between my thighs, my need to be touched so great that I moan into his mouth, biting his lip. He makes a sound that says he needs this, too, his erection pressing into my hip, the centering of his thickness as he nudges my legs wider with his knee making me hold my breath as he rubs up, just once, just right, just *there*.

"I've missed you," he hisses as his mouth takes my earlobe, sucking gently, then hard, the tip of his tongue flicking and laving, my clit spasming as it imagines him doing this between my legs. My fingertips dig into his shoulders, one hand diving down the length of his abs until I cup his sac, then ride the ridge of my palm up his long, thick, engorged–

"What are we doing, Parker?" I gasp.

"Whatever we want," he says, so steady, so sure, so unabashedly *here*.

"SKIP?" someone calls out from behind the door.

"PERKY?" Mallory whisper-yells, her voice breaking through as I clench, my whole body going tight, the core of me shivering with an orgasm that crashes over me as Parker's leg, his mouth, his very presence, make me lose my everloving mind.

And all my self-control.

Every shred of it.

"I want more of you," Parker says, so low that it's subsonic, my thighs aching and shaking, my slick juices a testimony to how much I want him right back.

"What did we just do? I shouldn't want this."

He recoils, the change in demeanor the first thing that cuts through my post-climax haze. "What do you mean?"

"It shouldn't be so easy. Why is it so easy with you? It was always natural. Like we were drawn to each other by some unnamed force that only affected us."

"That's exactly it, isn't it?" he confirms, brushing my hair away from my face. Slivers of light shine through cracks in the door frame, his eye color like confetti on a sandstone background. "You're a force of nature."

"No. Not me. Us. We…"

"Yeah. I know. You don't have to try to explain. I feel it, too."

"PERKY!"

Mallory's voice is so close, I make an *eep!* sound of surprise. A tentative *tap tap tap* makes Parker let out a long, frustrated sigh as he reaches into his pants, adjusts himself, then smoothes my hair one more time.

"You ready for primetime?"

"No."

Mallory opens the door, the light blinding me.

"Too bad," he whispers before turning to a stunned Mallory and Will, smothering a grin.

"We are *sooo* talking about this later," Mal mutters in my ear, the same one Parker was just performing unspeakable pleasures on.

"I need another drink," I mumble, pulling ahead of her, passing Parker.

Stumbling back toward the main room, Parker on my heels, Mal and Will behind us, I see exactly four people in our private dining room now. Raye, Hasty, Fiona, and Chris Fletcher, from our high school graduating class. I know Will has two more groomsmen who are stuck in traffic, so while the balance is off, it's better than nothing. Raye is talking to Fletch while Fiona is doing her best to peel every inch of skin off Fletch's body with her eyes.

I haven't seen that expression on her face since twelfth grade.

Five years after she dropkicked him in an epic fight.

She marches over, hands Parker his phone, and turns her back on him.

"Ah, Skip–the police want to talk to us." Will turns his gaze just behind me. Two uniformed officers are standing on the threshold between the main dining room and our space, Saoirse Cannon and Hasty chatting them up. Hasty's eyes are darting all over, scanning the room and making calculations on how to be relevant and use this to her advantage.

Mallory rubs the space between Will's shoulder blades with a tender touch that makes me wish my conversation with Parker had gone in a different direction. Then again, I'm pretty sure Parker got exactly what he needed.

Guilt floods me as I realize, um, *I* got something I needed. But he didn't. The angel on one of my shoulders feels seriously bad.

The devil on the other whispers: *Heh. Serves him right.*

Without a word, Parker nods and stiffly moves off with Will. Mallory and Raye move to me as Fiona comes over, the four of us huddled like football players planning their next move without a coach's signal.

"So much for a low key, zero-drama wedding rehearsal rehearsal dinner. Now Will and Parker are being interviewed by the *Boston Globe* and the police, and NECN has a camera crew here," Mallory says.

"They do? For this?" I'm stunned.

"There happened to be a grand opening event a block away for some community health center. While you and Parker were 'talking,' they came around. They'd heard the sirens." Mal's finger quotes make Raye and Fiona give me the hairy eyeball. I squirm. My panties are soaked.

A flash of super-bright light from the main dining room makes it clear they found Parker.

"You okay?" I ask Mallory, who looks like she's about to cry.

"I'm even worse after finding you and Parker having sex in a coat closet!"

Fiona's eyebrows shoot above the rim of her enormous pink glasses. "What?"

"We weren't having… sex. Not exactly."

"How do you 'not exactly' have sex?" Raye asks, her nose wiggling like a witch doing a tiny spell. She's so sophisticated compared to high school, her hair long and smooth, eyes clever and amused behind her glasses.

"We didn't… you know." I make an O out of my thumb and index finger and stick my other index finger in there.

"You didn't use a strap-on?" she asks sweetly, making Fiona spray half her cocktail all over the wall.

"WHAT? Who said anything about strap-ons? Besides, it's not like I carry one in my purse in case my asshole ex-boyfriend accidentally turns out to be a groomsman in my best friend's wedding and I see him at the rehearsal rehearsal dinner and want to peg him!"

Red and white lights flash in the parking lot, the repetitive glow reminding me of the seriousness of what happened just a few minutes ago.

"Then how did you have sex 'not exactly'?"

"I came, he didn't," I say bluntly to Raye.

"Leave it to Perky to find a way to single-handedly even out sexual behavior statistics," Fiona jabs.

"Can we stop talking about sex?" Mal says, suddenly serious. She looks at the ambulance. "I'm worried about Will. He and Parker–what if they hadn't been able to save that guy?"

We breathe together, all quietly acknowledging the shared thought, the pulse between my legs feeling tawdry. Disrespectful. Parker went from saving a dying man to giving me an orgasm in a coat closet within fifteen minutes. I do not know how to process this.

So I drink more. My martini glass was right on the table where I left it.

Raye squares her shoulders. "But they *did* save him. The man is fine. Paramedics just took him to the hospital."

"Wish I'd been here to help," Fletch says, interrupting. He's a paramedic, I remember, the haze of overwhelm making me pluck details out of my memory like I'm skimming a dirty pool with a net.

Fiona turns her back to him and stalks off. He frowns her way and says, "Just got here, and already I need a beer." Ambling off, he heads for the bar, the opposite direction of Fi.

"Parker said it triggered memories of giving CPR to Congressman O'Rollins," I tell Raye and Mal.

Mallory's stricken face makes me feel guilty for mentioning it. "Oh, God! I can see why!"

"He's fine," I assure her.

A member of the staff appears and tells Mal they're ready for our salad course. Mal and Raye head to the table we're supposed to sit at.

Out of the corner of my eye I track Parker, half my attention on my friends, half on him, a silent, invisible self at his side.

One who is suddenly edged out by Saoirse, whose side boob is practically shaking Parker's hand.

"She's a stage-two clinger, isn't she?" Hasty's whisper in my ear damn near makes me hit her, my startle reflex engaged. I jump. She smirks.

"What?"

"Saoirse. Going after Parker like that." Hasty's eyes dart around my face, then narrow. "You're still in love with him."

Someone this ambitious and this cutthroat isn't worth lying to, but she's also not my confidante. Tread carefully with Hasty, I've learned:

Here be dragons.

"You know they're dating, right?"

My inner dragon roasts my liver with a roar.

"They're *what*?"

"She got him to take her to some big journalism dinner in DC a month or so ago. *She's* already picking out the engagement ring and the house in Georgetown."

"Are they seriously dating again? *Engagement?*" I choke on the word.

"What? God, no. Someone as ambitious as Parker Campbell wouldn't be caught dead marrying a journalist." Her eyebrows bounce as she looks at me, telegraphing every judgmental thought she's also thinking about me.

Which is that Parker Campbell wouldn't be caught dead marrying *me*, either.

She frowns. "Wait. What do you mean, 'again'?"

"Saoirse is Parker's college girlfriend. They dated before I met him."

"Oh! So there's a history."

Standing on tiptoes in her Manolos, Saoirse places her manicured hand on Parker's shoulder and whispers something in his ear that makes him laugh, a genuine sound that turns heads, incites smiles, changes the energy in the room. Even the cops sense it, Parker's charm potentiated by the beautiful rising star in the news industry.

"She's gunning for a newsmagazine anchor position."

"But she's with a newspaper."

"And she's on every major Sunday news show where she can book a spot. Watch some of her clips, Perky. Saoirse Cannon is going for it." A pause. "*Again.*" Hasty's tone is a knife to my spinning head.

I watch the way she whispers in Parker's ear.

Oh yes, she is.

Parker walks up to Mallory and Will, speaking in dulcet tones designed to calm and reassure. Assured and suave, he oozes earnest genuineness. A natural peace maker, Parker seeks to understand you. Figure out what makes you tick, then meet you where you are and welcome your best self to the table to talk and open up and create the ultimate solution to make the world better.

It's a quality found in the highest echelons of business, academia, and government.

It can also be a bit sociopathic.

But not in Parker.

And that's what makes him dangerous.

Because he really means it.

"No, stay," Mallory says reluctantly to Parker, looking to Will for the right answer as the three of them finish talking, Parker pulling away. Rarely so deferential, she's clearly overwhelmed and seeking her soulmate to give her an anchor.

Will, like Parker, has an intuitive ability to read people. His gaze locks on Parker, trying to find the b.s.

Except that's the problem: even Parker's bullshit is the kind that makes you feel like he's rooting for you to join his team and prevail together.

He's the ultimate drinking buddy. The guy who you call when you're moving and need help. The man who will build a deck with you.

The guy who writes legislation that saves at-risk kids.

"I don't want Mallory to suffer because you turned me into an unknowing wingman to help you weasel your way back into Perky's life," Will says evenly.

I really underestimated him.

"I don't want that, either," Parker instantly replies.

"Then we're in agreement. Good." Regret leaks out of the protective shield Will's wearing, a forcefield that extends to Mallory, whose face tightens, tiny wrinkles between her eyes showing emotional pain. After what he's done to me, the tug of remorse at sending Nice Guy Parker away just shows how damn charming he can be.

Will cracks the knuckles on his left hand, three in a row, the fingers going *pop pop pop* before Mal lays a hand on his elbow and he stops.

But he doesn't back down.

It's not just me, then. Whew. Maybe I can give my past

self a break for still being in love with a guy so captivating, he can make really smart, highly functional people like Will rethink their boundaries.

"And you." Parker's attention focuses on me. His hand goes to his chin, rubbing the bottom of it, that space where the bone can be hard to navigate with a razor. Parker has a small scar there from slicing it open on a fence when he was a kid. If he pulls the skin up just so, you can see it, shaped like a thin canoe.

"Me?"

"I apologize. Deeply." He smiles and laughs through his nose, the sound teeming with instant self-reflection that makes you realize in real time how stupid you were just an hour ago and wonder why your wiser, present self couldn't have been in charge then. "When I arrived and understood that Will's Mallory was *your* Mallory, I got stupid."

He steps closer. Behind him, a team of police officers appears, clearly looking for him. Two men in suits, dark like undertakers, chat casually with them. I'm guessing they're connected to Parker somehow, but have no idea why.

"That is the most honest thing you've said all night, Parker," I inform him.

"No. It's not."

"Then what is?" I ask, the words too taunting. I'm baiting him, doing whatever I can to keep him in my orbit at the same time I want to run screaming from this place, away from him.

One step closer and I feel his breath on my cheek as he leans in and whispers, "*This* is the most honest thing I've said all night, Persephone: I'm still in love with you, too."

$$\text{❧}\quad 5 \quad \text{☙}$$

"He did it again!" Mom screams from the kitchen, the smart-home device picking up the sound and spreading it through every speaker in the house.

Mom doesn't shriek like that. *Ever.*

I leap out of bed and collapse, legs unable to support me.

Because my body is still nothing but pure alcohol.

The back of my skull feels like a shot glass slammed into a polished wood bar after being slobbered all over by sorority girls doing Bailey's blow jobs. Only the side of my mattress holds me up.

My phone buzzes like a vibrator in the women's room stalls at a Magic Mike live revue.

"Uhhhhh." That's all I can manage. The room is spinning. My phone says it's 10:21 a.m., which means Mom has been up for exactly fifty-one minutes because she gets up at 9:30 a.m. like clockwork.

And I've been asleep for about three hundred thirty. Metabolism doesn't work fast enough to clear the volume of liquor I consumed after Parker left in only three hundred thirty minutes.

Maybe one hundred thirty *hours.*

"PERSEPHONE!" Mom gasps, live and in my room now. I'm sitting on the floor, slumped against the bed. "What is–

oh, whew! Hoo! You smell like a distillery!" Her hand goes to her throat, fingering the lapis lazuli and crystal charm necklace she got from some shamanic healer in Taos, New Mexico on one of her 'meaning journeys.'

"I should. I drank one last night." My face rubs against the duvet on my bed. Wait a minute. I'm in my old bedroom. In the main house. How did I end up *here*? This isn't my cottage by the pool. The room is bronze and teal and denim, a color combination that seemed so very *edgy* in high school, but now it just makes me think of the bargain rack at the local St. Vincent de Paul thrift shop.

Narrowed eyes, bare and naked without a stitch of makeup, meet mine. "Why? Wasn't Mallory's rehearsal dinner last night?"

"Rehearsal rehearsal *rehearsal* dinner." I actually hiccup, like we're on a movie set and I'm playing the part of Drunk Teenager.

"Why are you saying the word 'rehearsal' three times?"

"It's like Taco Taco Taco, Mom." Invoking the name of my favorite Mexican restaurant in town, the one we locals just call Taco Cubed, makes my stomach lurch like there's a Mariachi band in it, with two tequila worms in a dance-off.

"That makes no sense. Why would you get drunk like this? You're not a drinker–wait. Wait a minute." One eyebrow arches like the Nike swoosh. "Did a man choke at the restaurant you were at last night?" Mom fingers a strand of her long black hair.

"Yes."

She gasps. The sound of air ripping down her windpipe is like nails on a chalkboard.

"Parker was there!" she says, her voice climbing so high, she might as well be sucking helium.

"I know."

"You know? How do you know?"

"Because, uh, *I* was there." Am I the only drunk person in this conversation? Maybe not.

"Did he approach you?"

"Will invited him to be a groomsman."

"WHAT?"

"It's a long story."

"It is 10:23 in the morning, Persephone. I have all the time in the world."

"I thought this was your 'be present' time."

"I am being present with *you*."

"But my liver is five hours behind, Mom. It needs to crawl out of the past." Or maybe it's in Paris, eating a pain au chocolat and some raspberries while watching the ziplines off the Eiffel Tower.

"Why would you get so drunk?" she demands.

I give her the best cold look I can muster.

"Are you having a stroke?" Her palm goes flat against my forehead, as if that would make a difference.

"What? No. That's a glare."

"One side of your face is slack."

That's my version of a stinkeye. I let my mouth set with a grimace. "Why do you think I got shitfaced?"

"Because you saw Parker for the first time in five years?"

All I can do is touch my nose and point to her. "Bingo!" I finally whisper.

"Oh, Persephone. Going to your best friend's pre-wedding party to discover that dog turd found a way to get into your life is–"

"*Congressional* dog turd, Mom. Use his honorific."

She snorts. It feels like a herd of elephants was released in my head.

"How do you feel?"

I give her a thumbs down.

"In your heart."

My thumb goes lower.

"Your pancreas?"

My thumb reaches the Earth's core.

"Do we really need to do organ inventory?"

"You know the healer says it's a vital way to manage emotions that are stored in the body."

I give her the middle finger. "Ask the healer what's stored in this body part."

"You know that joke is never funny."

"Mom, it's always funny." I giggle, then burp. "It's especially funny now."

"Your entire face just turned the strangest shade of green."

"That's because I need to puke." Somehow I stand and do my drunk version of sprinting, making it to the bathroom just in time.

"It's all over the morning news!" Mom yammers in the background as I empty myself of too many blood orange martinis and pale ale. I mixed beer and liquor, didn't I? Amateur. "Parker Campbell saved another life. That man has a very suspicious propensity for saving people in dire, mortal danger. Do you think he stages these events?"

Stages?

"It wouldn't be hard. Now that we have money, I know exactly what you can get away with to make the world look like whatever you want."

"You think Parker asked a guy to choke on a piece of steak so he could look good?" My cheek is drawn like a magnet to the side of the toilet bowl. So cool, so smooth, like the gentle touch of a mother's hand when you're sick.

My toilet is more maternal than my mother, who is doing her best imitation of a prosecutor.

"I wouldn't put anything past that man. Honestly! Did he harass you?"

Does that hot kiss count? I wonder.

"No," I say carefully. "I punched him."

"What? Why? Because he harassed you?"

"Because he *kissed* me," I blurt out, hating myself for revealing the truth.

"That is assault!"

"Assault with a deadly tongue?"

"PERSEPHONE!"

"What? He kissed me. I punched him. We're even." I don't mention the orgasm he gave me. On that, we are *so* not even.

"Good. That man needs to learn boundaries!"

"Pretty sure I committed a felony by punching a member of Congress."

"No jury of your peers would convict you." She pauses. "And besides, what good is the money if we can't spend it on lawyers to get you off?" Mom whispers the words "the money" like we're in Harry Potter Land and she's saying Voldemort's name.

Nine years ago, my mom went to a convenience store to buy a pack of cigarettes, a King Size Reese's Cup snack, and a lottery ticket. Just one. Like clockwork, she dutifully bought a ticket twice a week, letting the computer decide her fate.

Fate chose her one day.

$177 million dollars later, our lives were upended. Numbers, ordered in a certain sequence, made everything we knew obsolete. Money changes everything, sure, but you don't realize how important your *everything* is—even the crappy parts—until you can't have it anymore.

And everyone wants to be *you*.

Hissing "the money" is Mom's way of distancing herself from it, as if she's not responsible. As if she doesn't want to unleash some unacknowledged entity attached to it, like there's a demon ready to pounce if she says the words too loud. Conjuring good luck was too easy, I think.

She's terrified of a universe that seeks balance.

Always.

But that doesn't mean she won't spend it.

"Moooomm," I groan. "Can you get me some ginger ale?"

"Ahead of you, honey," she says, handing me something in a mug that smells like chicken and ginger with cumin and the squeezed-out sweat of a hockey player's game jersey. "Here's a tonic for you. Much better than–"

The smell makes me retch again.

By the time I'm done and can stand on shaky legs, I realize Mom has switched on my tv and is watching some kind of video. A quick face wash with cool water and a toothbrushing session with more excavation than a spelunker, and I'm fifty percent sure I can walk to the bed of my own accord.

I open the door.

To find Parker Campbell standing on my wall.

Not literally, but the ninety-inch television makes it easy to think he's there.

"Look at that man." The acid tone Mom uses makes the same words I'm thinking come out in a very different manner.

Look at that man.

I sure am. And I hate myself for it.

That kiss. That hot moment in the coat closet. The way he looked at me. How he pursued me.

How he made me come.

How I let him.

No—how I *welcomed* it.

Yes, he was wrong. Yes, he owned up to it. Yes, he did the right thing by leaving after he did the wrong thing by semi-lying to Will.

But all those *yeses* are just my mind making busy work to cover up the pain in my heart.

The pain of still wanting him. The pain of knowing he still, after all these years and all my rejections, wants me right back.

If I give in—and that's what it would be, a giving in—then who I am changes. It would be cheap and easy to lie to myself about how he betrayed me. Life wouldn't be so hard if I accepted his open arms, his invitation to bed, his beguiling offer to be back in his life. I would be loved and admired, sexed up and sated. I would be the partner of a powerful man who has loved me all along.

But has he?

Does true love involve leaking an intimate picture, awkward and hilarious in private but scathingly horrifying when sent out on the internet to become a meme people mock? Is that love?

I know it's not.

So if it's not love, and if Parker won't admit he did it and beg forgiveness, then what is this relentless come-on? Is he playing some mind game that gets him off? Am I a toy, a plaything, a vehicle for his amusement? Does he get his jollies coming in and out of my life, kissing me?

God, my head hurts.

And it's not just the hangover.

"Here." Mom thrusts the stinky witch's brew at me. I turn away and she sets it down. The overly polished words of the young newscaster telling the story of last night's choking incident are the backdrop of our conversation.

Parker is, of course, the hero of this story, with Will his second.

"Look! There you are!" Mom points. I see myself in the background, chugging my drink. I hold the empty out to someone I don't recognize and walk off. Replaying the next few minutes makes my liver wave a small white flag.

Because three minutes after that video, I came away from the bar double fisted, and that wasn't my last round. My goal: to get drunk enough to forget Parker.

Turns out there's not enough alcohol in the world for that.

Believe me. I tried to find the dosage.

Bzzz.

My phone is plugged in on a side table next to a round chair that faces the television. I ignore it. It buzzes again, then again in rapid-fire succession.

"Aren't you going to get that?"

"I'm not Pavlov's dog."

"I thought your entire generation was Pavlov's dog when it comes to your smartphones."

"Now you're going to dump on millennials? Come on, Mom, that's too easy."

Her laughter makes me smile.

"There's my girl," Mom whispers, coming in for the kill. "Just a sip."

"NO!"

"Hirsenia made it just for you." Mom's chef, Hirsenia, came to the United States twenty years ago from Macedonia. She's about eighty years old and makes some of the best dumplings you've ever tasted, but uses her cooking skills to create Old World "cures" that Mom is convinced are better than modern medicine. I half expect a heated castor oil and mustard pack to be delivered shortly.

For my tongue.

"Hirsenia made that god-awful balm that gave me hives all over my legs for weeks," I argue.

"Who knew you had a skin sensitivity to gluten?"

"Mom, I have celiac disease. Anyone with a brain knows that."

"She used non-GMO heirloom wheat!"

"I'm not drinking that." I eye my aloe vera plant. Maybe I could pour it in there, but that would be vegetation abuse, right?

"It's better than the shit you put in your body last night. You'll drink alcohol but not a soothing, nutrient-rich—"

"—so proud of my son."

My head jerks up at the new voice from the television, a cultured voice that makes my innards freeze in terror and revulsion. Mom looks, too, eyes narrowing.

There stands Jennifer Tanager Campbell, her name in big letters moving under the video as she speaks.

Parker's mom.

"She was *there*?" my own mother squeaks out just as someone taps on the door. We both twist to find my dad standing there in a robe.

"No," I croak through my paralysis and fury. "Look at the background. She's being interviewed at the statehouse in Boston."

"What's going on?" Dad asks.

"*Shhh!*" Mom points at the television. "Dolores Umbridge is on!"

"This isn't Harry Potter," Dad says, confused.

"Close enough," Mom mutters, pointing to Jennifer, whose pinched smile and bright eyes are a pretty good imitation.

Dad snorts, walks closer, and does a double take at me.

"*–from the bill my son has put forth in Congress to reduce the use of fossil fuels and increase green energy initiatives while helping oil companies with transitional tax breaks, his support for fair-trade coffee, his push for tax relief for small businesses, to his quick action in saving lives in emergency situations, as a mother, I could not be more proud.*"

"Proud! *Proud* of that slimy little beast," Mom rants. She looks at Dad and says, "Bart, I think we need to call Sally again."

I groan. Sally is the family therapist. She makes house calls. Until a month ago, she actually lived here, in a guest cottage (not mine–yes, we have more than one...) behind the main house. Sally got married and is currently three months pregnant, so she decided to leave her position as full-time Palace Therapist and become an on-call emotional Band-Aid for the Tsongas family.

Bzzzz.

That better be Mallory or Fiona, because I need a rescue text.

To escape my parents.

"Sally's in training this week. Remember? Something about tapping."

"Tapping?" I can't help myself. "Is she becoming a sex therapist now?"

"PERSEPHONE!" they both thunder.

"It's a technique for processing trauma," Mom says in a tight voice I don't understand.

Dad eyes the television as the screen clicks over from Jennifer and moves on to a gas explosion in Stoughton. "Huh. She's well preserved."

"Condescension is a more powerful biologic than Botox," Mom sniffs, making Dad laugh and pull her in for a hug. He kisses her temple.

They look at me.

I grab my phone.

It's Fiona.

Did you remember to drink sixteen ounces of water with lime in it and take three ibuprofen before going to bed? she asks.

I didn't even take my shoes off, I reply.

You are impossible. She adds a middle finger emoji.

I've heard that before somewhere. Oh, yeah. From everyone I know. I add a derp smile.

"MOOOOMMMM!" The screech from down the hallway tells me Ditie is up. My nineteen-year-old sister comes running in, holding her hand over one eyebrow like it's about to fall off. "The microblading hurts!"

We're becoming the Kardashians here. I'm hung over, my ex is an eligible bachelor with an eye on the White House getting tabloid attention, and my sister tattoos her face in beauty regimens designed for Instagram. Her goal in life is to have a successful YouTube channel where spilling the tea means something different than you think.

Mom's phone buzzes. She ignores Ditie, who turns to Dad as a sounding board.

"Our communications people tell us Parker is trying to text you again. They caught five texts going to your phone," Mom says, her head whipping up from whatever she's reading to catch my eye.

"He's blocked, Mom."

"I know that. They said so. I cannot believe the gall of that young man!"

"He's thirty-one. When do you drop the 'young' part?"

"Anyone younger than me is 'young,' Persephone."

"Perky."

"I hate that nickname. That's one thing Parker and I have in common. But only one. He always called you by your proper name, even when he was relentlessly texting and sending notes and emails and stalking you."

"*Calls*. He did it last night."

Our conversation manages to pique the interest of my sister, whose real name should be Gossip instead of Aphrodite. "You saw Parker? In real life?" Ditie is working hard to become an Instagram influencer. Knowing I was in the orbit of one of Congress's Most Eligible Bachelors must make her flip through twenty-three different filters in her mind and try on hashtags like shoes.

"No, Ditie, I carry a foldable cardboard cutout of him and pretend it's him. It's great for being able to drive in the high-occupancy lane in the city."

"Shut UP!" she hisses, but doesn't look away. "Are you taking that sleazeball back?"

"How did you get from 'saw him' to 'taking him back'?" Dad marvels.

"Because Perky *saw* him, Daddy." The words come out like the world's most obvious *duh*.

"I did more than see him," I whisper, my filter obliterated by alcohol and family.

"What?" Mom, Dad, and Ditie all ask the same question.

"He kissed me." I'm absolutely *not* mentioning the coat-closet climax.

"What did you do?" Dad demands.

"I punched him."

Mom grins. "Good girl."

"I get praised for punching a member of Congress? Fiona told me she thinks that's a felony."

"Then we'll use the money to get you out of jail. No jury of women affected by revenge porn would ever convict you," Ditie says brightly, echoing Mom.

At the words "the money," Mom flinches.

Dad's more affected by the word "porn."

My phone buzzes.

Hangover tacos? Lunch at eleven?

My stomach rolls up like a cockroach burrito.

Not ready yet, I text back as Ditie regales Mom and Dad with her tale of woe involving one eyebrow. It looks like the Very Hungry Caterpillar dipped himself in an inkpot and took up residence above her eye.

Hurry. We might be forced to include Mallory if you don't speed it up, Fi texts back.

I shudder. Mallory has this OCD thing about tacos. Eating at Taco Cubed (aka Taco Taco Taco), our favorite local Mexican joint, is like a piece of tastebud heaven.

Unless you're there with Mallory, who turns it into the food equivalent of an IRS audit. Her "perfect ratio" of meat, veggies, salsa, guac, and sour cream is an endless source of calibration she narrates and dictates.

Narrates while she's doing it and dictates that we should adhere to her protocol, too. Who the hell has a protocol for eating tacos?

Mallory. That's who. The woman who can't keep her cellphone charged above six percent is a cumin drill sergeant.

Noooooo, I type back, the sound echoing in my pain-filled head like a rabid raccoon flinging rocks at the back of my eyeballs.

Then hurry up. 11?

I look at the clock. That's in twenty-six minutes.

Just then, Mom sits on the edge of my bed, nudging Hirsenia's concoction my way. "Honey," she says, with that look in her eye. You know the look. The one that says she doesn't view me as a capable, competent twenty-nine-year-old.

Subtract two decades.

"Persephone, Dad and I are worried about you."

How about NOW? I text back.

Sofia and Bart driving you crazy? she answers. I ignore the text and stand up, my stomach flopping out of my body to slap against my toes, the top of my head leaping up into the sky to collide with a jet out of Logan.

Pick me up? I double thumb as I pretend I'm fine, plastering on a smile for Mom and Dad. Behind them, the news cycle restarts the Parker story, his big, aw-shucks grin making my panties melt.

Be there in five, Fiona texts back.

"I'm going out for tacos with Fi," I tell Mom, who looks to Dad as if asking permission.

"Tacos? You were just throwing up. Are you really in any condition for tacos?"

"They're the great hangover cure," Ditie says in the voice you use when you know nothing but want to pretend you're an adult.

"How would you know? You're only nineteen," Dad grouses.

See? She totally walked into that. Ditie disappears.

Mom and Dad follow. Little sisters aren't good for much, but right now, she's saving my ass.

So is Fiona.

Which means I owe them both, big time.

This is all Parker's fault.

And as I get dressed, it hits me.

Revenge is a dish best served cold, right?

With salsa and guacamole.

"You smell like my four-year-olds got their hands on some old, rotten apples and a can of Sterno and turned it all into a finger-painting mural," Fiona declares as I crawl into the front seat of her car, squinting.

"Jesus! Could you take that crystal off your rearview mirror? I'm blind!"

"It's to keep energy vampires out of my car." Mercifully, she reaches for the piece of fishing line that loops the damn Pink Floyd album cover imitation over the mirror. As it slips into the cupholder, I avoid looking at it.

"Return it to the store where you bought it and ask for a refund. It just failed."

"It doesn't work on *emotional* vampires," she says dryly, eyes cutting my way, mouth tight with disapproval.

Fiona adjusts her sunglasses, then slips them up over her forehead, perching them on top like a headband. Her hair is streaked with ombré lilac and she wears zero makeup. Thin, arched eyebrows frame a strong bone structure that is inexplicably delicate, too. My mother once described Fi's skin as "porcelain with steel underneath," and damn if she isn't right.

She smells like peaches and sandalwood.

"Taco Cubed!" I groan as we lurch forward. Fiona drives an electric car, a putt-putt vehicle that feels like we're riding an amusement park's tram service. If Disney ever goes into the automotive industry, they've got competition.

"You need some hair of the dog that bit you."

"Hairy oranges sound disgusting."

"I cannot believe how many blood orange martinis you sucked down. And then that beer Parker brought you! It was like watching my brother after the hot-dog-eating contest at the Dance and Dairy festival when he was in eighth grade."

"Shut up." An image of Dale in 2001, projectile vomiting all over the dunking booth after his fellow baseball-team players got in there, doesn't help.

"You're really hurting, aren't you?" She pulls out a small spritzer. "Spray this on your throat chakra."

"Why?"

"It detoxes you."

"What's in this spray? Some new medical treatment?" Putting the nozzle to my nose, I sniff.

"Flower essences."

I stare at her. Hard.

"What?" she finally asks.

"I pray for the children of our country if you're the one teaching them in their tender years. Unless this contains the real tears of children, collected in the moment they're told there is no Santa Claus or Easter Bunny, nothing in that spray will help me deal with detox."

"More like distillery. And what do you mean, there's no Santa Claus?" Mock outrage fills her features, then disappears quickly. "And you're never, ever subbing in my class again. Who would joke about harvesting the tears of emotionally traumatized children?"

"Me."

"And I am an excellent preschool teacher!" She points to the spray. "And that makes an outstanding monster spray."

"You just told me it detoxes my liver."

"It does."

"You're spritzing kids with liver-detox spray? Do their parents know?"

"I spray it on the monsters."

"Do the monsters know their livers are being treated?"

"Shut up, Perk."

"I'm imagining Bigfoot walking around with jaundice, desperate for Miss Fiona to come along and spray him so he'll survive."

"I would if I saw him," she huffs. "It would make him go away AND give him a hepatic boost. Betcha Bigfoot abuses his liver as badly as you do." She turns the nozzle and spritzes me.

"AUGH!" I open the window to get fresh air. "I need coffee."

"No."

"No?"

"Tacos first, coffee second. You know that's the ritual." She sniffs. "And if you'd listened to me about the lime water and ibuprofen, you'd be fine now."

"I'll never be fine. Not with Parker here."

"I assume he's gone by now. Mallory told Will he had to find another groomsman."

"She did? When?"

"Somewhere between your fourth and fifth drink."

"You were counting?"

"The last time you drank that much, you tripped and dropped my car keys down a sewer grate, so yes."

"That only happened once!"

"We were on the Cape. In August. The day before school was starting."

"I got you new keys!"

"Two days later."

"Picky, picky."

"No. Perky, Perky." She laughs. She doesn't want to, but she laughs. "Even half shitfaced, you're adorable."

"You make me sound like a golden retriever puppy."

"Your hair's close to the same color."

She grabs the crystal and holds it up, blinding me again.

"What the hell?"

"You know how this works." The last thing I see before closing my eyes is Fi waving a Y-shaped stick in the air, her lips moving with words I can't hear.

Pulling into the parking lot behind Taco Cubed, Fiona finishes her parking-spot magic and eases into a non-metered space. It's a four-block walk, but free parking in our area is as rare as a Yankees hat.

"How do you do that? You always find free parking wherever you go!"

"I am geopathically sensitive. I use the dowsing rod to find the Earth's magnetic lines and the rest just happens. It's abundance mentality. You should try it sometime."

I pat my hips. "I think it misses sometimes and hits here. If you ever have to actually *pay* for parking, you'll know I've gained five pounds and your abundance spell needs a GPS fine tuning."

"Shut up, Picky."

"Don't taunt me, *Feisty.*"

We head down the street in the direction of the restaurant.

"Hey! Fancy running into you two!" A bright and cheery Mallory appears just as we get to the entrance, hopping toward us with so much energy, her auburn curls bounce.

I give Fi a sideways glance that says everything.

"Hi!" Fiona's eyebrows climb over her forehead, into her hair, and try to rappel down her ears. "Mallory! What are you doing here?"

Oh, no. Taco recovery time has just turned into a culinary engineering lesson where the professor grades us with her eyes.

Mal thumbs toward the insurance agency next door. "Mom and Dad are doing something with their life insurance and I had to drop some papers in the mail slot at the insurance agent's office."

"Are they okay?"

"What? Of course they are. Sharon and Roy are just crossing all the t's and dotting all the i's. You know how they are." She makes a huffing sound, dismissive. "Some people can be so particular."

"Right." Fiona and I nod in unison, thinking the same thing. Taco Hivemind is real.

"If you're standing here, it can mean only one thing! Let's all have lunch at Taco Cubed!"

I stifle my groan.

No, actually. I don't. Mallory gives me a questioning look.

"You can just sip water if that's better. You're probably not feeling great today."

"No," Fiona says with a sigh. "She needs calories she can't drink."

Threading her fingers together in front of her, Mallory looks like a professor ready to ask a class hard questions. "So. How are we going to approach this?"

"This?"

"Lunch." Conveniently ignoring the fact that we've repeatedly told her we don't like eating at Taco Cubed with her, she soldiers on.

I see. We're playing Let's Pretend. I can do that, too.

"We're going to move our feet and walk into the store and Pedro Jr. will take our order and Pedro Sr. will cook it," Fiona says while I allow a small battalion of blood piranha to destroy my circulatory system.

"Ha ha." Mal's tone makes it clear nothing we say will make a difference. "The last time I was here with you, you ate like rabid dogs." She bares her teeth. "You disrespected the taco."

"That sounds like something you complain about after a one-night stand from Tinder. He disrespected the taco!" I blurt out.

Mallory blushes. Pay dirt. "You're comparing tacos to sex?"

"I'm joking about the vertical taco."

"The what? Oh, gross," she groans as she gets it, rubbing her eyes as if trying to smear the image out of her mind.

Victory!

Fi gives me a glare. "You're still hung over, aren't you?"

"No. But the longer we stand here being lectured by Mallory the Taco Engineer, the pornier I'm going to get."

Mal shuts up and instantly turns to the double doors, opening them. A wave of chile relleno hits me smack in the face. I ride it, inhaling like it's a cure, like I'm surfing on a salsa ocean. Fresh tomatoes and spicy beef can erase the memory of Parker's presence last night, right?

If anything can, a trip to Taco Heaven in my mind can wash away the residue of Parker on my body.

And if it can't, I'll just eat my way into a taco coma.

"You're drooling," Fiona says dryly, stepping up to the counter. There's no line, the lunch rush well over. I look at the wall clock. 11:25 a.m. Huh.

Then I realize it's Sunday.

"I'll have the special," she says to Pedro Jr., who has no surface of his skin that is not covered with tattoos, none of which are tacos.

"Soft or hard?" he asks.

Mallory clears her throat meaningfully.

"SOFT," Fiona says loudly, making Mallory wince. It's not the noise that bothers her. We're well aware of her opinion on soft tacos. Like mayonnaise, soft tacos sit on a throne in hell where they allow lesser devils to walk the Earth, marching into our mouths and destroying civilization as we know it.

But the devil sure does know how to make evil taste so *good*.

"It's like ordering a hamburger at a five-star restaurant," Mal says, unable to help herself.

"*Shhh*," Fiona snaps back, paying for her tacos with her debit card. I pat my pockets. I forgot my purse. One eye roll later and Fiona hands me her card.

"I'll pay you back," I promise.

"You always do," she says, completely sincere. Last month, Fiona's car had a powertrain malfunction—whatever that is—and $800 later, she could drive again. I make more than enough from my trust fund and my Beanerino paycheck, so helping her out just makes me a good friend.

I hope.

Pedro looks at me and shouts something to the kitchen line. Immediately, one of the workers changes his gloves.

I smile. "Thanks. I'll have the special, gluten free, on hard tacos."

A toothy smile matches mine, gold glinting off one of Pedro Jr.'s back molars. "No problem, Silly Yak," he says with a funny laugh.

A few years ago, after I was diagnosed with celiac disease, I came in for my first taco, armed with new nutrition knowledge. Pedro Sr. talked to me, then pulled out his phone. He typed the words Silly Yak into the translator. That's my nickname now, whenever Pedro Jr. has time to poke at me.

His father thinks that is my actual name.

"*Mi hijo* was just diagnosed, too." He thumbs to the back. "*Mi papi* wants to strip the store of everything gluten and use that to get more customers."

Mallory shoves her way past me. "You would stop carrying soft tacos?"

"No, we'd just switch to *maiz*, corn." Pedro looks at her hand, one corner of his mouth turning down. "Nice ring."

"Thanks!" she says brightly, his subtle but still obvious cues whooshing right over her head. Mallory may have been our high school valedictorian and may be smart, but she can be really, really dense when it comes to living life outside her bubble. Will Lotham's return to Anderhill after ten years of being gone saved her from the endless stream of bizarre dates where guys got through the dinner and then used (probably) invented excuses to get away from her.

I'm her BFF. I don't have that luxury.

We sit down in a booth and I elbow her as she starts stuffing her face with chips and queso. "He was flirting."

"Wha..?"

"He wasn't flirting," Fiona argues. "He was expressing his

disappointment that Mallory will no longer be a potential booty call."

A gagging sound comes out of poor Mal, who is now so far from Taco Heaven, she'll need an air conditioner for the rest of her taco life.

In hell.

With me.

A huge swallow and half her water later, and Mallory sputters, "I would never, ever be a booty call for Pedro!" At least her damaged throat makes her go quiet, the words coming out in an enraged hiss.

"I didn't say booty call," Fiona soothes.

"Yes, you did!"

"I said *potential* booty call."

"What does that mean? I am a happily engaged woman!" Looking at her left hand, Mallory caresses the giant diamond, mouth quirking into a distracted smile.

"We're *all* potential booty calls," I remind Fiona. "Anytime we talk to a straight guy, I mean."

She nods.

Wiping the corner of her mouth, Mallory looks up at us from her napkin with withering condescension. Or maybe disgust. It's hard to tell.

"I disagree. Straight men can look at women without wanting to sleep with them."

We hoot. Oh, the hooting. Fiona and I were owls in a former life. We're a flock of owls delivering howlers at Hogwarts.

"Stop!" she whisper-growls.

We hoot more.

Fiona wipes the corners of her eyes, chest hitching from rollicking laughter. "Oh, Mal. You're hilarious."

"I wasn't kidding!"

A long sigh escapes Fiona, who looks at her through those oversized glasses she always wears. Fiona looks just enough like a character from a children's fantasy novel to leave you a little unmoored, trying to think which one she is.

Before she can speak, I say, "Mallory, every straight guy evaluates every straight woman who isn't his mother's age. They all do. There's a mental calibration that goes on. It's a connection between eyes, brain, and–" I make a hand motion like I'm whacking someone off. "Not necessarily in that order."

"No way!"

"Ask Will."

"I can't ask Will that!"

I nod. "Because he'll lie."

"He would never lie to me!"

We hoot again.

"STOP THAT!" Her shout makes my headache hurt more. My mouth closes around the straw in my water. I take a sip and push the pieces of my taco around, carefully covering the refried beans. I'm done.

And this is the last time I'm coming to Taco Cubed with Mallory ever again. Screw this. I like sushi better, anyhow.

"Ladies." I look up to find Parker standing there, a grin on his stupid face. He's wearing khakis, loafers, and a navy polo shirt. It's the uniform of private school boys, golfers, and– apparently–young congressmen. It should make him blend into the background, but the simple clothes have the opposite effect.

He stands out.

Polished and suave, he manages to stay very real and accessible while balancing that out with a model-hot body and a smile that makes your panties melt–whether you're pushing policy or a hotel room key into his hand.

Throb. My head *throbs*.

So does a distinct spot between my thighs. It remembers the coat closet.

Fiona looks around. "You see ladies?"

He gives a polite chuckle, then goes serious, looking at Mallory. "I wanted to apologize again for last night."

"I'm not the one you need to make amends with. We're good. I know Will talked to you again."

My head jerks up. "He did?"

"I was going to tell you. After tacos." Her attention moves to her taco, where I swear she's calculating the exact number of grams of cheese to get her perfect formula.

Shoving my basket away, I give her a glare. "It's 'after' now."

"Will and Skip—er, Parker—went out last night. After the craziness of the choking incident. They talked it out." One spoonful—just the tip!—of guacamole. Mal removes about one-third of the shredded lettuce. She pauses. She eyes it.

She removes exactly one diced tomato.

"Talked *what* out? The fact that Parker is a sleazy stalking dog who lied to his friend to weasel his way into the wedding party and make my life a living hell?" I demand.

"I see you still have a way with words," he says with a cough.

"And I see you still have a way with getting exactly what you want, no matter who you hurt," I toss at him, furious and feeling betrayed by everyone.

Mallory puts her hand on my elbow, the other hand holding her taco like it's a Fabergé egg. "Will's not hurt."

"Are *you*?"

One side of her mouth twists in contemplation. Auburn curls bounce as she shakes her head. "I was. I am on your behalf."

"Don't give me your vicarious pity."

"My... excuse me?" The taco moves closer to her body, like she's protecting a small child.

"Vicarious pity."

"You think I enjoy feeling pity toward you?"

"Isn't that what vicarious means?"

She touches my forehead and looks deep into my eyes. "You're still drunk."

"God, no. This would be so much easier if I were."

"May I have a word with you?" Parker asks me, his own pity loud and clear in those bright brown-opal eyes. "Maybe our own table?"

"How about I have my own table and you have your own table and Mallory gives you a grad school seminar on the perfect taco ratio?" I snap back.

She brightens up, as if she's actually considering it.

"Easy, girl," Fiona whispers in her ear. "That was sarcasm."

"If that was sarcasm, then I'm the butt of the joke! Not Parker! Why am *I* being dragged into this mess?" Mallory protests. I'm pretty sure she's less upset about being made fun of and more upset at being deprived the opportunity to enlighten Parker on her ratio to enter the pearly gates of Taco Heaven.

"Because feelings."

"That is not a valid reason." Narrow eyes take in her taco again, like a painter on the Seine contemplating the aesthetics of sunlight bouncing off the water.

"Feelings don't have to be valid."

"Maybe my feelings about tacos are hurt. That's valid."

"A great reason never, ever to come to Taco Cubed with such insensitive besties again," Fiona says in a soothing, placating tone. "You are well within your rights never to forgive us. I sense a disconnect here, and–"

Mallory's right eye twitches.

Parker's hand lands on my shoulder. "One minute? Please?"

"Parker?" A woman's voice goes up at the end as if she carries her own exclamation point in a pocket to pop into place.

I go cold.

His hand on my shoulder feels like a piece of stone.

Then he squeezes me with a camaraderie I intensely appreciate.

Because that's his mother, Jennifer Tanager Campbell, standing in line, two customers away from Pedro Jr. at the counter.

"Not now," he mutters under his breath.

Not *ever*.

"Why, Persephone," she says, eyes like lasers taking me in, scanning like an X-ray machine at the airport, a faux-pas detector that always catches *something*. "How amusing to run into *you* here."

I make a sound that is supposed to be friendly but comes closer to a dying whale.

"Hi, Jennifer," I finally cough up. Parker and I were together for nine months, and Jennifer was part of eight of them. Once Parker told her we'd moved in together–after just a few months of dating, if you can call screwing like bunnies whenever he wasn't working "dating"–she practically moved in. Casually "stopped by." Requested weekly lunches with us. Showed up to fundraisers and city events in the city where Parker and I were living, and made sure to generally insert herself into whatever we were doing.

I now know why.

Because I never measured up.

When a weed finds its way into your perfect garden and starts to sprout, you remove it.

Immediately.

Roots and all.

And if that doesn't work, you pull out the poison.

"Are you all right, my dear? You look positively ill." Her eyes narrow, mouth turning down and up at the same time, the expression intended to convey sympathy.

"I think I let the wrong thing into my mouth yesterday," I reply.

Parker stiffens, his hand going still.

It's a great comeback, but now all I can think about is the taste of his tongue against mine.

While staring straight into the eyes of his mother.

"Mmmm. Food poisoning?" Eyes darting about, she bends down. "You didn't eat *here* yesterday, did you? I've heard they have the best Mexican food in the region, so I decided to try some of the local flavor myself."

"Really? Like mother, like son."

Parker's whole body turns into a marble statue.

Mallory spoons some salsa from her ramekin, digging in three different times to get just enough juice and chopped tomatoes. A cilantro shred tops the dollop. It pleases her.

"What are you up to these days, Persephone? Are you a professional protester? You must have an arrest record longer than Parker's resume by now."

"It's not quite the size of your ego, Jennifer, but this isn't a competition, now, is it?"

Her eyes go flat.

"I work in the coffee business."

"Drive-thru or counter?" she asks sweetly, not blinking.

"Actually," Parker says, "you and Persephone have something in common."

"We do?" We answer in unison, equally disgusted.

"Yes." He bites his lower lip, trying not to laugh. "Mom's in town to help plan her thirty-fifth Harvard reunion," he starts.

I pretend to count on my fingers. "Fifty-seven? Jennifer, you don't look that old."

"Thank you," she says tightly.

"–and," Parker continues, as if I'd never interrupted, "Mom is working on literacy and education projects on coffee plantations in Central America. With Will's dad, actually. They're helping to promote a wide range of school initiatives for the children of coffee farm workers." He turns to Jennifer. "You remember how Persephone and I met."

"What does that have to do with my literacy initiative?"

"Persephone works for similar causes. Her efforts in the coffee industry come from an ethically driven approach. She donates to organizations that improve the lives of workers and promote fair trade."

One eyebrow arches. She's impressed, but doesn't want to be. "Good for you," Jennifer grudgingly says to me.

"No. Good for the kids."

She softens.

But only for a second.

"I saw the clip reel from yesterday, Parker," she turns to him. "Impressive."

"Clip reel?"

She ignores me, but Parker doesn't. "It's a collection of all of my appearances on film," he explains. "Gets sent to my office every day. Omaia makes sure."

"Omaia?" I ask.

"My EA."

"Executive admin," Jennifer says pointedly, as if I'm too stupid to know what EA means.

"And *you* watch it?" Mallory asks Jennifer in that affable way that makes it seem like a compliment, but I know what she's really up to.

"Of course! I'm so proud of my son." She grins at him. "And you and Saoirse looked wonderful together."

Shrugging my shoulder, I make Parker's hand slip off as I scooch a little closer to Fiona.

"She's a good journalist," he says in a casual tone I know is covering up something.

But what?

Jennifer just winks. "She's good at more than that, Parker," she says before turning to me and winking.

Again.

The little bit of food I've managed to eat turns into a fidget spinner in my stomach. Am I being played? Are Parker and Saoirse together again and he's stalking me because he wants a piece of ass on the side? Does he get some weird cheap thrill out of tormenting me?

Was my mom right? For a split second, everything I know dissolves in a paranoid soup. Mom's conspiracy theories skip through my mind until my face, hands, and feet are on fire, emotion converting into chemicals that race through my blood and bring the leftover alcohol back to my head.

I'm woozy.

Woozy, nauseated, and done. So, so done.

Mallory's spoon hovers over the sour cream, the tip

dipping in once, twice, three times–but it's the fourth that makes me stabby.

Suddenly, the soft paper of the condiment cup is pliable under my fingers, the sour cream lifting up as I squeeze from the bottom. Flinging something so light with precision is harder than you'd think. Unwieldy, the unbalanced load veers to the right, nailing Parker's heart. A glop of sour cream slides down his chest, looking like shaving soap.

Jennifer's face is a perfect O, her polished edges all raw.

As I storm out, the last thing I hear is Mallory.

Screaming, "YOU RUINED THE RATIO!"

✺ 7 ✺

See that guy over there, sitting at the table up against the giant fern by the picture window? He's about to get dumped.

He has no idea. Poor sap.

You spend enough time in coffee shops watching a barista serving up double-skim mochas and breve macchiatos to the sophisticated palates of coffee snobs who think the place that starts with an S is the McDonald's of coffee, and you become a romantic anthropologist. Not that I'm a romantic.

Far from it.

But I know a pending breakup when I see one.

She walks into the store with a resolute look on her face, scanning the crowd for him, her shoulders hunched a little, spine straightening as she makes eye contact.

He stands.

He dumps his hot decaf chai all over his lap.

This guy is having a bad day.

And it's about to get worse.

"Reveling in other people's misery again, Perk?" Mallory asks as she comes around to my side of the counter and plucks a cup sleeve from the box of extras we keep. "And you're shirking your duties."

I look at the cream and sugar station–damn. They're out.

Again.

Cream and sugar are, too.

Someone really should take care of that.

"It's a fringe benefit," I whisper, grabbing a handful of sleeves and shoving them in the empty slot on the counter where they go. Every so often, well-intentioned environmentalists complain that we're using too many paper products, but they're recycled and cut down on the energy use and detergent of washing, so it's a compromise.

"You have a sickness."

"I'm innately curious about human nature. And coffee shops are the perfect environment for observing humans in their natural habitat."

"Overcaffeinated, wearing earbuds plugged into laptops, and camping at tables for hours without speaking to another soul?"

"Welcome to the 2010s, Mallory." I squint. "She's breaking up with him because..."

This is an old game of ours. Stranger watching and guessing. No way to know whether we're right or not. It's just a harmless way to mock people we don't know, and the stakes are super low.

"Because he punched one of the groomsmen at their wedding rehearsal rehearsal dinner." Mallory clears her throat after that, as if exorcising some awful taste.

Or a catty hairball.

"What are the chances someone other than me would do that in the same week?"

"Perky."

"You want to *taaaallllllk* about it, don't you?"

"Parker is here. You've been avoiding him. Will thinks he didn't do it, by the way." She sips primly.

"Didn't do what?"

"Post that picture."

"WHAT?"

"And she's really dumping that guy because he's an

orgasm whinnier." Mal nods in the direction of the dumper and the dumpee.

"WHAT WHAT?"

"I can't tell what you're whatting, Perky."

"I'm whatting every word out of your mouth, Mallory. What the hell are you talking about?"

"Which what?"

"What?"

"You two are like those old black-and-white-tv comedians. The ones who do Who's on First," a breathy voice chimes in.

"Dean Martin and Jerry Lewis?" I ask, completely stumped as Fiona reaches for a honey straw and starts chewing on it.

"You have to pay for those now. A buck each." I reach into my back pocket and peel off a dollar. Fi just smiles a thanks and keeps chewing.

Mallory sips her latte like she didn't just dump that big pile of horse manure into the conversation.

"Fiona, what's an orgasm whinnier?" I ask, totally sure she'll be as shocked as I am.

"A guy who makes that weird sound at the end. You know. *Neiggghhhh.*"

Mal and Fi fall apart laughing.

"It's like sleeping with Mr. Ed," Fiona giggles.

"Who's that?"

"You don't know who he is? Some old black-and-white-television show featuring a horse."

"Owned by a guy named Ed?"

"No. The horse is Mr. Ed."

"Who names a horse Mr. Ed? And how the hell would I know all this stuff from the black-and-white-tv era? And shut up. Mallory was just telling me about guys who are orgasm whinniers."

Fi nods and grimaces. "I've had one of those." Her nose wrinkles. "He was also terrible in bed. Went down on me like he was eating an apple."

Now we *all* fall apart laughing.

"I wonder if that's a tag on YouPorn," I say aloud as Raul turns a corner. His father owns Beanerino, and Raul is a big, cuddly guy made of muscle and smoking-hot eyes the color of one-hundred-year-old Scotch that make you want to dip yourself in them. He has dreadlocks that go down to his hips unless he pulls them into a lazy ponytail. Not much of a talker, Raul has a deep presence that makes you feel grounded around him.

But most of all, he loves coffee as much as I do, and he tolerates me, two character qualities in people I can never, *ever* get enough of.

He holds up a palm. "No laptops. You're banned from bringing a laptop into the store, Perky. Dad said so."

"I know."

Mal and Fi exchange a look that says I'm about to get roasted.

"Banned?"

"After the porn incident last year. You know. *Your* porn?" I say to Mallory, who blushes.

"It wasn't *my* porn! Beastman and Spatula were the ones who–"

I grab my phone and pull up the famous photo of Mallory, on her knees with an oiled-up, naked porno star named Beastman behind her, her now-fiancé Will in front of her, her mouth in the shape of an O and a set of anal beads poking out from between her legs (but not, thankfully, inserted).

"At least I was having a great hair day."

"We could crop out the impromptu spit-roasting part and use it on social media."

"Don't you dare!"

"Besides," Fiona says as her teeth make quick work of the honey stick, "it's already been done."

"Someone's using my head as their picture on Insta?"

"Not your head. Your ass. It looks like you're six beads in, Mal. Pretty sure if you make it to seven, you win free colonoscopies for life from some of the adult-film production companies."

"Those beads were never inside me! I was just sitting on them! I swear it's the camera angle!"

"They *all* swear it's the camera angle," I say with a snicker, knowing it'll drive her into a self-righteous frenzy.

"Don't you have a nicotine patch you need to dissolve into a macchiato or something?" she mutters my way.

"No, but we are experimenting with CBD-infused lattes. I'll add nicotine to the list of legal drugs we can blend into caffeinated abominations because *someone* wants to be trendy," I counter, my voice rising loud enough for Raul to hear.

"Hey," he says with a shrug. "Can't be a purist to the point of not paying the bills."

"Coffee is meant to be enjoyed. Savored. Put on a pedestal and revered."

"You make it sound like a woman," he says.

"Or a really, *really* good vibrator," Fiona whispers.

Raul flinches. "I heard that."

The house phone rings. I'm on the clock, so I answer.

"Beanerino! How may I caffeinate you?"

"Um, hey–I'm looking for the booking manager? Perky?"

"That's me."

The guy sounds like he's twelve. "Yeah, so, uh, I'm calling from Subterranean Paradigm Productions, and–"

That's code for *I Made a Studio in Mom's Basement.*

"–we're working on booking live shows for one of our bands."

"Yeah? What kind of music?"

"Celtic ska."

"*Okayyyyyy.* Tell me more."

As the kid–who is probably actually twelve–describes this new three-person band, Mal and Fiona chat up Raul, who is giving Fiona googly eyes.

Caramel, rich, strong googly eyes attached to a body that won't quit and a head of dreadlocks that are so sexy.

Not that I'm attracted to Raul.

But I'm not dead.

"Sure," I finally say, cutting the kid off. "We take a chance on new bands once a month, on Thursdays from five to seven p.m. You get to experience the after-work rush. We don't pay, but you get a tip bucket."

"SERIOUSLY?" the guy says in four syllables and three octaves.

I grin. "Yeah, kid. You booked a gig. Congrats." *And all before you even got pit hair.*

I don't say that last part aloud, though it's tempting.

"I–uh," he drops back to normal baritone range. "Thanks. What do we need to do now?"

I give him the secret URL for booking, where all the paperwork for the coffee house lives. He thanks me profusely, until I finally get off the phone to hear Fiona say:

"I just don't understand why hazelnut coffee went out of style. I really like it."

"That's because you are a reincarnation of some shoulder-pad-wearing woman from 1985," I say, then shudder.

"I am not! My quantum healer says that based on reading my past lives, I ran a camp in northern Canada and died in a polar bear attack."

Raul is shocked. "I died from being mauled, too!"

"Mauled by a band of horny women?" I crack.

"Watch it," he says in a voice of warning.

Fiona looks like she's eager to volunteer for that band of horny women. I flip through my memory banks to find the last time she went out on a date. Hmmm. It's been a long time.

Too long.

"Who was on the phone?" Fi asks.

"Some kid." I look at Raul. "I gave him a new-band slot in January."

He nods. "What kind of music?"

"Celtic ska."

He laughs, shining white teeth and full lips making it

impossible not to join in. "These kids. They mix in creative ways. Dad's gonna love it." Raul's father, Thiago, opened Beanerino about five years ago, right around the time I came home from Texas licking my wounds. After a year of protesting and working on fair labor practices in the coffee industry, and being appreciative of a good pull (Ristretto! Get your mind out of the gutter!), I waltzed into the store and was hired on the spot.

Thiago is an expansive guy with an open mind and an even broader heart. I love working here because with Raul and his dad in charge, you see the good in variety. How life gives you a richer experience when you fling open your emotional doors and let people find you.

"But the gospel Eurotech was horrid," Fi notes. "I didn't know whether to pray or start humping a post."

Raul happens to be sipping some sparkling water at that moment and nearly spit takes all over us.

On the television, a new installation Thiago insisted we add so he could stream concerts, the news comes on. Parker is front and center.

Every molecule in my body shifts.

Fiona takes me, gently, to a booth, Mallory waiting as Raul starts making coffees. I stare at the screen like a robot with a depleted battery source. Time changes when you're suddenly confronted with your past on a fifty-inch television screen at work.

Mallory appears with three drinks and a heaping swallow of regret on my behalf.

They settle in, asses firmly planted in the booth across from me, big eyes staring over the curved brims of their black plastic coffee lids as they sip. I pick up my macchiato and chug it, the heat burning but the caffeine oh, so loving.

"I don't want to talk about it." Two macchiatos in a row is going to be a big mistake, but I don't care. As Mallory looks up from her tall cup, her eyes fill with concern and the deep empathy you feel when you've experienced sorrow with another person, walked alongside them on the journey, gotten drunk with them and held their hair while—never mind.

Let's just say she gets it. She gets why I don't want to talk about it.

"You did everything right," Fiona interjects, twisting in place to look at Parker's image as he is interviewed in the lobby of the State House in Boston, "when the picture started making the rounds and the memes were coming up in the middle of online video games, and Facebook should have been renamed Perky's Tits."

"Hey!" I cut her off. "That's doubly insulting. You know I hate that word."

Mallory kicks Fiona's ankle.

"Sorry," Fi concedes. "But when that happened, your parents jumped in so fast. That first month was insane."

I guess we're really doing this, huh? Parsing Perky's past with Parker.

Say that five times fast without two shots of espresso in you. Good luck.

"No kidding. I think I still have carpal tunnel syndrome from that month. Delete-delete-delete. Cry-cry-cry. Block-block-block. Ignore-ignore-ignore. It's a blur." I get up to grab a sparkling water from the case and pop it open, making a mental note to have Thiago take it off my paycheck. The topic is somber, but this needs to be said. Rehashing the past with Parker isn't something I can avoid anymore.

The past is the present now.

"I remember when your mom reached out to me, and I told Tim what had happened," Fiona says.

"What are the odds that Fi's brother would be working in reputation management just when you needed it most?" Mal ponders.

We all look at each other, the silence comfortable and deep. What *are* the odds? What are the odds that I would have two best friends who were there for me through the hardest time in my life, *and* one of them would have a brother who could step in quickly to help?

Being naked and vulnerable in front of someone you love is an act of trust.

Being naked and vulnerable in front of billions of people on social media, turned into an object of ridicule and scorn, is an act of *war*. The masses turn your picture into a battlefield, covered only in your own blood.

"Thank you," I say to them both, reaching for their hands. Mallory grasps mine back while Fiona just pats the back of my wrist.

"You were the one who came up with the crazy idea to solve it, at least partly," Fiona says. "Who knew you could copyright your own dog-humping nude picture and then sue website owners for violating your copyright?"

"All those web hosting companies, too. Your parents were ferocious. They had so many lawyers working on it all. And you won!"

"It was never about the money."

"Of *course* it wasn't about the money," Fiona exclaims. "It was about the principle. I remember Tim telling me how hard it was to get people to stop using the meme. Once you went after those big websites–once you proved that you owned the rights, suddenly the morality shift—"

I stop her. "There was no morality shift. There was nothing about *morality* involved in what happened. Companies don't act based on a moral code. They act based on survival of the fittest. I had the law on my side and my parents had deep pockets. That's how we were able to shut down so many of those pictures of me, and so quickly."

"But you had to copyright a picture of your own ti–uh, *boobs*, to protect yourself from massive public shaming. And it took a while to figure it out."

"Yep."

Mallory snorts. "And then Parker was the one who bene-fited the most."

I give her a wry, sad grin that twists the same lips he kissed just yesterday. "He was an assistant district attorney when it all happened. The idea of running for political office at the national level was just a little seed inside his mind. If word had gotten out that he was the one who took the picture and uploaded it, it would have ended his political career before it really got started."

"But that's not why your parents got it taken down, or why they kept his name out of it. That's not why Tim did it," Fiona objects.

"Of course not."

"Instead of Parker being collateral damage from his own stupid, juvenile, jerk-faced act, his internet reputation was left clean as a whistle. So a few years later, when the congressman he was working for had a heart attack and Parker saved him, he could be lauded," Mallory spews, her face going red with indignation.

"So he could be *elected,*" Fiona fumes.

They're both angry. I can hear the bitterness in the way Mallory is raking through the past, trying to separate the trash that needs to be discarded from the treasures that need to stay.

I flatten my palms against the table and lean forward, my friends reflexively leaning in, too, as I whisper, "I'm tired of being angry at him."

"And you're wondering if he really did it," Fiona whispers.

"I am. I am, now. I'm so confused, guys," I choke out. "I just want the guy I loved five years ago. Before he did this to me."

If he did this to me.

The phone rings again. Raul gives me a look that says *I was being nice but now you need to actually work.* I get the hint and jump up, bottle in hand, shrugging at Mal and Fi like I need to apologize for letting work intrude on our talk.

"Beanerino! How may I caffeinate you?" I answer.

"I'm calling for a Per-purse-phone Ta…"

"I'm Persephone Tsongas. What can I do for you?"

"Oh." Relief fills her voice. It always does when I help someone with the mouthful that masquerades as my name. Per-SEF-uh-knee is harder to pronounce than ASS-hole.

"This is Katie Bollinger from New Start Booking."

"The bands?" I gasp, unable to keep my normal cynicism percolating along. I've been trying for a while to get live bands from New Start to play here. They're *way* above Celtic-ska-dude's level.

"No, sorry, not bands," Katie says. The rustle of papers she's obviously shuffling through sounds like disappointment. "I'd like to schedule a short appearance to announce a new fair-trade coffee bill," she says, her voice halting and robotic. She's clearly reading from a script.

I chuckle to myself. While Thiago was originally reluctant to bring new music talent into the place, he's always one for politics–especially politics involving fair-trade coffee. All of the roasting companies in New England know that if they need space for an event, Beanerino is it.

"Is this for an author who's written a book about coffee?" I ask her. "Or PR for one of the roasters?"

"No." More pages are rustled. "This is for, um, a politician? He's a senator? Or no–wait. Some kind of politician from DC. Sorry. I normally book bands, not suits. That's a different division."

Hoo boy.

"I just wanted to confirm the date and time tomorrow. He's not a sen—"

Click.

She hung up on me.

Raul gives me a strange look. "What the heck was that?"

I stare at the phone like it's going to bite me. "Someone giving millennials a bad name."

"How is that any different from *being* a millennial?"

"*We're* millennials, Raul," I point out.

The phone rings again.

This caller could not be more the opposite of the last one. Before I can say a word, she jumps in with:

"Hello. This is Janice Contell, with Congressman Ouemann's office. The congressman represents your district and he's co-sponsoring a fair-trade bill for coffee, in an effort to promote–"

"I know who Ouemann is and I know what fair trade means. What can Beanerino do? Carry the coffee? Help hand out brochures? We're active in the community and internationally," I inform her.

Her tone changes instantly, the pivot smooth and professional. "Excellent. You obviously care about the cause."

"I care so much, I've been arrested and detained for it."

I can practically hear her lean in. "And *you* are... ?"

"Perky. My name is Perky."

"Great name for someone in coffee."

"It helps."

We laugh together. Political staffers are like this. I should know. Parker was one of them. He didn't work for Congressman O'Rollins while we were together, but Janice is cut from the same cloth. Smooth, charming, and sharp as can be.

Which I admire in anyone other than a guy who screws me over.

"The congressman would like to use your coffee shop for a press conference."

"Oh?" This is a new one. Thiago is going to puff up like a popover when he hears this.

"Yes. We knew Beanerino was more than just a local place to get your four-dollar shot of caffeine. And now you've confirmed it. Congressman Ouemann is preparing to announce he's co-sponsoring a bill, and would like to root it in the community. Can we use the store tomorrow, from ten to eleven? About fifteen camera crews will be there, regional press, probably a few reporters from the big papers. It'll be chaos for a couple of hours, and there's no fee, but it will give Beanerino national spotlight exposure it wouldn't otherwise get. Bring in lots of new foot traffic, too."

"Yes, of course!" I know I have tacit permission from my boss. Maybe this will make up for the Bluetooth-porn-speaker incident last year, the one where I accidentally made Mallory blast the audio of a Beastman porn video throughout the coffee shop. Thiago had to give ten customers free coffee for a year to make up for it, and I'm pretty sure a certain customer's four-year-old gets free hot cocoa for life.

This could get me out of the doghouse.

Maybe.

"Should I speak with the owner directly? Or are you the booking agent?"

"I am." I give her my contact info. Within seconds, an email notification appears on my cellphone.

See? Political staffers get shit done. Immediately.

Like Parker climbing into bed with me back in the day, my first orgasm over before my panties were off.

Or what happened yesterday in that coat closet...

I cough, realizing that's *not* where my mind should be during this conversation. Why the hell am I thinking about orgasms with Parker while organizing this fabulous coffee-news opportunity?

"Excellent, Perky. See you tomorrow at nine. The congressmen both appreciate this."

Click.

I get off the phone and look over to find Raul staring at me, one eyebrow up as he wipes down the counter.

"Who," he asks, "was that?"

"Congressman Ouemann's office."

The sound of Raul's laughter is rich and full. "Ha ha. Very funny. What's the band really called? Because that's a *terrible* name."

"No. I mean it." Excitement gets the better of me. "That was a staffer from his office. He wants to do a press conference here, tomorrow, at ten."

"No kidding?"

"I'm completely serious." I pull up the email from Janice on my phone and forward it to the Beanerino business email. Raul's phone pings.

"Look at your email."

He reaches into his counter apron, a copper-color canvas

that sets off his eyes, which bug out as he reads Janice's email.

"Holy shit!" Raul rarely cusses. "Papá is going to lose his mind!" Craning his neck, he gives me an evaluative look. "*You* did this?"

"I, uh..." It would be so easy to take credit, right? "She cold called. Said she heard we were more than just a place to grab a cup of joe."

"We are." A true smile, one I don't get often, flashes my way. "But don't be modest. I know how much marketing you do in the region. The open mic nights have become a huge hit and we're getting a ton of new customers. And your advocacy work for fair trade and literacy in Central American coffee plantations plants the seeds for these kinds of calls."

"Thank you."

"It more than makes up for what a crappy employee you are."

"HEY!"

"Am I wrong?"

"How am I a crappy employee?"

"Mal? How big a tub of popcorn do we need for this conversation?" Fiona whispers as they settle in, Fiona propping her feet on a chair, both watching with the eager eyes of friends who love seeing me in trouble.

"One: You're late for every shift." Raul actually flattens his left palm, fingers splayed, and starts ticking off his answers.

"But I stay over if needed!"

He ignores me. "Two: You make sexually inappropriate comments all the time."

"I promised your dad I'd stop."

"Only after he made you take online training."

I start to protest, but he cuts me off.

"Three: You never refill the cream and sugar station without a customer pointing it out."

Mallory smirks at me before I can answer.

The giant silver ring on Raul's fourth finger glitters in the sunlight, like it's detonating. "Four: You parked in my parking spot three times last week."

"It's not marked!"

"It says Manager."

"I *am* a manager!"

"You are not."

"Well, I *should* be!"

"Five," he says, voice dropping. Oh, no. I know what's next.

Mal and Fi snicker.

"You played *pornography* over the sound system in the coffee shop. With customers here."

"It was an accident!"

"A porn star named Beastman went ass to mouth over *our speakers*." He frowns at the one in the right corner, as if it were an errant child. "Papá made me go back to canned radio in the store. Now I have to listen to Coldplay at least once a day."

Fiona makes a sound of mourning. "Oh, Perky. I had no idea. You're downright abusive to poor Raul here."

"And Raul is running out of fingers," Mal adds.

He opens his second hand. "Six—"

"Okay! Okay! Got it! I'm the worst employee ever. But I got Congressman Ouemann's office to do a press conference here."

His eyes narrow. "I thought you said it was a cold call."

My turn to ignore.

"This is going to make Beanerino a madhouse," I chirp, giving him a grin that I hope erases the last three minutes of conversation.

He sighs. "Papá will want to handle everything from here. You know how much he likes this." Raul gives me a look I know. "We'll take over. Just be here tomorrow before they come. Nine a.m. *sharp*."

"Of course." I know Thiago will fall apart at the last second, so I'll come and pick up the pieces.

And pull the best shots of the whole crew.

He starts tapping on his phone. "We need every barista on hand tomorrow. Start calling everyone in tonight. The store needs to be spotless. I'll make a list of extra supplies we'll need. And if we can get the deliveries increased in time, we'll..."

His words fade out as Fiona looks at me, impressed.

"You got Raul excited."

"Yes."

"*You* look excited."

"I am."

Weeping sounds make us both look around, the hitched breath of someone in distress cutting through the air. We turn in unison, a herd of attuned gazelles finding a loner in need of attention.

It's the guy from earlier, his girlfriend staring at him with eye-rolling contempt. He has drying chai stains on his shirt sleeve and leg, and he's holding a recycled-tan napkin over his eyes.

"Ouch," Fiona whispers.

"Poor guy," Mallory chimes in.

The woman looks up, catching my eye. If I look away, I acknowledge we're gawking.

So I give her a sympathetic smile.

She flips me off.

"What the heck?" Mallory gasps.

"Someone get Perky a container of sour cream," Fiona whispers, looking at me. "If anyone deserves a glop to the head, it's that bitch."

"Hey, hey, non-violent preschool teacher!" Raul says, looking at her with new appreciation. "What you got against sour cream?"

The weeping man makes sounds that start to resemble an orgasm whinnier.

"Ah," Fiona says, turning red. "I see."

"You see what?" Raul enquires, confused.

The sounds get louder; Mallory grimaces. Raul gives us major side eye until his face takes on the most extraordinary look of realization, mouth twisting into a grimace.

The woman storms out, shaking her head. Raul walks over to the dude and slides him a bottled ginger tea, speaking in a voice men reserve for other men when they're down.

I guess. I wouldn't know. No one's ever talked to *me* like that.

"No one likes being dumped," Mallory says in a sage voice.

"You ever dump anyone?"

She chews on a honey stick. "No."

"Me, neither," Fi says.

"Same."

"You dumped Parker."

"That doesn't count."

"Technically, it does."

"*Technically*, Parker dumped *me* by turning my boobs into a logo for teenage boy wanking."

They sigh, the long-suffering sound of besties.

As Dumped Dude falls to pieces, Raul struggling to help a stranger in pain, we look at each other.

"Thai or Indian?" Fiona asks.

Before Mallory can suggest Taco Cubed, I jump in. "How about Greek?" I quickly add, "Not my mom's cooking. Please."

"Take out from Athena's?"

I nod.

"Mallory's place?"

We all nod.

Parker's in town. Mallory's getting married. Fiona's paired with Fletch in the wedding. Hasty's part of it all.

We need to talk.

And eat.

❧❀❧

"I DON'T UNDERSTAND WHY YOU DON'T GET YOUR OWN

place," Mallory says as we lug the take-out bags from Athena's Delite into her perfect apartment. The scent of baked apples, sweet puff pastry, honey-gooey goodness, and roasted chicken makes my drool turn into tzatziki sauce before I've even opened a single container.

I haven't gotten my own place because I have a cottage next to the big house *and* my old bedroom. Why leave? After Parker and I split up, I came home, tail between my legs, and never moved out. Mom and Dad went into protective mode and my time was taken up with all the legal maneuvers needed to get that damn half-naked picture of me off the internet.

And I was heartbroken, okay? I took the path of least resistance.

"Are you offering this place up?" I ask, trying to change the subject.

"No. Will likes it." She gets a satisfied smile on her face that makes my antenna tingle.

"He's moving in?"

"Maybe. He prefers his condo, but agrees this apartment has appeal."

Fi and I look at each other. "You told him the energy in his condo is draining, didn't you?" Fiona says lightly, pulling out packages of roast chicken. My mouth waters at the thought of the lemon-coated grilled potatoes coming next.

"It *is* draining! I've rearranged that place countless times, and–"

"Will got tired of having his place rearranged, so he's agreed to move in with you."

"That's not how it is!" she protests. "He's just finally seen reason."

Fiona and I hoot. We're close to being used by Hogwarts as Uber drivers.

"Mallory," I say slowly, "Will has more than enough money to stay in his condo and not squeeze into a one-bedroom in-law apartment that you rent."

She reddens.

Fiona frowns, picking up on the same signal that has my radar pinging. Something's off.

"Wait a minute," Fiona says, setting down the styrofoam container in her hand. Sensing an out, Mallory's eyes alight on it. A lecture on recycling and environmental ruin via take-out containers is cueing up in her head as a possible distraction technique.

Mallory is good.

But Fiona teaches preschoolers.

She's a master.

"You're buying the entire house, aren't you?"

Mallory makes a sex-doll face. You know the kind? Mouth dropping to form a perfect O, the hole just right for, um...

Protesting.

"I heard the Bajerians were considering leaving town."

"Who told you?"

"Your mom."

"When did you talk to my mom?"

"She asked me to help her pick Himalayan sea salt for the custom-blend scrub you want at the bachelorette spa weekend."

This is the first I've heard of it.

"Sharon called you about that?"

"Yes."

"Mallory."

Her hands go up in protest. "I didn't pick it! Mom insisted!"

"Apple didn't fall far from the tree."

"What's that supposed to mean?"

"You had a wedding rehearsal *rehearsal* dinner, Mallory. Now you're making custom-blend Himalayan sea salt scrub for the bachelorette spa weekend. Do you hear my words?" I point to my lips. "It's like you're a walking wedding-satire account on Twitter."

"Am not!"

"Is the wedding cake vegan?"

Her eyes fly wide open.

"No. Wait! Don't answer that." I press my temple. "You have a vegan cake, a paleo cake, a keto one, and a—"

"Gluten free! Don't worry. We covered you. Turns out Fletch has a gluten-intolerance issue, too, and five people answered the pre-wedding survey with gluten-free options as a request, so—"

"Pre-wedding survey?"

"Didn't you get the Doodle poll?"

Fiona's lips curl in as she bites them.

"Can we change the subject?" Mallory whines, pulling out a souvlaki stick and shoving a piece of lamb into her mouth, chewing furiously. "Ooor oouining dah ooood."

"What?"

Fi pushes my container toward me. "Eat."

We do. It's good. Mom sniffs like we're the caterers at the Red Wedding and "The Rains of Castamere" is playing whenever we get take-out from Athena's, but it's the closest thing to Mom's cooking.

My grandma came here from Greece in the late 1930s and she taught Mom everything she knows. The gene broke somewhere in me, DNA strands snapping like weak branches on trees in an ice storm. Ditie is a born cook, but I can barely heat up a tray of grocery-store spanakopita without angering the gods.

"Please tell me you're not issuing instruction manuals for your wedding," I choke out. "Like the ones they make fun of on Instagram."

Mal's eyes get huge. For a split second, I worry I'll have to do the Heimlich.

Which makes me think of Parker.

Which makes me remember that kiss.

Which makes my body conjure that orgasm.

Which makes me want another one.

I shove a stuffed grape leaf in my mouth and chew.

"It won't be an instruction manual," Mallory says primly,

eyes shifty like she's giving congressional testimony. "Just a helpful welcome packet."

"I pity your obstetrician," Fiona says around a mound of potato spear.

Mallory starts choking. "What obstetrician? I'm not pregnant!"

"Your future one." Shaking her head, Fiona fans her mouth to cool down her food.

"Why?" Mallory peeps, holding her mouth open and blowing out hard, the piece of meat too hot.

"Your birth plan is going to be epic. Have you started choosing the colors on your Excel spreadsheet yet? It'll have a legend, won't it?"

"And you'll use pivot tables," I add.

"I would never use Excel to build a birthing plan!" Mal scoffs.

It's hard to hoot with rice pilaf (made gluten free for me by Athena, bless her) in your mouth, but Fiona and I manage somehow.

"I wouldn't! That's what AirTable is for!"

"Point made."

"Point not made."

"Mallory, what are you going to do when you realize you can't plan for everything in the world?"

"I didn't plan for Will." The satisfied smile on her face makes me happy. Happy she let him in. Happy her wildest dreams really did come true.

Happy we get to hear about the real Will and are forever spared the never-ending stories about Fantasy Will.

"No. You didn't."

"And you didn't plan for Parker." Mallory licks her fingers.

Acid fills my mouth. "Sure didn't. What he did to me five years ago was–"

"I mean *now*, Perk." Searching the counter for a napkin, she doesn't make eye contact.

"Huh?"

"He's back. You *have* to face it." Her eyes meet mine, unblinking.

"I am facing it! How am I not facing it? He kissed me and I punched him and–"

"He's still in love with you."

"I know. He told me."

"He did?" Fiona jumps in, the conversation more compelling than a piece of grilled pita bread, and that's saying a *lot*.

"Yes."

"What? Why?"

"I think because I said it first."

"So much happened while I was changing my dress!"

"You didn't tell me you got back together!" Fiona says, accusatory.

"We didn't."

"Wait wait wait. You told each other you still love each other?"

"Yes."

"And you kissed."

"Yes."

"And you punched him?"

"Uh huh."

"Then by Perky Relationship Standards, you're back together," Fiona declares.

"He *has* always sworn he didn't do it." Mal licks her fingers and grabs a potato wedge. Again.

"Creepy narcissists always say they didn't do it and then the police find the woman's head in a fifty-five gallon drum somewhere," Fiona muses.

"You are cut off from those true-crime podcasts," I inform her.

"They make me feel better about my life choices!" She bites into a piece of baklava I can't touch. "And I've learned never to get married because it's *always* the husband."

"Perk." Mallory finishes chewing and takes a sip from a bottle of flavored sparkling water she pulled out of her fridge.

"How are you handling all this? It's a big deal to have Parker in town."

"I'm fine."

Huh. Didn't know Mallory could hoot, too.

"I am fine!"

"You're in denial."

"Then I'm you, one year ago."

Mallory's offended. Good. I hit a nerve.

"And you and Fiona are the ones who told me I was holding myself back from being who I really am by refusing to believe Will really was interested in me."

"So?"

"So–you're doing the same with Parker."

"You're–you actually think I should take that sleazeball *back*?"

"I think you should talk to the guy. And I don't mean talk as in play Hide the Sausage in a coat closet at my wedding rehearsal rehearsal dinner."

Fiona stops, mid-chew, to gawk at Mallory. A thin line of honey slowly rolls down the corner of her open mouth.

"You think Perky should actually meet with Parker and have a conversation about what happened five years ago? After blocking him on all social media and on her phone? After having her parents hire teams of tech experts to strip that picture off the internet? After suing four different websites, claiming copyright violation on a photo of her tits?"

"Quit saying *tits*," I grumble.

"After years of social media bullying, you seriously believe the guy?"

A big gulp makes Mallory's throat move.

"Yes," she says with a little sniff that shows she's feeling the fear and doing it anyway.

"Why?"

"Because Parker Campbell has spent the last five years protesting that he's innocent. And he still loves you."

"Not a good-enough reason."

"And you love him right back."

"Still not a good-enough reason."

"Really?" The fire in Mal's eyes morphs into something worse than the righteous certainty she displays when she's dug in and convinced she needs to make me bend.

I can handle that kind of conflict. I know how to beat her.

What's radiating out of those earnest brown eyes right now is a weapon she doesn't even know she's using.

It's the love from a bestie who is a true friend. In Ancient Greece, my mom explained to me a long time ago, the concept of a true friend meant someone who would call you on your stupid shit. No, the philosophers didn't use the phrase "stupid shit," but they might as well have.

Mallory and Fiona are true friends. They tell me when I'm being a dumbass.

Like now.

"Perky, what Parker did to you was atrocious. But what kind of guy sticks to the same story year in and year out? What kind of guy realizes that coincidence made him come to our wedding rehearsal rehearsal dinner and then uses that time to plead with you–and tell you he still loves you?"

"And saves the life of a slimy jerkface who looked at your tits on the internet," Fiona adds.

"*Not helping*," Mallory hisses out of the side of her mouth.

I'm softening, though. I am, and I hate myself for it. Every word Mallory says makes my heart do jumping jacks. All these years, I've wanted to believe Parker was telling the truth.

Now Mal is saying I can crack that door open? Really?

"Remember, Mal, how you didn't want to take the job as a consultant for Will's company? How when he came back to town and found you on a porn set with a string of anal beds on the floor next to you and an oiled-up–"

"I remember."

"Remember how he offered you the home-staging gig to sell his parents' house?"

"Of course."

"You argued you didn't want to take the job because you didn't want to go back to being the person you were in high school. That you couldn't handle turning back the clock."

"I did. Is that what holds you back? You don't want to be the person you were five years ago, with Parker?"

I shake my head, finally giving in to my tears.

"No," I say as one drops on top of my hand. "That's the thing, guys. I *do* want to be the person I was with Parker. I do. And if I let myself go back and be that person again, then what have I done for the last five years?"

Fiona grabs my now-wet hand, Mallory clasping the other.

"Oh, God. What if I've been wrong all along? And what if Parker really didn't do it?"

❧ 8 ❧

Seahorse Cannon is *allll* over Parker.

Okay. Fine. That's juvenile. It's Saoirse. But she's attached herself to him like a barnacle on a hull, and *barnacle* doesn't work with her name.

She's at Beanerino when I walk into work this morning–at nine a.m. *sharp*–the place teeming with media and staffers from Congressman Ouemann's office.

And Parker.

What the hell is Parker doing here? This was supposed to be Ouemann's show.

"Congressman Campbell would like to make sure the lighting is..." someone behind me says in a high voice, the squeaky anxiety of a young woman who was adjusting her graduation cap just a few months ago piercing the air between me and the back counter. No one knows who I am, so I dodge my way through the cameras, careful not to trip on microphone cords.

Scratch that.

Someone knows *exactly* who I am.

"Persephone Tsongas?" Saoirse's voice has no twang this time, no inflection, and no warmth. "What are *you* doing here? You were at the restaurant the other night when Congressman Campbell saved that man's life."

"I work here. Have we met?"

"No. But I've seen you everywhere." Her smirk makes it clear *where*. That damn meme.

"Mmm." The noncommittal sound isn't my usual tactic, but people like her seek attention. It's painful for them when you don't hand it out freely.

"I've heard plenty about *you* from Jennifer." The emphasis on *you* makes my back teeth ache.

"Funny. I never heard a word from her about *you*." It takes everything in me not to smile.

All pretense of decency melts off her face. "She's here, you know."

My heart jumps into my throat as Thiago appears, running around like a man juggling crystal goblets. "Perky! We need you in the back. Some of the Sumatran turned and the shots are spoiled. We need a new dark roast!"

"Barista?" Her snide tone is so condescending.

"Mmmm." No use in trying to prove myself to someone like her. Been there, done that, have the lingering bitter taste in my mouth from my tenth high school reunion last year.

"Saoirse?" Jennifer Tanager Campbell's voice sends shivers down my spine as she approaches us from behind, the air hug she gives Saoirse careful to avoid smearing her on-camera makeup. "I thought that was you!"

What we have here, ladies and gentlemen, is a set up.

A big fat set up.

They turn to me just as Parker appears, tall and sleek and in a bespoke suit, cut to fit his fine, muscular form. My mind goes AWOL for a moment, the small coffee shop overrun with people who don't fit in, the memory bank of how this could have happened hopelessly jammed.

"Persephone," he says, lips twitching, eyes smoky and full of promise. "Give me something good to taste before I go on camera."

Being in close proximity to someone who has had his face between your legs is heady when he says *that*.

It's intoxicating, really, because unlike an emerging relationship where the possibility of all-things-new lets your imagination run wild and your heart and clit dance the samba, when you've already been with a masterful lover, there's nothing imaginary about what you know they can do with tongue, hands, lips, and... ahem.

Attention.

Being someone from Parker's past is hard. Being someone who is not part of his future is even harder.

So how do I handle right here, right now–the present? I'm present with him.

But I'm not present *with* him.

All the selves inside me–Past Persephone, Present Perky, Future Perky, and Horny Perky (hey, she's *very* real) are colliding, slipping and sliding against each other in a mud bath. I'm propping myself up on Past Persephone, who is bent on hands and knees to help out her sisters. But Future Perky wants desperately to stand on tippy toes, using Present Perky's scalp as a footstool.

And all of that is happening inside me as Parker Campbell looks me dead in the eye and says, "Make the mouthfeel perfect."

My eyes drop to his crotch. So do his, the decline of his head slight but noticeable.

The grin's even more obvious.

I turn away and start a shot for him, the grind of the grounds bringing me back to center.

"Ah, Persephone. You have not changed one bit."

I load the espresso and pull. "I've changed plenty."

"Really? How?"

"I no longer let guys I sleep with take naked pictures of me."

His jaw tightens. Did those deep speckled eyes just turn green? Aha. I've hit a nerve.

"Good policy," he grinds out.

"How about you? Your change log must be huge–" I jerk my eyes to his crotch at that word, then back up to his face, "–by now."

"I'm not going to talk about my sex life with you."

Handing him a tiny white espresso cup, I don't bother with the saucer I'd use for a regular customer. "Why not? Your sex life with *me* was made public by you, Parker. I would think you'd be less prudish after blasting my boobs all over the planet."

He downs the shot fast and easy. I've never wanted to be coffee so badly.

"We've been over this countless times." Placing the cup on the counter, he leans in.

"I'm not over it, though. It's not the kind of thing you just get over."

"Every conflict can be resolved," he whispers until I shiver.

I force myself to snort. "This isn't a committee meeting. I'm not a bill you're trying to convince people to vote for."

"No. You're more like pork."

"Did you just call me *fat*? A fat pig?"

The way he takes in my curves makes it clear he appreciates what he sees.

"Pork. As in politics. When we put a funding provision into a bill for a pet project that benefits a tiny group of people."

"I'm your pet project?"

"You're a project I'd fight hard to get."

"Because you'd directly benefit?"

A flash of energy lights up his eyes. "You could always do that."

"Do what?"

"Get my point in an instant and unabashedly call me out on my ulterior motives."

"If you're being ulterior in your pursuit of me, Parker, you're failing miserably."

"The ulterior part, yes. The pursuit part?" Questioning eyes meet mine.

"Failure." My mouth says that.

My clit screams, *She's lying!*

"Didn't seem to fail when you came in my arms after a few minutes of making out like frenzied high school students the other day," he whispers, oh, so casually.

"Congressman Campbell," Saoirse says, inserting herself between us like a razor blade on a callus. "They're ready for you."

He nods at me, but leans in. "I can't talk to you like this."

Saoirse smirks.

"We'll finish this conversation later. Over dinner?" he adds.

Mouth firmly set, Saoirse's eyes go dead.

I nod.

He turns away, walking slowly to the podium, standing next to it as Congressman Ouemann begins the presser.

And I die a little.

I should have known when Ouemann's staffers called to ask for the event. I should have put two and two together, knowing Parker's interest in fair trade.

But I didn't.

And here I am now, blindsided.

Crowds are my thing. I know it's popular to be a geeky introvert who hates other humans, but I've never been popular. The energy of too many people in a small space, all focused on the same thing, is divine. Almost indescribable, it's a palpable sense of potential that spills over into action and emotion.

In other words, it's a bucketload of feels.

All the feels.

Add caffeine–the truly good stuff, hand crafted to make each shot a work of art–and you have my idea of nirvana.

Minus the Barbie doll newscaster.

And Parker's mom, aka Dolores Umbridge.

Congressman Ouemann talks my lingo, with Thiago and Raul taking turns being recognized as community leaders, immigrants who created jobs on the North Shore of Boston, people forming a moral core in the community. Ouemann branches out, using fair trade and labor policy as a cornerstone of freedom, and soon the swelling crowd has me filled with a sense of purpose.

This.

This is why I protest.

This is why I donate.

This is why I travel to coffee plantations in Central America.

This is why I work here.

This.

"And now I'd like to present my co-sponsor, the newest member of Congress and an all-around incredible man, whose dedication to improving the lives of others is reflected in everything he does. Let's give a round of applause to Congressman Parker Campbell..."

The rest of the introduction is drowned out by cheers.

Parker clears his throat. Instant silence. The man really does grab everyone's attention. He could raise an eyebrow and part the Red Sea.

"Everything Congressman Ouemann said is so important, when we look at our values and how..." The speech is smooth and pitch perfect, exactly what I would expect from Parker. At the edge of the jam-packed room, I spot two familiar heads, one covered in red, curly hair, the other platinum blonde with a new pink streak on the left. Mallory and Fiona wave, the journey across the cafe nearly impossible to make.

It's like Coachella, only with politicians.

But my friends are masters at weaving through drunk left-over hippies and Instagram influencers who don't realize they're irrelevant. In under a minute, they slice through this crowd until they're standing next to me, half behind the counter as I pull shots and smile at them.

Parker's words change, the tone setting my senses on high alert.

"I would also like to talk briefly about another bill I am co-sponsoring in the House."

Jennifer turns to him, surprised, her expression one of being impressed. Leading the crowd with good optics is smart. It's how Jennifer Tanager Campbell has made it as far as she has in political and philanthropic circles. Never elected to office, she's one of those Old Money people who finds a way to be noticed. She knows how to use expression and body language to hold the emotional and operational frame in any situation.

Parker is a pro as a result.

"In addition to the Fair Trade Literacy and Education Initiative with Representative Ouemann, we're also partnering, along with nine other House members on both sides of the aisle, on important legislation in our technologically advanced, twenty-first century world. I'm the lead on this piece of legislation–"

Jennifer glows so hard, she's a nuclear reactor.

"–which we're informally calling the Revenge Media Act."

Only a subtle twitch of the eyebrow makes it clear she has no idea what Parker's talking about.

Mallory nudges me. "Is media another term for porn?"

"*Shhhh.*"

"We're all aware of the bigger news stories around this issue, with well-known public figures and CEOs who have dealt with 'sextortion,' in which perpetrators use intimate or sensitive materials against them in an effort to gain some kind of advantage..."

"Oh my God, he *is* talking about revenge porn!" Fiona hisses.

"... and that is why I am leading a bill that criminalizes these actions with stronger penalties for sextortion, 'deep fakes' that use image alteration to create false images designed to embarrass..."

Everything turns to a buzzing sound, the edges of the room going white.

Parker is talking about making a law that increases the criminal penalties for what *he* did to *me*.

"He's either a blazing narcissist or entirely innocent," Mallory muses.

My stomach seizes. My hands shake. A copper taste fills my mouth.

Because she's right. He's either the biggest, craziest, most self-centered, the-rules-don't-apply-to-me megalomaniac, or–

Or.

Or he didn't do it. He didn't send those pictures of me to anyone else. He really is innocent.

That *or*.

That damn *or*.

In the cacophony that comes as the press pins him down, asking question after question, I can't focus on anything. Eyes dart from thing to thing, like I'm filled with hummingbirds.

Then I notice someone else is going through the same thing.

Jennifer.

Our eyes lock.

Normally, she has a veil. A filter. A cover. A wall. It's a forcefield that slides over her, as if nanotechnology had reached that point, something she could involve like moving a muscle, the subconscious kicking in to move the body.

But not now.

Now she's vulnerable and raw, struggling to get her emotions under control.

Why? Why *this*? What could Parker's announcement invoke in her to make her disassemble enough for me to see turmoil underneath?

"Holy shit," Fiona says under her breath, the sound peppered with little hitches. "He–Perky. Is it really possible Parker *didn't* do it? I mean, last night we were speculating, but this is a new level of wondering."

Mallory hits her, a gentle tap that's as strong as a gut punch. "Don't do this here. Now."

"I'm sorry." Fiona touches my shoulder. "Let's get you out of here."

"No. This is my place. Beanerino is my territory. It's my home. It's what I've poured myself into all these years since he–since–"

Just like that, I can't say it.

I can't.

Because it's truly possible he didn't do it.

And if *he* didn't do it, who *did*?

"To be clear: If you knowingly release a sexually intimate photo or video of another person for the purpose of embarrassing them or for blackmail or extortion, your actions are a *crime*," Parker concludes, the rhetorical tone in his voice making it clear he's about to end his speech and shift to another mode.

Thunderous applause fills the room, his mother's hands moving slowly, her mask back in place as she beams at him with a tight smile, the kind you use when you agree with someone but the subject is serious.

"He's doing this for you," Mallory says, her face twisted with something close to wistfulness, but with an edge I don't like. "It's a show."

"A show?"

"Why else would he come to Beanerino with Congressman Ouemann and make this big announcement?" Mallory is wearing contacts today, so as her eyes narrow with contemplation, she looks even more intense than usual. Younger, too. "He knew you'd be here–wanted you to be here. It's a plea."

"For what?"

"For you to believe him."

"Just a minute ago you said he's either a flaming narcissist or he really didn't do it. Which is it, Mal?"

"I don't know."

"I don't either," I say, turning toward the door. Fishing through my pocket, I find my nicotine gum. One by one, I pop the pieces in my mouth until Fi stops me.

"That's too much."

"If I could smoke, I'd be chaining them until I turned into a chimney."

"Don't over-nicotine yourself, Perk. The last time you did

that, your family therapist was really close to getting you to the hospital for rectal valium."

"Don't tempt me, Fi. Having someone shove valium up my ass sounds like a joyride compared to this." Pointing to Parker, who is surrounded by local news station reporters and cameras, I make a sound of disgust.

At that exact moment, he happens to look at me.

I swallow my gum. All of it.

"Perky! You can't do that!"

"Done. Did it." The bolus is stuck in my throat, just below my clavicle, and it hurts.

"Gag it up!"

"I can't do that."

"How many pieces did you eat?"

"Half a pack of Marlboro Light 100 Menthols in a box."

"That's not too bad."

I grab my triple espresso and chug it down to push the gum further along.

"Three shots of espresso *and* half a pack's worth of nicotine inside Perky," Mallory muses, studying me like I'm a lab rat. Or a bail jumper she's babysitting. "What could go wrong?"

Fiona lets out an exasperated sound and hands me a gluten-free protein bar and a small packet of beef jerky.

"What's this?"

"Your biochemistry will thank me later."

"He's good, isn't he?" I smell Saoirse before I see her, the odor of on-camera makeup so strong it cuts through the fine-brewed coffee that permeates the air I breathe.

"Yes."

"I'll take a triple espresso," she says coolly, looking at me like she's doing me a favor asking for one. I cross my arms over my chest.

"He's really good at working the crowd." We watch Parker, who is shaking hands and pressing his palm over his heart, then belly, the gestures of earnestness genuine.

Her eyes narrow. "He's good in other ways." Her smile

goes tight. "And he's headed straight for the top. He needs to be careful he's not dragged down by baggage."

"Like the load you have under your eyes?"

Reflex makes her reach up.

A stone-cold Queen Bitch heart makes her stop before touching.

"It's cute that your friend manipulated Parker into being in her wedding, but your desperation is obvious. It's not going to work," she whisper-hisses as Thiago gives me looks that say he's close to an emergency-level panic attack.

The house is packed tight.

"Persephone." Parker's voice makes me cough so hard, the wad of gum almost comes flying up out of my mouth. Instead, it sticks in my throat, a lump of despair and poor willpower.

"Asshole."

"Excuse me?" That's his mom, horrifyingly condescending to me, her eyes catching Saoirse's, the two communicating nonverbally.

"I said, passable," I enunciate. "Your bills. Both are going to help so many people in the world who otherwise would be left without justice or recourse."

A smirk tweaks Parker's lips. He knows damn well what I really said. So does Jennifer, but I'm not giving her the satisfaction of holding the upper hand.

"But if you're co-sponsoring bills that pertain to your life, Parker, why not add in an anti-stalking bill?"

Nostrils flaring, Jennifer turns away from the cameras and hisses, "I knew this was a bad idea, Parker."

"If I wanted to stalk you, Persephone, I'd have been on your ass for the last five years."

"You have a really porny definition of the word *stalk*."

Jennifer huffs off, Saoirse on her heels. Good. Mission accomplished.

He moves closer and whispers, "Last I remember, you loved it when I got porny."

"Don't do this, Parker."

"Why not?" The words come out bold and brash, cocky and so self-assured, as if he knows I'm putting up a front and desperately want him on my ass, indeed.

And the saddest part is that he's right.

But I can't let him know that.

"Because this is neither the time nor the place."

"You chased my mother off with that dirty mouth of yours. This is a great time to talk about getting dirtier."

"Congressman Campbell, you are a representative of the people."

"No. I'm just a man, Persephone. A man who wants you to give me a chance."

I swallow. Hard.

"One date."

"No."

"One *double* date, then, Persephone. One. Please. Give me a few hours to show you I'm not who you think I am. To make it up to Will and Mallory. To find a way through this with all of you."

"You know you don't want a double date. You're trying to weasel your way back into my life."

"Yes."

His candor doesn't surprise me.

"Your snow job won't work, but I'll take you up on the offer to watch you squirm trying to explain to my friends what you did."

"I'd rather watch you squirm under different circum-stances."

"You turn everything into sex."

"You used to like that about me."

"You're a congressman! You're supposed to be less vulgar."

"Have you looked at Congress lately, Persephone?" Laughter rolls out of him like tanks on a mission. Rugged and hot, he makes it hard to think.

So do the two hundred people suddenly jones-ing for caffeine.

"Perky!" Raul calls out. "We need help!"

The hiss of the espresso machines sounds like the rush of an ice-zombie army.

"Fine. One double date."

He grins.

"Don't look at me like that."

"Like what?"

"Like you got what you wanted."

"But I did."

"No. You got me to relent the tiniest bit."

"That's how conflict resolution works."

"We're resolving conflict?"

"I am."

"Then what am *I* doing?"

"Being you."

Across the room, I catch Saoirse and Jennifer in animated conversation just as Fiona whispers, "Uh oh."

"What?"

In front of Parker, she holds up her phone. It's one of Saoirse's Instagram accounts.

With a picture from last night of Parker and her, at an event, his arm around her waist, casual and loose.

His satisfied smile changes in an instant.

"I can explain."

"Don't bother."

Before I can move away from him, he's wending our way into the cooler, an ice-cold place where we mostly store dairy products. My elbow is firmly in his grasp, and it feels like I've lost seconds of my life, as if I blinked and suddenly I was in the back of the store. The cooler is the size of a walk-in closet and it's pitch black as the door snicks shut.

"Parker! What the hell?"

"I knew if I didn't contain you, you'd bolt."

"So y-y-you decided to f-f-f-reeze me in place?"

Warmth in the form of body-heated wool covers my shoulders, the scent of Parker filling my increasingly frozen nostrils as I realize he's given me his suit jacket.

Hot breath warms my ear as our noses bonk. I look up, lips grazing his, and then suddenly my hands are all over the fine cotton of his dress shirt, fingers tickling the waistband of his pants, the thick leather belt making me remember taking it off him, that one time he tied me to the bed with it, how he looked when his face shifted to intensity right before he came.

All of the memories of being naked together, of skin and tongues and heat, oh, the heat, rush through me, Parker's hands in my hair, his tongue in my mouth, his heart holding mine and begging me to let it go.

Let it pitch into his arms and trust him again.

"What are you doing?" I ask as I step back, my ass hitting the shelving, my mind spinning completely out of control.

"Kissing you."

"You're relentlessly pursuing me while you're doing Saoirse? That's a new low, even for you, Parker."

"It's not what you think with Saoirse. She invited me to some journalism event and asked me to play it up to make some guy jealous. We're old friends. Nothing more."

"Nothing is ever what it seems with you. You've spent five years telling me not to believe what I see right in front of my nose."

"What do you see now, Persephone?"

"N-n-nothing! It's pitch dark!"

"What do you feel?"

Everything.

I feel everything, Parker.

"I feel... confused. Conflicted."

"Then that's progress."

Light shines in the cooler suddenly, a very angry woman appearing in stark relief as the door opens.

"There you are!" Jennifer's chiding tone makes me feel like an eighth grader caught making out in her parents' basement. "Parker! CNN is looking for you."

"CNN can wait."

"CNN isn't going to wait so you can screw your ex-girlfriend in a coffee shop cooler. Good God, Parker, what on Earth do you think you're doing? She's tricking you into this?" Furiously looking around, Jennifer hisses, "Saoirse was right?"

"Right?" Parker shrugs back into his jacket. "About what?"

"Never mind."

"PERKY!" Thiago bellows. "HELP!"

I take my out.

I run to the front.

I become the Perfect Employee.

I pull espressos for so many hours, I subluxate my shoulder.

The pain is so much better than what my heart feels.

But you bet your ass I'm parking in Raul's spot tomorrow.

And suddenly, I know exactly how to handle Parker.

It's so simple.

I just have to sleep with him.

9

If a jellyfish covered itself in glitter and smelled like flower essences, it would be named Fiona.

Except I know better.

I know this isn't all there is to my best friend, the one I met when we were the same age as the little kids she now teaches. I remember her Doc Martens phase. Her shaved-head, henna-tattoo, baggy-jeans-held-up-by-a-rope phase. Her lean, muscle-bound phase, when she wore tank tops and looked like the "after" picture for a CrossFit gym that advertises on *Ninja Warrior* shows.

And then there was the kickboxing.

She might look like a rainbow in human form now, but she'll always be Feisty to me.

And right now, Feisty is standing at my front door holding a take-out bag from Thai Me Up, wearing a frown, the corners of her eyes covered by the enormous shell-pink glasses she's wearing.

"How can you look so sad when you have chicken satay in your hands?" I ask as I unburden her of the olfactory sensuality of an orgasm in a bag. Four orders of yellow-spice-colored grilled chicken on sticks are in there, followed by plastic containers of peanut-coconut sauce. She smells like curry, peanuts, and frankincense. The frankincense is just because Fiona is so *extra*.

Fi has come to my house to hang out.

"House" being a very fluid term. I spend some of my time in the main house at Mom and Dad's place, but this is the pool guesthouse where I mostly live, a two-bedroom cottage Dad jokingly called Kato's Chaos.

I have no idea what he means.

"Because I read your text about Parker. You *can't* be serious. You're *seriously* planning to sleep with him?"

Suddenly, the curry and peanut aroma smells like indictment.

"Yes. But I'm going to sleep with him for a *really* good reason."

Pulling containers out of the bag, I ignore her interrogation as she flops down on one of the giant soft cushions in my living room. Last year, I removed all the furniture and replaced it with enormous beanbag-like structures filled with broken coffee beans and buckwheat hulls. My house looks like a posh preschool.

And Fiona loves it.

Mallory may have the superior apartment, but my living room is a preschool teacher's wet dream.

"You're just planning to sleep with Parker so you can have an orgasm that doesn't involve batteries," she says flatly.

"What?"

"That was a vibrator joke."

I huff. "What makes you think we didn't use vibrators when we were sleeping together? Parker was *very* inventive."

The skewered chicken in her hand lowers, mouth puckering. "TMI!"

"*You* made the bad joke!"

"And you made it worse." Palm flat against her belly, she groans as she uses her other hand to guide the long, thin, pale piece of chicken toward her mouth, eyes crossing as it gets close. "And now, damn it, this looks just like a penis."

"If that looks like a penis, Fi, you're having sex with the wrong guys."

She chomps down. "I haven't seen a penis in the flesh in nearly a year," she confesses around a mouthful of meat. It's not much of a secret, because Mallory and I already know how long it's been. We track each other's dry spells the way you calculate a split check.

And we won't even mention *my* dry spell.

"Then perhaps you've forgotten, but I promise you, they don't look like *that*." I take the satay stick from her and start chewing.

"Ew!"

"And we need to get you laid."

"I want to talk about *you* getting laid. With Parker! Why on Earth do you want to sleep with him?"

"Revenge. Plus, he's got a tongue that operates with such wondrous precision, it's like he's part robot."

"More TMI. But get back to the revenge part. How is it revenge to sleep with him?"

"If I get pics or a video I can release to the media, it is."

"No. *No no no*. Perky, you can't!"

"I can. And I will."

"But he just introduced a bill to make revenge porn a *crime!*"

"Then I'd better hurry up and do it before the law passes."

"You've been carrying around this weirdly self-abusive attachment to him for five years. When are you going to let it go?"

"Weren't you the one who wondered if he was telling the truth all along?"

"I was," she admits.

"And then there's the whole Saoirse thing. She's posting pics of them together on Instagram. He's totally screwing her. He's screwing her *and* weaseled his way into Mallory and Will's wedding party. It's all a big mind game to him. Chase me down, get me hot for him, give me an orgasm, and play some sick little joke on me."

Getting over her chicken-penis aversion, Fiona gnaws on a stick and nods.

"Bet you're right," she says around a mouthful of yum. "The anti-revenge-porn bill is just a cover."

My heart sinks. I said that because a part of me wanted to hear *No way!*

Or *Of course not!*

Or *You're so much better looking than her!*

Instead, I get pragmatic confirmation of my worst fear.

Sometimes my friends are just a little too down to earth. Would it hurt Fi to shine me on a little?

Her phone buzzes. She ignores it.

"Mallory?" I ask, cracking open the subject.

A nod.

A wince.

A sigh.

"You're ignoring her, too?"

More nodding.

"At least I have an excuse. All her group texts about the wedding include Parker, but I've still got him blocked. It's a mess, but I just don't want to deal with him until I've strengthened my resolve to terrorize him with leaked sex videos."

"VIDEOS?"

"Yeah. I decided a video is way better than just a still photo. Social media algorithms really favor videos."

"Who told you that?"

"Your brother."

Fiona looks up like she's begging God for divine intervention. Either that, or she really likes my Swedish stars hanging from the ceiling. "This is an indoor hot springs conversation."

A few years ago, Mom and Dad upgraded the indoor pool to look like an underground cave. Natural hot springs don't magically run under our house–and trust me, Mom hired five different geopathically sensitive dowsers to search for anything–so instead, they went ahead with the design elements and just trucked in water from New York to recirculate in some sort of mineralized process that mimics nature.

Kind of like Saoirse's boob job.

"When you come over, *every* conversation demands the hot springs."

"That's because I have to talk to *you*."

Laughing, I munch to the end of my skewer, "Food first, mineral hot springs second."

"And your morality intervention third."

"My morality is just fine."

"Not if you're planning to stoop to Parker's level."

Bzzzzz.

"Ignoring our best friend doesn't exactly put *you* on high moral ground, Fi."

"She wants me to help pick a font for the wedding rehearsal dinner invitations! And she's talking about using Taco Cubed for the rehearsal dinner!"

We both grimace.

"It's that bad?" I gasp, calming myself with peanut sauce. It's like an EpiPen for dealing with Malzilla, the bridezilla of the North Shore.

"Pretty much. Hasn't she been bugging you about these details?"

"Only as they relate to coffee."

"That's not so bad."

"Except she wants me to find hypoallergenic civets for the Kopi Luwak coffee so that people with cat allergies can drink it safely at the reception."

"Kopi Luwak? Isn't that the coffee where the animal eats the coffee cherries off the bush, poops, and you scoop out the undigested coffee beans and brew it?" Fiona asks.

"Yes. And civets aren't even cats, but Mallory didn't like being corrected, so..."

"That's disgusting enough, but she wants *what*?"

"I got a three-page Word document from her about proteins in civets and asking whether people who were allergic to cats could still drink the coffee. She suggested I go to the CEO of that coffee chain the billionaire bought for his wife. You know, that one called – "

"She's..."

"Mallory," we say flatly, in unison.

"And the dance lessons! She's making us take dance lessons!" I protest.

"I actually like that part," Fiona says, suddenly defensive.

"You realize Fletch will be there? You're going to have to dance with him."

"WHAT?"

"The guys who are local are coming. Same with the women. So no Hasty or Raye. No Parker," I explain, voice going sad at those last two words.

"I knew Raye had to get back home, but Hasty?"

"She was invited to some mastermind in Micronesia where a Chinese billionaire built a manmade island. It's all about how to profit from climate change refugees," I inform Fi, thrilled that Mallory's overbearing sister is gone.

"Climate change *what*?" Fiona asks as she crosses her arms over her chest. "And I am *not* dancing with Fletch."

"You shouldn't have to."

"Thank you."

"Your foot belongs in his gut, not on the floor next to his."

"Stop it. I'm not that person anymore."

"Of course you are."

"No. I'm not."

"Yes, you are! The Fiona I knew in middle and high school was awesome!"

"I'm awesomer now."

"And so is Parker," I sigh, turning the subject back to him. The memory of his shoulders under my hands as we kissed makes my palms tingle. The feel of his breath on my neck. The tingling moves south. "Damn him."

"If he's so awesome, why would you trick him into sleeping with you so you can make a secret sex tape and leak it to the media to ruin his entire career?"

"And life. Don't forget the *ruining his life* part."

"Why?"

"Because that's what he did to me."

"And doing it back will make you feel better?"

"Yes! No! Wait... Damn it."

"Aha! There's a glimmer of morality in there! We have hope after all, ladies and gentlemen!" Her sigh comes out with a disturbing growl at the end. "Besides, Perk, if you make a video of him while you're having sex, you end up being exposed, too."

"I've thought of that! I'll just position the camera so you only see him and *his* naked body. Not me. It's perfect, and just like before, when I was the naked one – "

Fiona puts her hand on my shoulder. The warm, soft pressure of her palm makes me cringe. It should be comforting, right? She smells like fairy farts and popsicles on a hot summer day.

But that hand. The look on her face. I know what's coming next.

"You know what you need?" she asks, except it's not a question.

As she opens her mouth, before her tongue can form the first consonant against her teeth, I head her off. "No. Absolutely not, Fi. We are not doing the dowsers."

She shakes her head, negating my rational, one hundred percent grounded, not-at-all-woo response. "This is definitely a job for the dowsers."

"I am not sitting in a circle touching crystals and stirring herbs and holding sticks at various energy angles because I need my energy to shift. I have more than enough energy."

"All your energy comes from caffeine."

"Maybe I've invented a new form of energy. My potions don't involve eye of newt and toe of frog. They involve coffee cherry skins from Malabar and Kopi Luwak."

"You're comparing coffee to dowsing?" She's aghast.

"It's a good comparison. One involves summoning energy into your body using a shaking stick, and the other involves letting your hand shake to approximate energy."

She ponders this. "Huh. You're right in more ways than I want to admit."

"That describes our entire friendship."

"You need the dowsers. Bad."

"I need a lobotomy if I let you drag me to them. I wish my mom had never, ever let you come over the day the first one came."

"I am grateful to Tristania! It's because of her that I found the quantum healer who helped me discover my true energetic self."

"Three shots of espresso on an empty stomach can do that. And it's a lot cheaper." I grab a spring roll. "I refuse to go to your next dowsers group."

"Oh, absolutely not. I wouldn't take you back there. Not after the last time you went. You broke Janet's Y rod!"

"I thought you were supposed to use it like a wishbone. Anyway, those women were weird. Like witches."

"It's not a coven. It's just a gathering of women. But if it *were* a coven–and I'm not saying it is–you're not allowed in *my* coven of dowsers."

"Why not?"

"They all say you have bad energy."

"Hold on." It's one thing to choose not to be part of Fiona's mystical weirdness. It's another to be banned from it. "Bad energy? My energy is fine!"

"You're stuck. You can't let go of what Parker did to you."

"What does that have to do with energy?"

There goes that warm, comforting, insufferable hand on my shoulder again.

"Perky, you will never, ever find peace if you can't let go of this."

A long sigh, stretching back five years to the day I opened my phone and received the first of millions of notifications about my boobs with two dogs humping above my head, makes my ribcage expand until I am nearly levitating.

Opening my phone, I reluctantly navigate to the small folder I labeled Receipts.

Because I'm in receipt of so much pain.

Pulling it up, I tap the picture, forcing myself to look.

"Persephone," she says mournfully, "You don't have to do this."

My phone reflects the light above, the tiny flash as I rotate it for her to see like a portal to the past. "He sent *this* to the media, Fi. He thought it would be funny to send this picture to a cheesy website where some geek spread it."

We stare together at the impulsive split-second moment in my life that meant nothing when it happened. Nothing more than a laugh. A daring, bare-breasted shot of me after sex, my skin still pink with his touch, the scent of our lovemaking together filling the air. I remember how the door cracked open and suddenly Bunny and Billy, his mom's teacup Chihuahuas, leapt onto the duvet. Parker was sitting at the foot of the bed, on his knees, pointing my phone's camera at me.

And then they started humping.

Only I didn't know it.

Parker folded over, one hand on my thigh, the vibration above me making me sit up, turn around, and lose it.

We laughed together until our stomachs hurt.

But we did it *together*.

For what felt like an eternity, we created this little pocket of space, naked and sated, so comfortable with each other. We were at his mother's place in DC, the two of us staying in Parker's childhood room. The doggies were part of the household, Jennifer's pampered, precious twins, and the moment was too ripe, too delicious, too much a collision of competing interests not to be downright hilarious.

Until.

Until.

Casting my phone aside, I glare at Fi and point at it.

"Don't feed me that forgiveness bullcrap. Forgiveness is

what other people tell you is required to make *them* feel better. Not the victim."

"You are living life with a victim mentality."

"I'm more of a survivor."

"You're stuck," she says, withdrawing that hand with an irritation that makes me snap to attention. Fiona has a strange power about her. Unconditional love and acceptance ooze from her pores. To have her withdraw it means I've done something bad.

"How do I get unstuck?" I ask reluctantly, knowing the answer before she says it. It's worse than witches. Worse than labyrinth meditation. Worse than past-life regression.

Worse than master cleanses and fasting designed to achieve enlightenment.

Not that I'd know. Those programs involve giving up caffeine.

"Quantum," is her one-word answer. That's a big step up from the dowsers. It's the nuclear bomb of woo. "First we soak in the hot springs, though. Your energy grid is giving me a headache. I need to absorb soothing minerals."

"Mom has magnesium cream that can help."

She rolls her eyes. "I just like the hot springs, okay?"

"Fine. Hot springs first, woo second."

"It's all woo, Perky. You just haven't realized it yet. Science is woo people agree on, nothing more. Anyway, why not try it? You're suffering. You're stuck. It can't hurt, right?"

Darting to the side, my eyes are drawn to my phone. A bitter taste takes over my mouth, evicting the Thai food.

All right. Fine.

Quantum it is.

10

My finger shakes as Fiona drives, but I do it anyhow.

I unblock Parker Campbell's number on my phone.

I close my eyes.

I wait.

And... nothing.

Five years of blocking him has led me to imagine his texts as a pile of pent-up words all pressing against a wall I built, the pressure enormous, the sentiments pressed together like sediment to form immovable rock.

"What are you doing?" Fiona asks as we walk into Beanerino, on our way to some cottage in Westford where Fi says underground magnetic lines converge to create a clarity point that allows our healer to do her work.

"Refueling. I can't believe I let myself run out of my espresso at home."

"Not that! I know why we're here. But I just saw you on your phone with your eyes closed, pecking."

"I unblocked Parker."

A flat grimace is all I get, making the sparkle in her eyes dull, like I've unplugged her. "Oh. You're really going forward with this?"

"Forward with what? The double date he wants to have with Mal and Will?" I pretend not to pick up on her judgmental eye roll.

"You know what I'm talking about."

"My plan makes sense. It balances the energy. Isn't that what karma is all about?"

"You have a perverted view of energy."

"I have a perverted view of everything, so how is that any different?"

"Because you're talking about ruining an elected congressman's life."

"It's only ruined if he actually sleeps with me and I get it on video."

"Listen to yourself! Your amygdala terrifies me."

"You can't see it! Or even touch it! How can it terrify you?" I scoff. "And quit using Mallory science words." I wave her away like she's a gnat.

A myrrh-scented gnat.

"Your amygdala is a demented playground where bad ideas go to run themselves into the ground, unrestrained, exhausting their energy by running in erratic patterns until they wind down and finally collapse."

"That's what my mind does every night when I climb into bed. It's how I fall asleep."

"See? Terrifying."

"And also, you're getting the amygdala completely wrong. That's not how it functions," I reply, *really* sounding more and more like Mal every day.

Ugh.

"What's terrifying?" Raul asks as he starts up the espresso machine, knowing our orders by heart.

"The dark underworld of Perky's mind."

He shudders. "Oh, girl. You need a talisman? A sage stick?" he asks Fiona with a wink.

Her face splits with a huge grin, the dimmer switch inside her suddenly turned so far to the right, it's like Raul is her own personal nuclear reactor.

"Her third chakra is stuck. Won't move at all."

I hip check her. "I am seeking justice."

"You're turning it into revenge. That's not going to work well for you."

"Since when did *you* become the judgmental friend? That's Mallory's job."

Raul watches us, caramel eyes flecked with gold, the dark outer ring of his iris a boundary made stronger by his narrowed gaze. "You two are weirder than usual."

"I'll take that as a compliment," I inform him as he pours cream into Fiona's macchiato.

"Perky's out for revenge."

"Against who?"

I slice my finger across my neck. "*Shhhh.*"

One of Raul's thick eyebrows goes up. "There's a story here."

"It's *my* story," I insist.

"So now you're shy? In what universe do you not spew every detail about your personal life to every person you spend a nanosecond with?" Fiona challenges.

I open my mouth to protest indignantly.

"Date of last menstrual period," Raul recites, blinking hard. "Underwire escaped bra last week and stabbed her. Preferred brand of antiperspirant. Something about gaining weight and camel toe–" He curls his lips in and walks away.

Grabbing her hand, I pull Fi away from the counter and hiss, "I haven't told anyone here about the meme."

"You think no one who works here has ever figured out you're Two Dog Tits Girl?" The way she says it makes a minor chord explode in my head, like the beginning of every creepy horror film's final climax.

"Don't call me that!"

"I'm sorry! But that's–that's not even the worst of it. And sweetie," she whispers, complete compassion radiating out of every pore, "if you think Raul hasn't figured it out–"

"I know he has! I know everyone has! I just need to main-tain the illusion that they haven't, okay?"

Fiona frowns deeply, distracted.

She points outside to a red sedan, the kind of nice, upscale rental car you get when you're a preferred platinum member of every travel-rewards program and get upgrades for simply breathing.

Parker is getting out of the car.

"Oh, God! I cannot deal with him right now." I grab the finished drinks and hurry to the door, Fiona following in my wake.

"Why the rush?" Raul calls out.

"My ego needs fresh air."

"Perky, wait! He's coming around the–" Fiona gasps, hands on my shoulders, but I don't stop, can't stop, have to get away, ears closing off, her words dissolving into thin air. Blindly, I move, time divorced from my reality, my body just disconnected chunks of flesh that can't listen.

I shove the front door with my shoulder, twisting myself outside, and my face smashes into a t-shirt.

A t-shirt that covers a wall of muscled steel.

A wall that is now covered in splashed hot coffee.

"Oh, my God!" I shout. "I am so, so sorry!" Fortunately, Raul put lids on the coffee containers, so there's only a bit on the poor guy's shirt, but it's hot and–

"I'm fine, Persephone," says Parker, whose hand is on my hip, the other holding the door open. Coffee blends with his cologne, a whiff of shaving cream, and the all-too-familiar scent of plain old Parker.

Who is anything but plain or old.

"Did I burn you?"

Fiona moves fast, taking the to-go cups out of my hands.

"No. I'm fine. But what about you?" His fingers move, nimble and caring, to brush against the wet web of my right hand. "You look like you need to cool that down." Blowing softly on my hand, lips full, he meets my eyes.

I can't breathe.

Can't swallow.

Can't move.

But oh, how my blood can pump like an enormous fountain of lust crashing against my clit.

Bam! Bam! Bam!

My libido is the Bellagio water show, complete with flashing lights and a symphony score.

I'm wet and pulsing, all from his touch, his loose breaths and tight gaze.

"You burned him," a woman says in a low, offended tone from behind us, Parker's body going tense as a red-tipped manicured hand moves into my field of vision across Parker's ribs, over the coffee stain, a possessive grasp that makes me want to rip hair and claw eyes.

Saoirse.

Quickly, I step out of Parker's hypnotic orbit, my nether regions slow to grasp the reality of what I'm experiencing. They're together. Her hand is on his waist now.

I am just a coincidence.

They are a *couple.*

Fiona watches, eyes angry on my behalf, calculating the narrow truth of whatever we're witnessing.

"I'm fine. It's Persephone who was hurt when we collided," Parker responds, brow creasing as he frowns with concern.

False concern, I'm sure.

"If she'd watched where she was going, you wouldn't have–"

"We're just doing a newspaper interview," he says coldly to her. "No need to worry about optics."

She tilts her head, looks at him–but doesn't move her hand.

Peeling out of her hold, Parker stands before me, hands on his hips, eyes bouncing from me to Fiona. "Can I get you another coffee? Half of that one has turned my t-shirt into a Rorschach test." His laughter makes the chaotic feelings inside me all rush together, uniting in one huge, confused ball.

"I–I should be the one offering something," I say, clearing my throat around the feelings that are gathered there.

Anger is slowly building a three-story condo in the back of my throat.

"Indeed. I'll take whatever you have to give me." Eyes flashing, he turns the words into a pointed double entendre.

One Saoirse cannot let stand.

"You should pay to clean his shirt," she says smoothly, having discerned that hysteria and drama don't work on Parker. Never did.

Never will.

What works to charm Parker is connection. Authenticity. Being real and unguarded, genuine and, well...

It's hard to put into words.

How do you put magic into words? It's magic. It works outside of reason and description.

What works on Parker is the magic we had.

Have?

"I absolutely will pay to clean it," I announce as Fiona takes a sip from the wrecked cup, nonverbal signals telling me it's fine, we can go, we can leave, we can escape.

And later, we can *talk*.

Joking, Parker starts to strip out of it, his belly shown for the flash of a few seconds, Saoirse's outraged gasp enough to tell me everything.

They're really together.

She's controlling his image.

He's playing me.

So I bolt.

"Bye, Parker and Saoirse! Send me the bill for cleaning your shirt!" On my heels, Fiona's acting like a lady's maid doing the good work of serving the shamed. I pull open her car door and my phone buzzes as I sit on it, eyes cast down, ass humming.

Fumbling, I find it.

And read Parker's text. The first one allowed on my phone in five years.

See you tomorrow, it says.

Slamming the car into reverse, Fiona takes us the long way out of the parking lot, away from the building and prying eyes. The car is smooth as she accelerates, and soon we're on our way.

Away.

Which is the only direction that matters.

"I can't believe that bitch," Fiona mumbles as she makes a sharp right, two cars honking at her as she claims her lane like a Boston pro. Driving in this area is a contact sport.

And if anyone knows contact sports, it's a former kick-boxing champ.

"So it wasn't my imagination?"

"Is your imagination living in Westeros and do you have control over dragons? Because that woman needs to be flame roasted."

"They *are* together! Then why did Parker flirt with me?"

"Because he's a sociopathic pig who gets off on trifling with your emotions?"

"Seriously, Fi? *Seriously?* You think it's that bad?"

"I think it's pretty bad."

"I wish Mallory were here. We need a voice of reason. You're the woo chick and I've got a temper the size of the Green Monster. How can we figure out what Parker's up to without Mallory?"

"Call her."

"What?"

"Call her. Now." Through gritted teeth, Fiona makes another crazy turn and *bam*–we're on the road to Mallory's apartment.

"She's busy."

"I think this is a little more important than–"

Bzzzz.

I ignore my phone.

Bzzzz.

"Are you going to answer that?"

"It's Parker."

"Then *definitely* answer it!"

"All I can think about is texting him a picture of my middle finger."

"Photoshop two dogs humping above it."

The giggle starts in the back of my throat, the bitter tang of the past mingling with a sudden craving for a cigarette and a wish for Photoshop, Phone Edition.

Fiona grabs her phone, puts it on hands-free settings and gets Siri going. Soon it's ringing.

"Who are you calling?"

"Hey!" a voice cuts in. "Why are you calling me?"

"Mal? Emergency. We need you to come right now."

"That's what I just said," chimes in a deep male voice from Fiona's phone.

"Will! *Shhhh!*" Mallory says, giggling.

"Great," I mutter. "There goes the reasonable one."

"What's wrong?" Mal gasps.

"You're having sex and I'm not?" I say under my breath.

Fiona elbows me, the car swerving slightly. She looks like a cartoon character in a road race, clutching the wheel, intently focused.

"We need your brain right now," Fiona shouts as she winds the car down a narrow side road, a hedge suddenly disappearing to reveal a big swamp, all of the trees still standing but half dead at the tops.

"She's not using it. You can have it as long as I get the rest of her!" Will calls out.

"Oh, God. Turn it off, Fi. Turn it OFF."

"No, no! Wait!" Mallory says, the sound changing as she's clearly pulled away from Will. "What's wrong? Do you really need me?"

"Fiona's taking me to the Quantum Cottage."

A sound like one thousand bats being sucked into a vacuum cleaner fills the air. "She what?"

"*Right?*"

"And you let her?"

"You think I had a choice? We need you, Mal."

"Oh!"

Fiona fist bumps me and mouths, *Perfect*.

"This means a lot," Mallory says in a soft, slightly stricken voice. "You two, you know, lately, well... you do stuff together and don't invite me. I thought maybe you didn't like me as much."

"That's just for Taco Cubed. You're never allowed to eat there with us again," Fiona declares.

"But for everything else, we love you! And for this, we need your logical mind," I soothe, knowing Mal will be stung by Fiona's words, hoping my jumping in is like smoothing aloe vera on a burn.

"You do?"

"Yes."

"And you're going to the Quantum Cottage?" Trepidation fills her voice.

"It's time," Fiona says ominously. "Perky's planning to make a sex tape and we need serious intervention."

"MAKE A *SEX* TAPE?" Mallory shouts.

"SURE!" Will calls out from the background.

"*Omigod!*" she squeals. "NO! Not *us!*"

"But why *not* us?" I hear him say in a low, sexy voice that one should never, ever hear from one's best friend's fiancé, because Sex Voice is like O Face. You only reveal that to people who have mingled their juices with yours.

Even *I* have a line.

"You have ten minutes to be standing outside your apartment. And you can't smell like sex," Fiona adds.

"Why not?"

"The olfactory energy is part of the healing evaluation."

"Your quantum healer uses scent to find... auras?"

"What? No. That makes no sense."

"And the rest of this does?" Mal squeaks.

"Ten minutes!" I shout. "No Will sexfunk on you. And charge your phone! Bet it's under ten percent."

"How did you – "

"See you soon!" I shout. Fiona ends the call and looks at me.

I look right back.

"How," I ask with a long sigh, "did *Mallory* become the only one of us getting laid regularly?"

"True love."

"I want some of that!"

"I'd settle for True Sex."

Parker's chest comes to mind, the way his warmth felt against me just a few minutes ago, but then the creepy red fingernails attached to Saoirse ruin that.

And make me realize I'd settle for plain old truth.

11

The first thing I notice on Jolene's land is the hum.

"Why is everything buzzing in her driveway?" I whisper to Fiona, who gives me a blank look that makes it clear she can't hear it. We've picked up Mallory and spent the last forty minutes teasing her about her pink cheeks and relaxed body, drinking really good coffee, and musing on what Parker's balls would feel like if a rabid opossum got hold of them.

Okay. Maybe that was just in *my* imagination.

"If the opossum were rabid, wouldn't Parker need a rabies injection series?" Mallory asks, her brain clearly more focused on the science part than the revenge part.

"Did I–was I talking aloud?" I ask, burying my face in my coffee cup, taste buds screaming for a smoke.

"You muttered." Mallory fishes around in her purse and pulls out a blister pack. "Here."

It's nicotine gum. I'm dumbfounded. "You carry this in your purse? You don't smoke. Never did."

"I know."

"Then why?" The car dips into a rut. Jolene the Quantum Woo-man lives in the middle of nowhere. I didn't know Boston had suburbs with woods this thick. Her driveway is starting to feel like one of those access roads to a water treatment plant where no one goes on Friday and Saturday nights, so it's safe to hide there and smoke pot.

Not that I'd know anything about *that*.

"It's for you," she says as I take the gum gratefully and pop one in my mouth. "You left it at my apartment a few weeks ago and I've been meaning to give it to you."

"Thank you!"

"And for the record," she says with an uptight sniff, "if you're not a nicotine addict, one piece is like taking twelve NoDoz. I didn't sleep for twenty-nine hours."

"Why were you chewing my smoking-cessation gum?"

"I thought it was the regular kind!" Shifty eyes drift to the gum. "But I cleaned the apartment *so* well. Who knew you could remove the floor vents and use a Q-tip and hand sanitizer gel to get every speck of dust out of them?"

"Only you, Mal. Leave my nicotine alone."

"I promise!" She sips more coffee. "Caffeine is my favorite upper."

"What's your favorite downer?"

"Orgasms."

Fiona sighs, a sound that turns to a growl. "Can we please stop talking about all the sex you're getting? It's really unfair." There's a muddy spot in the driveway, forcing Fi to rev and lurch the car forward.

"How is it unfair?"

"Because I'm not getting any."

"It isn't a zero-sum game."

"No. It's a zero-sum orgasm, though. The sum of orgasms I'm having with anyone other than my hands and items made in China is *zero*."

I'm gobsmacked. Horrified. Chagrined and hurt. "You buy sex toys made in China? We've talked about this before! Women are enslaved in the factories!" A full-body flush takes over, all my emotions needing an outlet. Fiona's foot just went into her mouth anyway, so why not shove it all the way in and stretch those hamstrings?

Mallory and Fiona both groan. They sound like Fi and me when Mal wants to eat tacos.

"The factories use slave labor! The women are wildly underpaid to make the mushroom ridges on those jelly dildos. And the nickel in the tools is–"

"TOPIC CHANGE!" Fiona shouts. "Let's talk about your insane plan to screw Parker and make a sex tape that you'll leak to the media because you can't manage your inner emotional states and are fixated on revenge as a psychological coping strategy."

Can you tell she majored in human development in college?

"My plan is not insane!"

"*That's* the part you object to, Perk?" Mallory says with a head shake, her auburn curls a split-second behind her movement. I take a good look and realize the back of her head looks like a shredded pot scrubber.

Sexhead.

"My plan is perfectly rational," I contend as the idea of sexhead makes me think of Parker again.

"You're going to screw the guy and then ruin his political career!"

"It's not like I won't *enjoy* the revenge sex!" I sputter. "There's something in it for me. Pure pleasure."

"Why can't that be enough?" Mal questions. "Why can't you just hook up with him to see if you can work things out?"

"Because he betrayed me!"

"And betraying him right back is going to... *what*?"

"Make me feel better."

"No. It won't. An orgasm will. But not revenge."

"Would you two stop saying the same thing over and over?"

"Then stop *doing* the same thing over and over, Perk!" Mallory shouts.

"This is the opposite of what I did five years ago!" I slam the dashboard with both hands. "I was passive then!"

"*SHHHH!* Here it is!" The turn onto a dirt and gravel parking lot strip, the kind that holds three or four cars at the edge of a lawn, makes the car drop slightly, the tire settling into a deep impression that must turn into a small kiddie pool during spring rains. The land around the parking spot is rustic, to say the least.

No HGTV-obsessed owner lives here.

"Does she run an apiary? What's with all the buzzing?" I ask, my ears feeling like someone's blowing on them with a tiny fan.

As Fiona turns off the car, some of it stops instantly, but maybe twenty percent remains.

Mal and Fi look at each other, perplexed. "What buzzing?" Mal finally says.

"You don't hear that?" My ears pop, a high-pitched sound filling just one, the buzzing converted to something brasher, bolder, more specific. Looking around, I see a broken tree, glacial boulders, aged and moss-covered, the rocks jutting out at completely random spots in an overgrown yard. Every wildflower from daylilies to brown-eyed Susans to dandelions is blooming everywhere, and I really do start to worry about a giant swarm of bees or wasps.

"All I hear is you whining," Fiona grumbles.

An owl in human form greets us, descending from a small glass-enclosed deck off the house. Her thick, shoulder-length hair is grey and brown with tufts of white, and she wears big, round, black-framed glasses.

"Jolene!" Fiona gasps, folding herself into the mother of all hugs. The older woman's long hair, no strand the same color as the next, covers Fi's bare arms like a wing.

"Hello!" Jolene says with a hearty chuckle, voice firm and no-nonsense at the same time it exudes love. "How wonderful to see you again and for you to bring two insightful friends!"

Insightful?

Mallory's mouth quirks up at the comment, eyeing me like we're in on some sort of joke.

Jolene takes one look at me and goes dead still. You know why she's staring at me like that?

Because of two dogs humping on a pillow over my head.

Even Fiona's energy dowser intuitive healer has seen that damn meme.

Bracing myself, I get ready to explain.

"You hear it," she says, moving only her lips, the effect as disconcerting as the high-pitched sound ringing in my ears.

The one she knows I can hear.

"Yes."

"But you two cannot." She looks at Mal and Fi, whose eyebrows go in nine thousand directions, all of them confused.

No words comes out of her mouth about the meme. She doesn't recognize me.

At least, not for that.

"Do you live near an electrical substation?" I ask. "Because sometimes those high-tension wires–"

"Make you vibrate?"

"They hurt everyone's ears," I answer, confused about the question, pulling my hair back into a ponytail with nervous hands.

Fiona shakes her head slowly. "No, Perk. They don't." Mallory joins her, heads moving in sync.

A sudden awareness creeps over me, skin crawling as Jolene studies me, arms in the air like I'm doing the Macarena. Wise eyes take me in without judgment, though she has to be evaluating the who and why and how of me. She carries her thin frame with ramrod-straight posture, as if decades of proper training turned her into a caricature.

"Come in! Come in! Let's have some tulsi tea."

Now, my mother has steeped us thoroughly in the woo. We've had Reiki healers and witches and even a breatharian come to our house, all working to make life smooth and harmonious.

We're so well steeped, in fact, we're basically woo tea bags.

But I've never, ever actually *felt* the woo before.

This is new territory.

"Here." Jolene stops in front of the stairs up to the deck, next to a small patch of grass. She sits on the bottom step and starts taking her shoes and socks off.

"What are you doing?"

"You need to earth."

"To... earth? Earth is a verb now?"

She nods, thick hair shaking out in the wind, an agreeable entourage of keratin attached to her head. "Earthing. You're really distressed. Spending too much time disconnected from your roots."

"I am not disconnected from my–"

"Let's walk."

"Here? Barefoot? On your grass?"

"That's the point of earthing."

"What about ticks?" Mal asks. Lyme disease is endemic in our part of Massachusetts. Mallory can be anal retentive, but the question is valid.

"I have an amethyst foot bath for you when we go inside. No problem. We'll catch any that are out there."

Mallory has been out-OCD'd by the energy healer. Huh.

"Besides, the opossums do a great job in our containment zone."

Opossums?

"Containment?" Mallory gasps. Is she swooning a little?

"Opossums?" My bizarre mutterings on the drive here flicker through my mind. Why would I think about doing evil things with an opossum to torment Parker on the drive here and then have a quantum healer mention the very same obscure animal just a little while later?

Coincidence?

The second our bare feet hit the grass, I swear Mallory's shoulders drop six inches. Inhaling deeply, she tips her face to the sun. The gesture is infectious. I join her, like a group where one person yawns and the rest cannot help themselves.

And just like that, the high-pitched sound disappears.

"There you go," Jolene says, her hand on my shoulder as if steadying me. "Much better."

She's right.

I am.

One of Fi's eyebrows cocks high, as if to say *See? I told you so*.

I return the gesture, but barely holding back from using my middle finger instead of my eyebrow. I just needed to pop my ears. I'm sure that's all it was.

"Let's take a few cleansing breaths," Jolene begins, closing her eyes. All the muscles in her face go slack, the change as engaging as it is alarming. Watching other people shift their emotional states feels vulnerable.

Not for them. For me.

Instead of closing my eyes, I look at the three of them.

And *feel*.

We're standing on the grass, maybe fifty feet from the steps, a breeze blowing our hair. Mine is the color of honey, Mallory's a copper that shines like polished metal, and Fiona looks like spun sugar graces her shoulders. Jolene has the hair of a woman forged by time and woodland essence, greys and whites and browns mingling like a bird's nest.

We are all sisters of nature, the daughters of one mother who grants sunshine and rain, ticks and rainbows, wonder and torment.

Life weathers us. Time ages us. Love, though–what is love's role? It can't undo any of the bad. It can't protect us from the deep grooves experience etches into us.

What, then, is the purpose of love?

And when the hell did I become so philosophical?

As I let myself watch their faces, indulging in feelings and thoughts that are simultaneously familiar and *so* not me that I feel like another person, a deep vibration begins and centers me. My skin hums and stills at the same time. This stupid new-agey crap makes me sneer, but at the same time I am watching all of them–even the logical Mallory–communing with an energy that you can't see, touch, or taste.

Jolene is the first to open her eyes, an abrupt click that reminds me of a camera shutter opening. Pupils dilating like an aperture, she's otherworldly, making all the hair on my arms stand tall.

She does not smile. Her face does not move.

Energy between us, unnamed and amorphous, crackles.

I've felt this once before. Only once.

With Parker.

The ground I stand on is firm. The light touch of green grass beneath my feet, different depending on the season, both connects me to and divides me from the earth below. Fresh and growing in spring, summer, and fall; dry and lifeless in winter. Without saying a word, that's Jolene's message.

Revenge is death.

Moving forward is growth.

I can't, I want to say, the connection between us lost. My arms fill with pain, nerves on fire then suddenly extinguished by a force that isn't water but quenches the scorching madness. Only a familiar ache remains, holding me in the unending chaos of not knowing, never knowing.

A purgatory of Parker.

In my peripheral vision I see Mallory open her eyes, instantly registering the fact that Jolene and I are staring at each other. The wide expanse of white around her intelligent eyes gets bigger, a growing cloud that stretches across the sun. In her expression, I see the unguarded perception of someone who goes through life in a constant state of curiosity, like me.

Unlike me, though, Mallory doesn't feel this.

And unlike me, Mallory carries the scent of the love of her life in her hair, on her thighs, on the tips of her fingers.

Smeared on her heart.

"This is bullshit!" I cry out, forcing Fi to open her eyes, making all three of them face off against me like I'm an orc they must vanquish. But this isn't some female kick-ass urban fantasy where the dark, dangerous streets of an anonymous city are made safe by a spunky crew of underdogs-with-ovaries who save the day.

This is me.

This is my *life*.

And Parker Campbell just showed up in my coffee shop, my town, my world. He crashed the gates.

Saoirse in tow.

"He's relentless!" I shout at Jolene, whose expression never changes, head slightly tilted, eyes witnessing without judgment. An invitation if I ever saw one to talk and spill and get it all out.

"He won't stop trying! And he swears he didn't do it! But then he's here and he's winning Mal and Will over and there are pictures of his arm around Saoirse at one of those events where I'd be photographed by the press with my bra strap showing or get into a fight with a deputy undersecretary for international development over phthalates in flashlights and—"

"Let yourself love him."

Jolene might as well have slapped me.

Furious, I turn to Fiona and Mallory. "You brought me here for *this*?"

Slowly, with a grace and patience I'll never possess, Jolene walks across the grass, her hands kind and warm as she touches me. Magic doesn't quite describe it, but it's close. As her skin connects with mine, it grounds me. Not just the humming or the rage flowing through my veins, though.

It's like her hands are helping my swirling emotions find home.

Two fingertips go to my spine. "I don't need to do any evaluations on you, Persephone. Your pain and your energy are clear. You are stuck, here," she says, facing me, pressing hard against a spot above my sacrum, "and here."

She kisses my forehead, and her lips send a tiny shock through me.

Images of Parker flood me, except the word *image* doesn't do it justice. Words come easily to people like

Mallory, but I'm driven by something else, the rush of my body needing to move. It finds its way through time and space by touch.

A good coffee against the tongue, savored by your palate. The brush of a dandelion seed against the fine hairs of your forearm. The wink of a hot guy at a bar as you lean against the polished mahogany of the counter. The intuitive movement of your knee bending just so during sex so he can touch that place, that perfect spot as he's inside you, so he can join you there in the space you invent.

What washes over me isn't so much images as snapshots of emotion, flashing fast and furious. Like hot coffee after a hard night, a warm sherpa fleece blanket in a spot of sunshine during a nap, the stretch of muscles under a down comforter after getting sticky-sweet with, well...

Him.

Parker.

I am him. He is me. I let him in so deep, there is no core of me without him. It's empty, a hole I can fill, yes, with time. With effort. With forgiveness.

Not of him.

Of *me*.

What Jolene is telling me is that I need to give myself permission to love him. Because I do.

It's okay to love him.

I also can't let this go until I forgive myself for loving him so hard.

"THIS IS STILL BULLSHIT!" I shout at Fiona as Jolene's hands hold steady on me. This time, though, she laughs, a sound so free, I'm not quite sure it's even there.

Fiona shrugs, tears in her eyes. "This is why you're not allowed in my coven. You feel what you feel and deny it. You know the magic is there, but you repudiate it."

"No," Mallory says, her face torn by confusion and acceptance. "It's not magic for Perk. It's energy. You–you glow."

"I'm just really sweaty," I confess, airing out my damp pits.

Jolene chuckles. "If deflection were a form of energy, you would be a magnetic pole."

"Sounds about right," Mallory says seriously. "She attracts nothing but trouble and instead of dealing with her emotions, she's using revenge sex as a poor substitute."

"The word *poor* has no place in any conversation about sex with Parker."

"Let's have that tulsi tea," Jolene says, guiding us back to the house. We each retrieve our shoes. I'm suddenly self-conscious. I don't like it.

I also have a massive nicotine craving.

So what do I do? I deflect.

"What's next?" I ask as we walk up the stairs. "Voodoo dolls? I could get behind making some little felt figurines of Saoirse and stabbing them with clumpy mascara wands."

"You are a piece of work," Fiona says with a long sigh. "I bring you all the way out here to appeal to your higher self, and this is the result?"

"I never claimed to have a higher self."

"We all have one!"

"Speak for yourself."

"She's right," Jolene says pleasantly as we step into a two-story glass-enclosed solarium, like something out of a Regency novel. Or maybe the Amazon spheres in Seattle. It feels like a biodome, both modern and antique, the air so fresh. Each inhale feels like helium.

"I do not have a higher self. And if I did, it would be ashamed of me."

"For plotting to use revenge sex against Parker?"

"No. For letting myself be fooled by him."

Jolene turns on a tea kettle, taking out four steeping contraptions. Shaking loose tea that smells like basil, she apportions our drinks, then stops and gives me a penetrating look.

"You know what you need to do."

"I do?"

"Absolutely."

"What is it?"

"I can't tell you."

"You pay her for advice like this?" Mallory says to Fi out of the corner of her mouth.

"You're the one who won't let anyone position a couch under a support beam."

"Because feng shui principles make it clear that's madness!"

"Feng shui is just another form of geopathic sensitivity," Jolene says calmly. "Good to know I'm in expert company," she says with a nod to Mal, who blushes modestly.

Jolene knows how to work a room.

Am I supposed to feel two strong, contradictory forces inside me? On the one hand, I am cradling my rational mind in my cupped hands, simultaneously protective and yet also encouraging it to open itself to this possibility. Am I hearing and feeling energy no one else is?

Really?

It says no. Firmly. My mother buys into stuff like this. Not me.

On the other hand, there is a piece of me–the same damn piece that loved Parker with such abandon–with its arms open wide, facing the wind, embracing this revelation.

And the hardest part?

I'm pretty sure both are right.

Just like Parker and me.

He's here, whether I like it or not. And I do like it. Nothing I do makes him leave. His energy is in me, carried everywhere. Trying to shake him off is like wishing I didn't have my right thumb.

I can cut it off, but where does that leave me?

Bzzz.

With a look of apology to Jolene, who seems to be personally offended that I forgot to turn off my phone, I look at the screen, my finger on the power button to turn it off.

It's Parker.

Speak of the devil.

Nice seeing you today. Don't worry, I sucked most of that coffee off my shirt.

The words "sucked off" and "Parker" trip through my mind.

You sure that wasn't Saoirse doing the sucking? I type back. As I hit Send, Jolene's head jerks up sharply, as if she knows.

She can't know. I'm faced away from her.

I hold the Power button down. I see three dots on my screen as Parker concocts some sort of explanation, a denial, a *statement*.

The screen goes white, then black, before my eyes.

Like my heart.

Mallory was right. The restaurant is perfect.

A server carrying an enormous tray of chocolate and cream and cake and strawberries dodges her way around me as I walk into the small, brick-walled bistro. Mallory told me the place was basically nothing but food porn, and judging from the luscious spread I'm eyeing, the server's spin showing tiramisu and some kind of pavlova made with mango and grilled pineapple, it absolutely is.

A flash of red hair in the distance tells me Mal's already here for our double date.

She's sitting next to a button-down shirt wearing a big smile.

And yes, I'm here. I decided to attend this farce. Remember? I'm opening myself up to possibilities. Embracing uncertainty. Being expansive and namanasty and whatever…

Ok. *Fine*. I just can't stay away from him.

Plus, I have a video to make.

As the light shifts and my eyes adjust, I take in the sight of my best friend sitting with her fiancé, their hands together, fingers intertwined, the big rock on her finger gleaming in the light. They lean into each other the way that truly intimate couples do.

The casual crossing of lines between two human beings is

a sign of affinity, of trust, a sign of something more than just love.

Once upon a time, I leaned into Parker like that.

Once upon a time, I trusted Parker like that.

Once upon a time, I deeply loved him, just like that.

But that was a time long ago, and time can't be turned back.

Can it?

Whatever apology he's about to deliver tonight, he can't erase what's been done. Whatever goal he has for this double date is tainted by Saoirse. He'll say that they're not together. He'll say that he still loves me. He'll say that he never released that photo five years ago.

Parker says lots of things. It's what Parker *does* that matters. Actions speak louder than words, but only when they are authentic.

Only when they are sincere.

The anti-revenge-porn bill that he's co-sponsoring in Congress says a lot. His relentless–and I must admit, *endearing*–pursuit of me since the night of the wedding rehearsal rehearsal dinner says a lot, too.

The body can lie. It's only human, after all, right?

You know what can't lie? The heart.

And right now my heart is tap dancing under my ribs as I walk up to the booth to find Parker sitting with Mallory and Will, engaged in an amused conversation that fills me with a wistful sweetness and dread at the same time.

"Persephone," he says, standing quickly, stepping out of the booth so that I can slide in. His hand goes to the small of my back, as if we are as intimate now as we were in the past. It's also an electric gesture, almost transgressive, because my body and his body have not yet signed a treaty that defines where we can and cannot cross the boundaries between us.

"Parker," I say, turning to Mal, who stretches up for a hug. As I bend down, Parker's hand pulls away from me. The quick press of her cheek against mine makes me feel safe. I get a smile from Will, who can't reach me across the booth, and we all settle down.

Except for my heart.

Before I can say another word, the server appears. "Can I get you something to drink?" she asks in a too-chipper voice.

My eyes dart around the table. I take in Mallory's half-full glass of wine, Will's empty tumbler of something that was amber, and Parker's half-full pint of dark beer.

"A dirty vodka martini with three olives," I say.

She asks which brand of vodka, and when I name it, Parker chuckles. As the server skitters away, I turn to him.

"Something funny?"

"That's a brand made in Texas," he says with a slow drawl. "It's made from corn, gluten free." His parents weren't from Texas, so Parker doesn't have the accent ingrained in him, but he was born there. It comes out sometimes, a cadence that slips easily into his speech, from a culture so strong that it claims you forever.

My heart skips a beat.

It slips, too.

He moves, man-spreading slightly, shifting in the booth. His right thigh brushes against my left, and then he pulls back away, leaning with a casual elbow to the right.

"When did you start drinking dirty vodka martinis?"

Mallory looks at me as I answer with a laugh that doesn't reach my eyes, "The night you came into town."

"And there it is," he says simply, hands going flat on the booth.

A chill cools my skin, though it's not from fear. Even discomfort doesn't quite explain it. Mallory and Will go still. We're in close quarters, fully formed adults now, and the two people across from me are really in it with us.

I don't have to hide. I don't have to fake any feelings here. And neither does Parker.

"I've already apologized," Parker says, and those words coming from any other man's mouth would have a defensive tone to them, produced by bruised ego combined with salty regret. The server interrupts, appearing with my martini and sliding it onto a printed coaster right in front of me.

I do a double take at the logo.

The Energy Master, it says, with a small lightning bolt right under the edge of my glass.

Martini glasses are simple cones, but this one looks like a piece of Art Nouveau, a thin line of blue glass swirled in curlicues around the edge. The liquid inside is smoky, three fat olives with pimentos peeking out in a flash of red, like a bullfighter urging on a bull.

I'm ready to charge deep.

"And I'll apologize again," Parker continues after the server leaves, my mouth already tickled by the perfect blend of olive brine, vodka, and vermouth. The sip goes down smooth, like ocean water.

Like drinking tears.

Five years' worth.

There's a pause, a chance to catch my breath, as all of us take a moment to sip, to look away, to turn inside and regroup.

Then Parker says, "But I regret nothing."

Tapping on the edge of his glass, Will's first knuckle makes a thumping sound, fast and muted, like the underbeat of a song. He stops abruptly and looks at me.

Not Parker.

"How did you two meet?" he asks, prompting Mallory to sputter slightly. His obvious ploy for breaking the tension is a little *too* obvious.

Will's question is genuine, though. His blue-green eyes meet mine, the color of a dark robin's egg. Mallory wasn't the only girl in high school with a crush on him.

And for the record, the rumor someone started that I stole his jockstrap in ninth grade and huffed it every night was just a *rumor*.

In the seconds before I look away, I see all the Wills. This is what's wonderful about having lifelong friends. I see ninth-grade Will with broad shoulders, long, lean arms, and a self-assured walk. Twelfth-grade Will, the burst of testosterone adding muscle, the scruff of beard, the squared jaw, and the confidence to hold the frame in any situation.

Twenty-eight-year-old Will last year, returning to town, walking back into Anderhill to take over his parents' real estate company after his father's cancer scare (and, thank goodness, recovery).

And Will now, my best friend's fiancé, asking me this totally normal question.

"We met in jail," Parker answers simply.

I nod.

What? It's the truth.

"Which one of you was behind bars?" Will asks politely, cutting his eyes to Parker, who chuckles.

"Guess," I say, drinking half my martini, the crisp, cold mouthfeel grounding me.

"What were the charges against Perky?" Will asks, not even pausing to think. "Something involving assault, Skip? Er, I mean, Parker?" A rue head shake follows the slip of name, reminding me that Parker's had five years of experiences away from me. People know him who I've never heard of. He's a congressman for goodness sake.

And he's here. With me. With my bestie and her guy and we're being so *normal*.

Other than talking about me being in jail and all.

Squinting, Parker scratches his chin, a devilish smile making the pause feel delicious. Or maybe that's the martini. My mouth fills with salt and memory.

Olives always evoke sophistication, smooth and full. I can't really taste the vodka but it gives me liquid courage, a soul sister supporting me as I mourn for a relationship I never had.

But could have had, if life had been different.

If *Parker* had been different.

And what I really, desperately want more than anything (except Parker) is a damn cigarette. Olives may represent a worldly, cosmopolitan layer of life, but a nicotine stick gets shit *done*.

"If I recall correctly," he answers, "the charges against Persephone included unlawful assembly–"

"We had a permit!"

"–and you ignored the police order to disperse."

"WE HAD A PERMIT!"

Will's eyes light up with amusement. Mallory drains her drink and waves the empty glass in the air to signal the server.

"Resisting arrest–"

"We went limp! How could we be resisting when we exhibited the clinical signs of hypotonia?"

His hand goes to my knee, the fingers spread, a light touch meant to convey familiarity. To bridge a gap.

To right a wrong.

"They brought thirty-seven of you in that night. All detained in a cell intended for ten prisoners."

Squeeze.

"Back up, back up," Will says, laughing. Stretching his arm across the back of the booth, he pulls Mallory in, as if settling in for a story. "What were you protesting?"

Parker's hand doesn't move. I don't want it to move. I've spent five years not touching him. Now he's touching me. If I slough him off, if I shift away, if I scooch a few inches to the right, I break the contact.

I can't. It's as hard to separate as it would be to stop breathing.

Feeling energy others can't detect is my superpower, right? Jolene basically said so yesterday.

Who renounces their superpower?

"She was protesting the use of slave labor to make the AlwaysDoll," Parker says somberly.

A snort comes out of Will, casual and free. Normally, he's a fairly controlled guy, so maybe the alcohol loosened him up.

"You got arrested because of a *sex doll*."

"No! I got arrested because of the working conditions greedy corporations inflict on their female workers. The red dye on the dolls' lips contained lead! Can you imagine sticking your face in a set of labia two thousand times a day, day in and day out?"

Parker's grip on my knee tightens.

Will looks at Mallory. "I can," he says solemnly, nodding.

The hand on my knee is attached to a man who is shaking slightly, trying to control his laughter.

"You assholes," I mutter as the server appears with another glass of wine for Mallory.

"Perky was looking for a purpose after she graduated from UMass and her trust fund kicked in," Mallory says suddenly, eyeing me like she's decided to go for it and spill my secrets for my own good.

"Who wouldn't?" I ask, drinking a bit more.

Will frowns, as if the bridge of his nose is reacting to something but the rest of his face can't quite agree. "The lottery money?"

I nod. "I never have to work again. And it was unearned. I have an obligation to help people who can't help themselves."

"That sounds very noblesse oblige," Parker replies. I look up sharply, expecting a smirk, but instead I get a sort of admiration that shakes me.

"We're not exactly old money here, Parker. Not like you. Your mom's family has had money from the days of trading fake beads with the natives."

"The Tanager name carries its own set of obligations. Just like your lottery money." He finishes his beer and as he sets down the glass, his wrist angles down, flashing a Blancpain. Unlike most guys our age, Parker still wears a watch. A long time ago, he told me it conveyed seriousness to the older men he worked with. Gave him the gravitas a new law school grad really needed.

I also know it was a college graduation gift from his mom, handed down from his great-grandfather.

"Money is a weight," Will adds. "Managing Mom and

Dad's company comes with plenty of privileges, but responsibility, too."

"When you're me, being arrested is a form of privilege."

Eyebrows shooting up, Will cocks his head and gives me a look without saying a word.

His expression demands an explanation.

"I have money. I work in a coffee shop for fun. I don't need my paycheck. I feel guilty."

"So you protest and get arrested out of guilt?"

"Not only that, but sure–it's part of it. I have the luxury of being able to go out on the line and fight for the rights of people who can't do it for themselves. I won't lose my kids or my job if I'm arrested."

"That is crazy," Parker says, the hand on my knee stiffening. I remember these arguments from five years ago, our nine months together fraught with conflict over this one issue.

"You think the best way to defend the rights of others is to do it from within the system," I say lightly but seriously.

"And you think that shaking up the system is the only way to enact change."

"Tastes great," Will says.

"Less filling," Mallory laughs.

"We're never, ever going to agree on this, Parker," I say to him, moving my hand over his, patting it.

Until he flips his hand, grabs mine, and holds hard.

"That's what makes being with you so interesting, Persephone," he says, looking me in the eye.

The server sets down a basket of focaccia with caramelized onion, pan-seared rosemary, and salt chunks on top, breadsticks, and some sort of multigrain bread with whole pepitas in the crust. She drizzles olive oil onto a small plate, then leaves quickly. Mallory digs in. I can't touch it, of course.

And then she adds a smaller plate, with a different kind of bread, the plate lined with a red circle around the edge. "This is gluten-free," she says, offering a small separate dipping bowl for oil.

"Thank you," I say, grateful my friends said something to the server before I even arrived.

"We get a lot of ribbing for being together," Will says to Parker, jolting me out of my thoughts.

"We do?" Mallory enquires, holding her head in the universal gesture that warns guys to watch the next words out of their mouth.

Parker's smirk deepens, but Will? Will forges on.

"*I* do. You know. Hometown girl and guy, high school sweethearts, the whole nine yards."

"You have people claiming we were high school sweethearts?" Her voice notches up. Will takes a piece of focaccia and dips it in oil. I do the same, stifling a moan. Flavor explodes on my tongue, the top of the crust brushed with a roasted garlic concoction you don't see, only taste.

Parker, who isn't stupid, just leans back, ready to be entertained.

"Sure. And Philippe takes credit for bringing us together all the time, after we went to that dance lesson together at Bailargo on your failed dance date."

Parker grins. "What is a 'failed dance date'?"

"Don't ask," I whisper out of one side of my mouth.

"Perky made me sign up for a dating site. I met this guy named Dave, who asked me to a dance lesson for our first date, at a dance studio called Bailargo. It seemed like such a fun idea. Turns out, Dave is a salesperson for the corporate owners of Bailargo. He invites women on first dates, then stands them up and hopes a percentage of them will convert to paying customers," Mallory explains, mouth twisting with bitterness.

"That's genius!" Parker exclaims.

"Right?" Will chimes in. The side of his body next to Mallory jolts suddenly. "Ow!"

"You deserved that," she says with a growly sigh. "It's NOT genius," she adds pointedly to Parker. "It's cruel manipulation of a lonely woman's emotions."

"Right. Terrible," Parker adds with a grin. He looks at Will. "Why were *you* there?"

"My sister was getting married and I needed dance lessons."

"What a coincidence."

Will gives Mal a loving look. "The best."

"Who else ribs you for our being together?" Mal asks him.

"Mrs. Philomena claims she knew all along."

"She was our ninth-grade English teacher. How would she know?"

"She and her husband run that little farm stand on the north side. My mom thinks their raw honey is quaint," Will explains, digging the hole deeper. "I got an earful when I went there last week."

"Earful?"

Maybe Will's not so smart after all.

"You know." Will reaches for his glass of water and takes a sip, eyes unfocused, clearly trying to craft his answer carefully.

"No. I don't know." Mallory rests her chin on one hand. "Tell me."

"Are you blushing, Lotham?" Parker asks, leaning on the table. He's the masculine version of Mallory as he rests his chin in the web of his open hand, grinning with a deep amusement that carries so much sex appeal for me that I'm the one who blushes, hard and fast.

Between my legs.

"She said I should have dated you long ago. Back in high school. That I let you get away and I was damn lucky some smart local boy didn't snap you up."

"I always liked Mrs. Philomena."

"You hated her in high school!" I bark, amazed to hear Mal lying. "She's the one who never gave you a hundred on any of your papers."

"She never gave *anyone* a hundred," Will says bitterly.

"What you're saying," Mallory interrupts in an arch tone,

"is that lots of people in town think you're an idiot for not noticing me sooner."

"I noticed you," he says without protest. "I just..."

"What?"

"I left. I was gone for ten years."

"Were you planning to look her up when you came back?" Parker asks, invested in the conversation, feeding Will an easy lie if he needs one.

"Yes."

Mallory blushes. "No, you weren't."

"We talked about this. Remember?"

She blushes harder. That means they talked about it in bed.

"We'll never know. We met on that porn set, and the rest is history."

Parker snorts. "This, I've got to hear. I don't know anyone who has a relationship story that starts with, 'We met on that porn set.'"

"You two met in jail!" Mallory protests.

"But they're not together," Will points out helpfully, his words turning my heart into a lump of lead.

"Where are the menus?" I ask, needing to talk about anything but the fact that Parker and I are not together.

"We already ordered," Parker explains.

"What? How did you know what I want?"

"Salmon on a cedar plank, cooked medium, with roasted root vegetables and a sweet potato-fig puree," he says smoothly. "Made gluten free."

Drool forms in my mouth. The fact that he remembers my celiac disease makes me choke up a little. I suddenly understand the special bread plate.

"How did you–but I–well, damn," I say, shoulders dropping. "You *did* know what I want."

He leans in. "And I would love to always give you what you want."

On cue, the server appears and sets our plates before us, the luscious scent of Tuscan herbs tickling my nose and making my stomach groan for deliverance. My plate has that same red ring around it, a clear sign of a kitchen accustomed to food allergies. The added little extra touch makes me feel vulnerable and cared for at the same time.

Safe.

Our hands have to untangle, the cool air that rushes in at the absence of Parker's touch a relief.

For the next ten minutes, we eat and make appreciative sounds, Mal offering Will a bite of her chicken, Will declining. At no point do Parker and I offer each other anything.

We already have.

An olive branch has somehow been extended under the tabletop.

I'm just not sure who extended it to whom.

"How do your parents like Will?" Parker asks Mallory as we slow down, each of the four of us taking random bites of food.

"Dad loves him. They watch Pats games together." Mal wrinkles her nose. "Gives Mom and me a chance to go to the movies. And Mom adores Will. *Adores* him."

"She just wants grandbabies with my color eyes," Will says, clearing his throat.

"She actually said that to you?" Mal gasps.

"Sure. Complete with a wink."

"Sharon isn't subtle," I groan sympathetically, Mallory giving me a look that says, *Can you believe this?*

"Your mother hates me." My statement is a toss off as I nudge Parker.

It's also true.

"Hate isn't the right word. My mom doesn't *hate* you," he adds, but his words are diplomatically anemic.

"Fine. Loathe."

"She does not loathe you. She just–"

"Wants to see me eaten by a civet, shat out, cleaned off, and roasted, to be sold as Persephone Whole Bean coffee?"

"That's not exactly what I was going to say."

"But I'm close, aren't I?"

"You and my mother actually have a few pieces of common ground."

"Like what?"

"Coffee. A passion for fairness for workers."

"And you," Will points out.

Parker sighs. "Mom has her own ideas about who she wants in my life."

"Your mother has a rigid construct for what she wants your life to be," I correct.

"I'm my own man."

It's the way he says it that melts me. I stop, putting my hand on his forearm. "I know you are, Parker. You've never been the kind of person to change who you are just for her."

"Thank you." The tightness in his voice gives way. "I don't need your validation, but I won't turn it away."

"Of course you need my validation. Everyone needs my validation. The Perky Seal of Approval makes careers. Lives. Empires." I give him side eye. "Campaigns."

"I wish your validation included trusting me, Persephone."

"Excuse me," Mallory says suddenly, hip checking Will. "I need to go to the ladies' room."

They both get up, Will giving Parker a look. He goes with her toward the restrooms, leaving us alone.

"I wish for a lot of things, Parker. Doesn't mean they happen," I say through gritted teeth.

"You have total control over believing me."

"I wish that were true."

"What does that mean?"

"I—sometimes I want to trust you. To push away the horror of what happened. To think that it wasn't your fault. But I can't."

"You can."

"I can't."

"You mean you *won't*."

"It's—"

He turns to me, a tilt of surprise in the way he moves.

Something in my tone makes him react with less of a shell, the armor dropped a half-inch for reasons he doesn't quite understand logically, but reacts to emotionally.

And I get it–because that's me right now, too.

"–it's not simple."

"Quit deflecting. Tell me what you really think."

"Really?"

"Of course."

I take in a long breath and ask, "Do you remember that time I sucked you off so hard, you broke a bunch of blood vessels right on the tip of your cock and we called you Purple Mushroom for a month?"

"Wasn't expecting you to say *that*," he coughs.

"It's what I'm really thinking."

"I like how you think." His eyes drop to my lips, then he smiles, eyes wrinkling with amusement and memory. "Purple Stephanie gave me a Purple Mushroom."

Giggles consume me. I can't blame the martini, because I only had one.

"I still have the hat you ordered from the handmade crafts website, embroidered and all." He winces. "And a visceral memory of a week of chafing and pain."

"Worth it, though. Best orgasm you ever had."

"Until the next one with you."

I lose all of the air in my lungs, all the blood in my head, and all the will to hate him in a single gasp.

"I was on the campaign trail in a little town called Piddlewick, Texas," Parker begins, looking away. "And there was a restaurant called The Purple Mushroom."

"You're making this up."

He puts his hand over his heart and looks at me. "Not making it up."

"Liar."

"Do you want to hear the story or do you want to be right?"

"I can have both!"

"No, you can't. One or the other."

"What if you tell the story and it turns out I'm right? Then I do get both."

"After the fact, Persephone. Right now, you have to choose. Say you believe me before I finish."

"Fine." I cross my arms over my chest, not in defiance but so he can't see how hard my nipples are right now. "I believe you."

"If you believe my story about the Purple Mushroom restaurant in Piddlewick, Texas, why can't you believe me when I tell you I never sent that picture to anyone?"

Oh, no. I've walked into a trap.

I rally, fast.

Looking away, I say lightly, "Because I've got nothing to lose. If you're lying about a restaurant, my life isn't ruined. My heart isn't shredded to pieces, blowing in the wind like ribbons caught on an electric wire. Like a balloon that popped long ago."

So much for the *lightly* part.

"I didn't do it."

"You didn't eat at a restaurant called The Purple Mush-room in Piddlewick, Texas?"

"Actually, I did." Sad eyes meet mine. "It made my dick hurt the entire time, but I ate there."

"Why?"

"Why did I eat there, or why did my dick hurt?"

"Both."

"There you go again, wanting both."

"And there you go again, questioning–"

Before I realize what's happening, his hands are on my waist, my fingers are in his hair, and he's kissing me. My mouth melts against his, bodies awkwardly twisted in the booth, the tight space both intimate and constraining. Hip to hip, we turn toward each other, but still face forward, desperately trying to connect but the structure is working against us.

I taste the past in his kiss. I taste apologies and regrets, questions without answers, the fine-grooved sense of time making me relax and tense up at the same time. Meaning doesn't matter in this brief flash of touch. What this kiss *means* isn't important.

That it's happening at all *is*.

"Before they come back," he asks, smoothing my shirt sleeve, forehead against mine, "promise me you'll go out with me. On a real date. Not like this." Nudging his head toward the other side of the booth, he gives a wistful grin. "Mallory and Will are great, but I want you to myself."

"What about Saoirse?" I ask, the words escaping before I can reel them back in.

He tenses.

"What about her?"

"I see you in the news. The pictures with her."

"How many times do I have to tell you there's nothing going on there?"

"How many times do I have to ask because–"

His fingers press against my lips, eyes beseeching, begging–no.

Demanding that I believe him.

"One date. That's all I ask. Let me convince you."

"Convince me? Of what?"

"That it still matters, Persephone. It matters that we're still in love with each other. Whether you admit it or not."

I stand abruptly. "I can't do this. Not here. Not trapped in a booth with you." At that exact moment, both of our phones buzz.

"Come here," he says, standing, reaching for my hand and tugging me out of the booth, around a few tables, and into a dark hallway. We stand in front of the door to the women's room.

"Oh, no. I'm not falling for that again," I say, but suddenly, I have an *aha!* moment.

Maybe coat-closet sex is exactly what I need.

Complete with phone in hand.

Now's my chance.

"I just want to talk. Every time I try to get you to talk about how you feel, you shut me out."

"All you do is try to kiss me!"

"You're the one kissing me," he counters. "Not that I'm complaining."

I take a chance and open a door. It's a small storage room, dry goods on wide, tall shelves. I pull him in. A motion-sensor light comes on.

Perfect.

"Look," I say, emotions warring with my plotting brain, eyes darting all over the place as I try to figure out how to hold back the burning, greedy arousal in me, give in to it at the right moment, and manage to record this.

Whatever *this* is about to be, I know one thing:

I need to record it.

My question about Saoirse casts a pall over the moment, a bitter sense that everything's slimy and not quite clear. Why is she around at all? She makes me suspicious, and when I'm suspicious, I go into lockdown mode.

And then I get stupid.

Bzzz.

Our phones buzz again.

"Ignore it." His kiss gives me a headrush, the worry about Saoirse evaporating as his intent comes through loud and clear in his touch, his tongue, the way he holds me.

"I can't!" I lie, grabbing my phone. I've downloaded a special app for this, one that I can activate by voice commands, but suddenly–I can't do it.

I can't trigger Record. Can't say the words.

Fiona and Mal will be so proud of me. When push comes to shove, I just...

Can't.

I set the phone down on the metal-grid shelf behind me, propped up on the vertical bracket. There's no shelf above it, the space to the ceiling empty, clearly storage for enormous boxes. A lower shelf digs into the middle of my back as Parker stares at me, chest rising and falling, eyes taking in my face, my neck, the tops of my breasts–

All of me.

"You kiss me, Persephone. You let me touch you. But you're not *hearing* me." The air feels heavy. Charged and crackling, but with an intense feeling that's less playful.

The stakes are higher.

"I hear you."

"I don't want to just screw you. I want to love you. I want to talk to you. I want to... *everything* with you."

"Why?"

"You know why." He moves forward until my ass presses into the edge of the shelving. His hips are against mine, his hands on my shoulders, and he's sucking his lower lip in. "You feel it, too."

"I always feel this with you," I murmur. "Always. But why me? I'm scary and unpredictable and I'm weird and chaotic and–"

His mouth shuts me up. Ending the kiss, he presses his forehead against mine and whispers, "And you're always genuine. Never fake. I need how real you are. I need it in every cell of my body. Why you? Here's your why." My arms encircle him, the familiar leather belt making an image in my mind, and suddenly, I'm lifted up, my ass on the shelf, Parker leaning over me with powerful hands that know exactly how to possess me. Pushing against me, he half hovers, mouth on my breasts as he pulls my silk shirt down enough to take one nipple in his mouth, shifting my body.

Ka-thunk. Something next to my ear falls. I don't care.

I don't care because I'm with Parker and he smells so good, his head right below my chin, my hands on his broad shoulders. While the nice suit jacket he's wearing makes what he's doing with his mouth feel sophisticated and oh, so dirty at the same time, I wish I could reach down and touch the marbled skin of his bare shoulders.

"Hey. Seri–" he says, kissing me, voice dropping to a whisper. "–ously." Another kiss. "Record this in your heart. On your skin. Everywhere inside you. I just want you."

He rises up and slides his hands under my ass, lifting me and pushing me back, splitting my legs so fast. Something is under me as his fingers linger along my inner thigh, coming to the thin slip of panties that he pulls aside, soaking wet, all for him.

And then his tongue replaces his fingers and I arch up, his hands pushing my skirt up with an almost savage motion, my panties pulled down and off, his mouth on me again as he pairs the sensation with a finger, then two, inside me.

"Oh, God," I moan, fingers in his hair, cold steel on my ass as I lower my hips. With his free hand, he slings my right leg up over his shoulder, the changed angle moving my whole body to a new layer of sensation. What we're doing is so indecent, where we're doing it is so illicit.

And so *perfect*.

He's going down on me in a restaurant supply closet and as my abs clench and his tongue takes me up, up, up, I just want to live here forever.

Slowly, with aching precision, he moves his fingers in that curling, pumping motion he perfected five years ago. Color explodes behind my closed eyes and I am soaking his mouth, his hand, the shelf, my ass bucking against him. Whatever is under me slides, too, with a metallic sound, but water rushes in my ears like an Amazon rain and I am gritting my teeth, flushed with pleasure, riding and riding the wave of what Parker is doing to me.

He pauses, mouth still just as I'm about to come–*hard*.

"You like this?" he asks, the question nothing more than a cruel tease. I hate myself for needing more, but I do. If Parker doesn't get that tongue back on my clit right now, I'm going to die. Craving nicotine has never felt anywhere near as bad as this.

"Yes," I gasp.

"So do I. I've wanted to do this every day for the last five years, Persephone."

And then he finishes me off with three strokes of his tongue, three strokes of his fingers, and three strokes of the clock.

Wait. There's a *clock*?

As I come so hard, my mind holds two realities–the sins of the flesh and the sins of the phone. It's beeping, the sound right next to me, and I lose momentum, foiled by my own devious plan.

Distracted from the best orgasm of my life by my own need for revenge.

Damn it.

"What's that?" he asks.

"My phone."

"Why is it beeping?"

Knock knock knock.

"Seriously, guys? AGAIN?"

"Mallory," I hiss, pushing Parker away with my knee, sitting up fast. My left ass cheek, bare against the shelf, is resting on my phone.

I carefully climb down, aided by a gentlemanly hand from Parker. The movement pushes my phone to the ground, and I'm thankful for the rubber flooring. A light flashes as it falls, face down.

What the hell was that beep?

Parker wipes his mouth with his palm, laughing eyes meeting mine. "*Shhhh,*" he says, pressing his finger to lips that would taste like me if I kissed him.

Which I won't.

Because if I do, I won't be able to stop.

Bending down, I retrieve my phone and shove it in my skirt pocket, hitting the power button to stop it from pointing fingers at me.

The door opens. Mal and Will are standing there.

"Is this a fetish?" Will asks. "Not judging you two, but this is a pattern. If every time we go to a restaurant with you guys, you're going to have sex in a closet or a cooler or a coat-check room, we just need to know."

"We were talking," Parker lies.

Mal sniffs the air. "Mmm hmm. Smells like 'talking' in here."

"I smell none of our business," Will says, backing her out.

Taking in a deep breath, I decide I smell something, too.

The scent of confusion.

The scent of an abandoned plan.

And the sound of my heart, trying to sort out truth from wishes.

❧ 13 ❧

"**W**hy are we here, again?" Fiona asks as she sips the coffee I've just made her at Beanerino. It's the morning after my impromptu sexfest with Parker on our double date. I was too scared to look at my phone last night, so I've been waiting for this moment.

"To watch the sex tape Parker may have made with me yesterday."

Mallory's jaw does the O thing. "You were *recording* when you were having sex at the restaurant?"

"You had sex in a restaurant?" Fi squeals just as Raul walks by.

"In the supply closet," I clarify. "It was private. And the sex tape was an accident."

"You are hereby restricted from *our* supply closet," Raul declares.

"What? You can't do that!"

"Does Perky even know where your supply closet it?" Mal asks. "She never fills the sugar or cream or sleeves on her own."

I punch her arm as Raul fistbumps her. "Hey! And besides, we're not talking about that. We're talking about the sex tape!" I hold out my phone. Terror rips through me. "I didn't mean to do it. I think it's all Parker's fault."

Fiona and Mallory freeze at the same time, then look at each other.

"And how is it *Parker's* fault?"

"So, first of all, you need to know *I* did not record this. At all." I put my hands up in a defensive gesture.

"The recording fairy magically sprinkled dust on you while you screwed in a restaurant supply closet and that's how you have the video?" Fiona cracks.

"Basically."

"Ha ha. That's impossible."

"Says the woman who uses a dowsing rod to find free parking."

"That's energy, not fairy dust!"

I cue up the video on my phone. "All I know is, I did NOT record this. And there's a fifty-seven-second video on my phone. We were having sex and the phone suddenly beeped." I start to hit Play.

"Oh, no," they say in unison.

"She wants us to *watch* it," Mal groans.

"Of course I do! I can't do it by myself. I don't know what's on here!"

"How would Parker record it? Did he touch your phone? You think he's setting you up by recording sex on your phone?"

"I've thought about our conversation in the supply closet when his head went between my legs, and–"

"You talk during sex?" Mal asks.

I glare at her. "–and at one point, he said, 'Hey, *seri*ously.'"

"Aaannd?"

"I think it made Siri wake up. And then he said something that had the word 'record' in it."

"Parker's a formal talker, isn't he? Most guys just grunt about where to put your pinkie and call you by the wrong name," Fiona mutters.

"You are seriously screwing the wrong guys, Fi," Mallory chides.

"See! *Seriously* sounds like *Siri!* It's all Parker's fault!"

Mallory pulls out her phone and starts tapping. Eyes bouncing all over the screen for about ten seconds, she finally stops, giving me a troubled look.

"A quick Google says Perk might be right. There are voice-activated recording apps, and the sequence of words could trigger an app to start up, but–"

"You had a plan to get him on video, Perky, and now you have the video, but you're saying *you* didn't make it?" Fiona asks, clearly not believing me.

"Exactly! This is not my fault!"

"This is totally your fault," Fiona chastises.

I stick my tongue out at her and hit Play.

Mal covers her eyes.

Fiona leans in.

At first, it's just darkness, a handful of words between us audible but muffled. Parker's voice says what sounds like *heart*, then something else, then *want you*. Then the phone scrapes, a sudden, jarring movement. More shadowy motion, then the unmistakable sounds of two people getting it on.

Mallory plugs her ears.

Another scraping sound. More darkness.

And then some light.

"What is that?" Fiona asks, peering intently.

"Us! Having sex!"

"It looks like a spider."

"What?"

Her fingertip touches the screen. "See? Maybe you filmed a hairy spider in the supply room? Were there cobwebs?"

"No! That's me and Parker!"

"Oh, God," I groan on the video.

"Huh. That's *definitely* you guys having sex," Mallory announces. "Hear all the moist sounds?"

I shudder. "Don't say the word 'moist.'"

"Calm your *tits*," she replies.

Raul shuffles over and looks at my screen.

"What are you watching?" he asks.

"Perky made a sex tape."

"You know the rules, Perky! No pornography at work!" He's outraged.

"You never said anything about my *own* sex tapes."

"We shouldn't have to specify!"

"But you didn't. Plus, I'm only banned from watching pornography at work on a laptop. Phones weren't in that agreement."

"That is definitely a spider," Mallory concludes, finger on the screen like Fiona's. "See the fuzziness? It's hairy, and it–"

Raul stands up straight, hand over his chest. "That is not a spider."

"What is it?" Mal asks.

"That is a starfish."

"A what?"

"A starfish," he says in a strange gagging voice as he walks away.

"What does he mean, starf–"

"Are you kidding me?" Fiona groans. "Perky! You filmed your *butthole* the entire time."

"My *what*?" I try to grab the phone but Mallory and Fiona suddenly engage in an infuriating version of Monkey in the Middle.

"OMG!" Mallory snorts. "That is totally a butthole. I can see it now." She strokes the screen as Fiona holds it where I can't reach. "See the outline of the–" A mortified expression covers her face as she snatches her finger away, holding it like it's contaminated.

"*I* didn't film it! *Parker* filmed my butthole!" I screech.

"What did Raul mean by 'starfish'?" Mallory persists in asking.

"Brown starfish," Fiona explains.

Mal's blank expression makes it clear how she ended up on a porn set last year after applying for a fluffer job, assuming it was a real estate industry term for a house stager.

"That," Fiona says, finger quickly withdrawing from my

phone screen, "is fifty-seven seconds of nothing but Perky's bare asshole."

"Why would you record your butthole?" Mallory asks me, head tilted, red curls covering her shoulder like she's protecting it from my video.

"I didn't intend to! It wasn't me! I did not film my own butthole! WHO VOLUNTARILY MAKES A SEX TAPE OF THEIR OWN BUTTHOLE DURING SEX?"

"Apparently, *you* do," Mal says with a shrug.

Fiona cuts in. "Is this an aspect of the restaurant-sex kink you and Parker have? Is ass play–"

"An aspect?" Mallory giggles. "Get it? ASS-pect?"

I snatch the phone back and watch. They're right. Raul was right. That's nothing but a recording of my actual butt-hole. It clenches in solidarity.

"And someone needs a waxing session. Stat!" Fi says dryly.

"Hey! Don't judge my bits!"

"Your butthole looks like it could compete in a beard contest."

"And win," Mal adds.

"You two are such assholes!"

Mal slings her arm around Fiona and smirks. "Then take a video! That seems to be your YouPorn category."

I power my phone off and sigh. The memory of Parker's mouth and hands on me makes me shiver.

Fiona appears to be deep in thought before catching my eye. "Isn't this the second time Parker's given you an orgasm in a restaurant and you've left him hanging?"

"Left him *what*?"

"Or not hanging," Mallory snickers. "Bet he's hard and blue right now."

"What are you talking about?"

"For a guy who betrayed you, he's awfully generous with the orgasms. A selfish jerk wouldn't do that, you know?"

She's got a point.

"Maybe I can give him a blowie," I say, oozing sarcasm. "But how do you video that while using both hands?"

"A GoPro camera on your head?" Mallory suggests.

Fiona folds in half laughing.

"That's a great idea!" I shoot back.

"I WAS KIDDING."

I slump in my seat. "What am I going to do now? Parker– not me!–made a sex tape of us and it's nothing but fifty-seven seconds of my *butt*."

"Perk, you need to drop this stupid, immoral stunt."

"Nope," I say, shaking my head. I let out a long sigh. "I know what I need to do next."

"What?"

"I have no choice."

"WHAT?"

"I have to sleep with Parker again."

❧

BAILARGO. MALLORY DRAGGED US TO THIS DANCE STUDIO, insisting that the wedding party needs lessons. Of course, she's doing this while Parker is still in town. Of course, she is doing this while I'm still processing last night.

My blood is racing through my body at double time as I stare at the front door.

The Bailargo building is nothing but shades of red and black. Black trim, red walls. Red trim, dark grey walls. A perfect turret that looks like a bullfighter standing at attention. A multicolored door, if by "multi," you mean red and black.

There's a splash of white and a mural possibly done by Salvador Dalí… or Pablo Picasso. I'm not sure.

My mother calls this kind of building a "painted lady." It's a Victorian mansion that's been renovated, with wooden shingles and trim in all shapes and patterns. I've been here a bunch of times. This is where we learned to dance in middle school. Rachel Rabinowitz invited us to a Purim ball, and we took our first dance lessons… not that any of the boys actually asked us to dance at the ball. We just felt cool to know that we could.

The walk up the steps is filled with laughter and chatting as Fiona, Mallory, Will, and I enter the studio together. The entire wedding party couldn't make it today, but the gleaming floors of the ballroom beckon to those of us who could.

"Hey!" says a loud male voice.

We turn as a group to find Chris Fletcher standing there in front of big trays of cookies and a large lemonade dispenser. He waves, his hand halting in midair as Fiona inhales sharply and halts.

"What's *he* doing here?" she hisses in an accusing tone, all of it piled on Mallory.

"He's in the wedding party," Mallory says in a patient voice that only serves to escalate Fiona's wrath.

"I know he's in the wedding party," she snaps back. "But what is he doing *here?* You didn't warn me!"

"You require a trigger warning for Fletch?" Will pipes up. "I know we're millennials, but come *on*."

I shut my eyes hard. He just took a level-six situation and escalated it beyond ten.

"I don't need a trigger warning," Fiona practically growls. "But a heads up would have been nice."

"Why? He's just Fletch. Nothing to be afraid of."

"I'm not *afraid* of him!"

"Besides, you can take him. You did in seventh grade." Will crosses the line when he adds one word, two syllables, and sixteen years of baggage: "Feisty."

His whisper of her nickname causes Fiona's entire spine to stretch up along the curve of an S, a cobra rising up and spreading wide before it strikes.

"I don't have to defend the fact that I don't like him to *you*," Fiona says in a, well, *feisty* tone.

"And I don't have to defend the fact that my friend is going to be one of my groomsmen," he responds in kind.

Fiona turns to the right just as Will turns to the left, mirror images of misplaced anger and outrage. Mallory catches my eye and without another word, we take our positions.

"Will. Fi," we say, each of us touching our separate person's shoulder, each of us designed to neutralize. We are Switzerland. We are a United Nations field team. We are the backstage staffers of a Dr. Phil episode, trained to defuse.

Yet prepared for combat.

"Hello, hello!" says a man with an accent, his hands rising up in the air at forehead level for two staccato claps. "Welcome, welcome to the group DANCE lesson," he says, the word DANCE shouted as if in all caps. "I am Philippe! Many of you are here to celebrate Will and Mallory's wedding! How wonderful. The rest of us are here to have fun, too! You know they met here, yes? Bailargo is for lovers!"

"No, we… didn't?" Mallory says, her voice going up in a question, as if the suggestion itself violated her sense of order in the universe.

"You reconnected," he corrects, his left arm spread out, as if he's the emcee and we are but a circus act.

"No, actually, we had reconnected before that lesson?" Mallory says, her voice rising at the end even more. Uptalk is a sure sign of anxiety.

Meanwhile, Will and Fiona are shooting lasers at each other with their eyes.

"Hey, what's goin' on?" Fletch ambles over. He's a muscular guy, but not as big as he was in high school. Tighter. Leaner. More muscle than fat. More compact.

He's genial, and if you don't pay close enough attention, you think he's a little bit stupid. In high school, he hung out with Will, Sameer Ramini, and Michael Osgood, all four of them football players, the four of them inseparable. But of Will's three friends, Fletch was the nicest.

Not that that was saying much.

And of the four of them, he's the one I've had the most interaction with over the years. Fiona teaches his nephew now, but she pretends not to know what's going on with Fletch. He owns a small personal training and boxing studio in the next town over, and my mom told me he's a volunteer paramedic and firefighter, too.

You know the type. Hometown hero.

He's also entirely clueless when it comes to social tension.

"Hey, Feisty," he says, giving Fiona a shrug. "What's up?"

She pretends he doesn't exist. Which works.

For about three seconds.

"Hello?" He gets in her face, not in an aggressive way, but like a well-meaning church member at coffee hour who genuinely thinks you just didn't hear him greet you.

Eleven years disappear.

In high school, Fiona was a shit-kicking, ball-breaking, give-no-fucks *grrrrrllll* who was disagreeable, opinionated, and quietly seething.

But since we graduated, she's changed. Dramatically. Her first semester of college altered her, moving her closer to the sprightly fairy-like preschool teacher she is now, a free spirit with the emphasis on *spirit*.

Have you ever known someone so kind, so pleasant, so generous of heart that the very idea of their being angry or ungracious would shatter your world?

Well... here you go. Get ready to pick up the pieces.

"Go to hell, Fletch," she whispers. Don't mistake the soft tone for anything but strength, though.

Parker is suddenly beside me, holding two clear plastic cups of lemonade, wearing a confused expression. "What did he say to piss her off?"

"Called her Feisty."

"She *is* feisty right now."

"*Shhh!* Don't let her hear *you* call her that, either."

"Why not?"

"She hates it. In seventh grade, she dropkicked Chris Fletcher and earned the nickname."

"Isn't that guy's name Chris Fletcher? The same Fletch?"

"Yep."

He crosses his arms over his chest, biceps flexing. "Got it." His phone rings. With an apologetic look, he examines the screen. "It's Omaia. Have to take this." Pivoting, he walks near the door, speaking firmly and with precision.

CLAP CLAP!

I turn toward the sound to see Philippe standing next to a group of whitehairs, three women and one gnome masquerading as a human being, all looking at us eagerly. We're two generations younger than any of them, grandparents on one side of the room, grandchildren on the other. Nothing makes a group of late twenty-somethings devolve into children faster than a grandparent.

I suddenly crave a butterscotch candy.

And then I want a cigarette.

"Get your lemonade and cookies, my dears, for we are about to DANCE!" Philippe shouts as I turn to the cookie table, snickerdoodles a poor substitute for a Marlboro but I eat one anyhow. Parker comes back over, arms akimbo, big smile on his face.

"Call went well?"

"First one did. Follow-up on the guy at the restaurant who choked. He's doing well. I ignored the second one."

"Why? Was it your mom?" I crack.

His eyes widen, then peer at me with a strange fascination. "As a matter of fact, yes. How did you know?"

"I'd go out of my way to ignore her if I were you, too."

"It's the fifth time she's called in two days. I don't want to deal with her."

"Maybe it's important."

"If it were that important, she could leave a message. She just wants to give me her advice."

"I'm Sheila," interrupts a short, wide woman with close-cropped white hair in a pixie cut with long tapered sideburns that curl at the ends under her earlobes. She's talking to Parker, hand extended. "I would love to be your dance partner, Congressman Campbell."

Parker looks down. He has to. She's easily a foot shorter.

"Hi, Sheila," he says, giving me a look that almost includes a wink, but Parker is far too suave to do that. "I would love to."

"And how about you? You look like a nice prime steak in a world of chopped liver," says the gnome. When I turn toward his voice, I find myself the recipient of an amused grin from a bald man with a long white beard, our eyes level. The grin falters slightly, a bit of the color leaving his sweaty face.

"Is that a pick-up line? Because if so, it's really bad," I tell him with a smile as he sips his lemonade and gives me a shaky wink.

"DANCY!" Will shouts from across the room. "Mallory's best friends are off limits!"

"Which of you is Mallory's best friend?" Dancy says to the room.

All of the women raise their hands.

Good-natured laughter fills the room, Sheila calling out, "But he's a damn fine dancer."

Proving her words to me seems to be Dancy's mission. He grasps my hand in his and pulls me close–but not *too* close– as people pair off. Everyone else in the room seems to know what to do, though Fletch looks at Fiona, then Mallory, and finally settles on Angie Muriano, whose family has run Muriano's Farm Stand and Storage for more years than anyone can remember.

Including Angie, if my mom's stories about her creeping dementia are right.

"We will work on the basics. You are all here for wedding dances, yes?" he asks me.

"Yes," I say, realizing he's peering at me with a look I know too well.

Great. Some dude born before television was invented has seen my damn meme.

"You look familiar," he says.

They all start that way.

"Uh, people say I have one of those faces. You know." If

the old dude's eyes drift to my chest, I know he's seen the meme.

"No. I don't know. I have a face that reminds people of someone who works at The North Pole."

"Santa?"

"No. Rusty, the mechanic who keeps Santa's sleigh going. No one talks about him, but Donner and Blitzen sure do appreciate his work."

His hand is clammy in mine, and as the music starts, it finally occurs to me to really look at the dude, even as I'm laughing politely at his joke. First of all, he's old. Like, so old that the collagen in his skin just decided to defect outright and make a run across the border without waiting for a visa.

Second, it's increasingly clear he is super nervous right now.

But even if he's a bit anxious, his footwork is incredible. I suddenly realize that I've never danced with someone who knows exactly what he's doing. As Dancy gathers me in his arms, he's light as a feather with his touch but uses a hard-to-pinpoint firmness in how he guides my body through the steps. I look over to find Sheila giggling, looking up adoringly at Parker, who seems to have the same sure-footedness as Dancy.

A pang of regret rings through me.

I've never danced with Parker. Ever.

CLAP CLAP!

"Change partners!" Philippe shouts. For a comical moment, Fletch and Fiona are next to each other, a natural pair until she storms over to Dancy, grabs his hand, and shoves it onto her waist.

"I like a woman who takes charge," the old man says as Parker chuckles in my ear, his hands touching me, his scent filling me before I can think.

And then he moves me, taking control, guiding my body in ways that enhance my experience of being human. The tactile sensation of being in his arms, carried through in tempo to the swelling Spanish music that is soulful yet quick, is too much.

And too little.

"Why are you still in town, Parker? Don't you have a country to run?"

"I'm working with Ouemann on the new bills we're sponsoring."

"You can't do that from Texas?"

His fingers stroke my back. "I can't do *this* from Texas."

I must be the color of a fire engine. So much heat races through me at his touch. At the casual sense of his body against mine. At how unbelievably good he feels. *Perfect* is such an anemic word to describe how it feels to be in his arms, and yet it's as close as I'm going to get using my mouth to explain this feeling.

"Are you turned on?" he asks.

"What? No!" I lie.

"Your face is really flushed. And you're breathing hard. Like yesterday, in the supply room." His grin makes it clear he's enjoying every second of this.

"It's an allergic reaction to your belt buckle. Maybe it's nickel?"

"My belt buckle misses you." He nudges with his hips.

"That is *not* a belt buckle!"

"And you're not having an allergic reaction to anything except your own stubbornness."

"Ah!" Philippe says, one hand on each of our shoulders. "I love the passion between you! The tension in your steps! Your hips are so wanting!"

"So is my fist," I mumble.

Parker's eyebrow arches. "Kinky."

I punch him.

But before my knuckles connect with his washboard abs, he catches my hand.

And puts it on his shoulder.

"Your propensity for violence is troubling, Persephone."

"So are your reflexes."

"You never minded them in bed."

I swallow my tongue.

It doesn't taste nearly as good as his.

Damn it.

I'm in his arms and here we go again.

Not *again* as in dancing. We've never, not even once, danced together.

Again, though–*again*. Yet *again* I find myself in his arms. I find who I am when he touches me. I don't have to seek an identity. Or dig under layers of other people's expectations to find the core of who I am. When I'm with Parker, I know.

I know instantly.

I know who I am.

It's more than that, even. I am who I am when I'm with him. His gaze, his breath, his smile, his attention, all seem to change the lens of the world so it gives me clarity. I've never met anyone else who tethers me to the truest version of myself and tugs gently on that line, giving me just enough room to breathe.

Being near him is oxygen.

Being beside him is power.

Being with him–oh, how we moved mountains together. We explored universes without ever leaving our bed.

And he explored me, in full, as if I were an uncharted land waiting patiently to be discovered.

Once you've been loved so thoroughly and centered so swiftly by another soul, how do you live without that?

The last five years have been a sad experiment for me.

One with no acceptable outcome.

Parker's hand presses my rib line, one of his thumbs in the divot where my spine rests between two thick lines of muscle. My nose brushes against his lapel. He's still wearing his suit jacket, the light wool infused with old cologne, woodsmoke, and the scent of a man who once took his time letting me learn how to be me, wholly me, in his orbit.

While he revolved around me in return.

We're twinned by circumstance, by gravity, by some

unnamed force that makes me breathe him in. His charged air is a nutrient I'm so deficient in that now—as I take him in freely, his foot moving surely, his thigh brushing mine, his belly beckoning—I see how much I need him.

How weak I am.

Giving in to what he's told me would be so easy.

Dropping over the edge of the precipice of his truth would be the surrender I need.

"I'm sure there's a coat closet here," he says into my ear. Teeth nip at my lobe, making me shiver.

"I'm not having a quickie with you in a coat closet at a dance studio, Parker." Then again, maybe I could get my video here? Hmmm. Warmth floods my entire body at the thought.

"How about a longie?"

I glare at him.

He's relentless. "Then where, Persephone? Name your location."

Someplace with a video camera, I almost blurt out, but don't.

Because I don't really want that.

I want the impossible.

I want the last five years back. I want them all with Parker.

I want to reverse time.

Before I can answer, Fiona lets out a surprised grunt, then a sound of alarm that crescendos as Dancy melts into a puddle at her feet, right in the middle of the dance floor.

"Dancy!" Mallory gasps as Philippe, Will, and Fiona all flock to his side, Mal reaching for her phone, ever the pragmatist. I can see her press 9-1-1 as Parker jumps to Will's side.

"I'm—I'm fine," Dancy gasps before his eyes roll up and he collapses on Will's arm and the tops of both his feet, pinning him in place on the gleaming ballroom floor.

"WHERE'S YOUR AED?" Fletch shouts, looking at Philippe and rushing to Dancy's side.

"DANCY!" Philippe shouts, leaping across the floor to a large cabinet, pulling out a portable defibrillator machine. Mallory runs to help him, ashen but in control, the two rushing back.

I stand and watch, frozen.

Parker dips his ear down and listens. "He's not breathing."

Will holds Dancy's wrist, then checks for a pulse at the neck as Fletch rolls something to put under his head. He lets out an expletive and gives Parker a wrenching look.

"NO!" Mallory's seen it, too, and drops to the floor. "He has a heart condition!"

"I know," Philippe says, moving like a high-speed robot to get the defib machine out and ready. Fletch grabs the device from him as Philippe calls out, "He was just telling me he's having a pacemaker installed next week, so this should be safe."

"I'm a paramedic," Fletch grunts. The difference between a terrified bystander and a trained medical professional is astounding. Fletch is not tentative. His movements have an economy of energy, each designed for maximum efficiency. Time is of the essence, and as I hold my breath, heart pounding in my chest and eyes on the not-breathing Dancy, a running mantra takes over my mind.

Don't die don't die don't die don't die don't die don't die don't die.

Sirens start in the distance, but *too* distant. How long has Dancy gone without a breath? Every second is too long.

The doors to the studio burst open, and in runs Saoirse Cannon of all people, wearing a camera-ready red sheath dress, white tennis shoes over her pantyhosed feet.

She's speaking into her phone and giving a blow-by-blow description of everything about the scene.

Scratch that.

Everything about *Parker*.

Parker rips open Dancy's shirt. "No excessive chest hair," he says to Fletch, who nods and pushes a button on the small AED.

189

What does chest hair have to do with this?

"You're sure there's no pacemaker?" Fletch says loudly as Parker uses a handkerchief from his pocket to wipe down Dancy's sweaty chest.

"Definitely," Philippe snaps. "I wish he'd gotten it sooner, the stupid, stubborn old–" His voice breaks as Fletch ignores him, Parker moving the sides of Dancy's shirt aside to expose space on his chest. Carefully, Fletch places one sticker from the machine just under the collarbone and one just below the heart.

"Back!" Fletch says, Parker's hands going up in the air, Fletch sliding on his knees away from Dancy as he presses a button.

"What's happening?" Fiona asks as the sirens get so loud, it's clear the ambulance has arrived in the parking lot.

Dancy starts to cough, and Fletch answers her but remains completely focused on his patient. "The machine is analyzing whether to shock his heart."

A flurry of activity and scuffling behind me makes our group look up as an onslaught of uniformed paramedics rushes in, recognizing Fletch and coming to a near-comical halt.

Dancy makes a groaning sound, rolling to his left, enough to make tears spring to my eyes.

"He's breathing," Mal chokes out. Fletch ignores us all and begins speaking in medical terms to the guys who are here to take over, the AED set aside as they confer.

Fiona just blinks, over and over, watching Fletch without a word.

Off to the side, Philippe is on the phone, his hands shaking, lithe body so tense, it looks like he would snap in half if you blew on him. Will and Parker stand up and walk over to me, where I just gape at them both.

Slowly, with a long breath in followed by a huge exhale, Mallory looks at Parker, her eyes increasingly weird, like she's watching something distasteful unfold before her eyes.

"What?" I finally choke, creeped out by her expression.

"Why do people always nearly die around Parker?" she asks.

A bright light blinds us, the *click clack* of camera crews setting up a tripod making us turn. A flash of red fills my field of vision, and then we hear:

"Texas Congressman Parker Campbell just assisted in saving the life of..."

"Oh, God," Parker groans as Saoirse positions herself in front of him, arm extended as she's about to ask him for a comment. He's sharp, though, and knows he can't escape. She's fine-crafted a situation that leaves him the loser if he does.

But no one actually wins in this situation.

Other than Saoirse.

"–it's Chris Fletcher who is the real hero here," Parker says, pointing to Fletch, whose look of grumbling astonishment makes him look even more like a bear than usual. "Chris is the one who stepped in and saved Mr. Dancy."

"It's just Dancy!" Dancy weakly gasps from the gurney as he's taken away.

Mallory laughs with relief, then claps her hands over her mouth, mortified by what she thinks is impropriety.

Just a few minutes ago, Parker's "belt buckle" was stroking my belly, and now Saoirse is stroking his ego, ignoring his attempts to divert attention. She's connecting this newsworthy bit to the last and back to Congressman O'Rollins, then ending with the two new bills he's co-sponsoring.

Instead of looking weary, Parker goes grave, serious and concerned, adding a comment about the importance of AED devices and how public health initiatives and education can save lives.

It's perfect synchronicity.

Saoirse thinks so, too, but not in matters of policy, her hand going to his elbow as the camera snaps off, full attention on Parker as a man.

Not Parker as a news subject.

"You're just a one-man lifesaving show, aren't you, Parker Campbell?" she asks rhetorically, her Texas drawl coming out in a sultry flirtation that makes me want to choke her to death with an oversized homecoming mum.

"What are you doing here?" he asks flatly. "You rushed in the building like you were stalking me."

"Stalk? What a strange word to use. I'm a journalist. We report the news."

"You report on Parker like you're a bounty hunter on a reality television show," I crack before I can stop myself.

She ignores me and returns her attention to her target. "You weren't complaining when I took you to that reception and hooked you up with the envoy you needed for–"

The rest of her words become Silly String in my mind, because she said everything I needed to hear with the words *I took you to that reception.*

They're still socializing.

Together.

Every shred of sympathy I had for Parker, every wavering bit of my mind that wondered whether maybe–just maybe– I've been wrong all these years, disintegrates.

Poof!

Before I realize it, I'm stomping out of the ballroom, away from the chaos of women comforting each other, of Philippe gathering Dancy's coat and what appears to be a cane, of Mallory and Fi calling out for me. Fletch looks up as I leave, and I swear he's the only person with a face that isn't judging me. A throng of camera people blocks the path behind me as I leave, crowding around Parker, Will, and Fletch, the sound like the past whooshing forward.

I need a cigarette.

I need a body-sized nicotine patch.

I need a break.

14

I *would like to take you out to dinner*, the text from Parker says, the cursor for my reply winking at me like it's hitting on me, too. I just got a text from Mallory that Dancy is fine, recovering at a Boston hospital, and I'm glaring at my nemesis.

No. Not Parker.

Worse.

I'm in my cottage behind the big house, staring at a pack of Marlboros, willing myself not to touch them.

Yes, real cigarettes. My generation is *all* about the vaping, but there's something about a good old-fashioned cancer stick shoved between your tight, angry lips that a vape pen just can't replicate.

Parker's text couldn't come at a worse time.

I would like world peace and to eat 5000 calories a day and not gain weight, I reply, grasping the ciggies, flipping the hardpack's lid up. The tangy scent of slow, painful death triggers all my cravings.

Mmmm. Inhaled poison. I have mastered the art of self-sabotage.

I'm working on the world peace part, he replies, my eyes cutting from the cigarettes to the phone.

That's not the part I care about, I answer, forced to let go of the pack to double thumb it on my phone.

What do you care about?

The question stares at me like it's a person, every O in the words a tiny eyeball, unblinking, judgmental.

Aren't you texting the wrong person for a date? I answer. *What about Saoirse? You two are a hot item.*

I am asking you on a date.

That's not an answer to my question.

Which one? I answered you.

Are you sleeping with Saoirse?

RING!

Startled, I drop the phone.

Parker, is all it says on the display. How can a simple name elicit such complicated emotions?

Sighing, I pick up the phone and answer.

"No."

That's all he says.

"No... what?"

"No, I'm not fucking Saoirse." The f-word makes my vulva tingle.

"I didn't mean right this very second," I counter, the sudden image of the two of them naked and breathing hard together making me go dry everywhere.

"I think I'd sound a little different on the phone if I were in the middle of sex with someone, Persephone."

"Maybe you're a master manipulator and you can fake emotion."

"Do you think I ever faked it with you?"

"No."

Silence fills the air. His no, my no, our no.

Lots of no. So much *no*.

"Tonight. Dinner?" he asks, except it's not a question. Commanding me is something Parker used to try all the time. It was a game. Could he make me do anything?

Only in bed.

Always–in bed.

"You're not safe to be around, Parker."

"What?"

"People drop like flies around you. Heart attack. Choking. Another heart attack. You're a walking Grim Reaper. Did Saoirse ask you to date me so I'll get hit by a bus in front of you and you'll have to perform emergency neurosurgery on me in the street using an iPhone and your shoelace?"

"Don't joke about your dying." The easy banter turns serious.

"I'm not joking. You're really starting to freak me out with the saving-lives thing."

"Am I supposed to *not* save them?"

"No. But it's weird."

"It is." His voice changes, a strange tone of relief in there. "It's really, really bizarre, Persephone. I can't explain it. Trust me, I wish it didn't happen. My staffers are starting to call me The Boy Scout behind my back. Pretty sure Grim Reaper is next."

"My mother thinks you're paying actors to pretend to die so you can save them and get good press."

"If I recall correctly, your mother also thinks she can find free parking spots by waving a dowsing stick along the dashboard."

"That's Fiona. Not Mom."

His genuine laugh makes me shiver, the delicious feeling so, so welcome. "When strange events happen to me, your mother wonders if I'm faking it. But when strange events happen to her, it's divine?"

"No. Not divine. It's energy."

"Give me *your* energy, Persephone. All of it. Tonight at seven. Dinner."

"I'm scared." The words come out of my stupid mouth before I can stop them.

"Of me?" Voice turning up with alarm and surprise, he doesn't say another word, the sound of his breath as it hitches like a long, curling finger straight down my bare spine.

"Of... me."

"Oh." Compassion and victory radiate from his voice. "Well, you *are* scary."

"I scare you?"

"No. Not me. But plenty of other people. That's what I love about you, though."

I growl at him. "I'll go out with you on one condition."

"What is it?"

"You have to sleep with me."

Victory takes laps around my ear as he says, "If you think that's going to turn me away, you need lessons in negotiation."

"I'm not *that* easy."

"You just made sex a condition of having dinner!"

"On *my* terms, Mister. You know the hardest part about the last time you make love with someone who hurts you and the relationship ends? It's that you don't know it's the last time. There isn't some flashing red alarm that says, 'Savor this while you can because you're never doing this again. Ever.'"

"Oh, God," he groans. "What does this have to do with a dinner date?"

"The last time you make love with someone is random. It's not planned. It's as average and commonplace as any other sexy time, and yet–suddenly it isn't. So you don't make it last. You don't stretch it out. You don't give it the depth and soul it deserves, because you don't know, Parker. I didn't know. I didn't know that the last time we made love would be that day."

"Persephone," he says, voice strangled, as much emotion in that one word as in one hundred of mine.

I made sex a requirement because it needs to be. How else will I get video of him to use? But hot tears fill my eyes as I tell him the truth.

The whole truth, and nothing but the truth. Mostly.

So help me Parker.

"If you pursue me, you're going to catch me. And if you catch me, you have to–"

"Love you."

"*Make* love to me."

"Done."

"If you had sex with me that fast, Parker, you're either a superhero who moves at lightning speed or you have a wet belly and need a washcloth right now."

"This is why I love you."

"Because I talk about your hypothetical premature ejaculation?"

"Because you talk to me like I'm a real person."

"And quit saying you love me."

"It's the truth."

"If you loved me, you wouldn't have done what you did."

"A person who didn't love you would have stopped trying to get you back."

"A person who didn't really love me would use that as a tool to manipulate me into going to bed with them."

"YOU are the one who asked ME for sex!"

He's got me there.

"Only once. For old time's sake. Because while you might be a total asshole, you're a good lay, Parker Campbell."

"I think you just wrote my re-election campaign slogan. Parker Campbell: Because Congress Needs a Good Lay."

"PLEASE tell me you have staffers for your public relations, Parker," I sputter. "Because you seriously suck at writing slogans."

"I think it's good! And I have to give you credit."

"As long as I'm the one writing it, and not Saoirse, we're good."

"Are you jealous of her?"

"Should I be?"

"Absolutely not."

I pause. "Then I won't be."

"Just like that? Where's Persephone the Hothead I once knew?"

"She's wondering why we're still on the phone when you could just come over here and climb in my bed." I walk into my bedroom and stare at the bed, imagining Parker on it, sexy and beckoning. My pulse starts to gallop, a familiar warmth igniting in my belly, settling in for a long, hot ride.

"That's not how dates work."

"That's *exactly* how ninety percent of our dates worked!" I laugh, a low sound that ends with a sigh that leaves nothing to the imagination.

He makes a sound I can't translate. "I don't want to go out with you tonight just to sleep with you," he finally says, surprising me.

"Then why?"

"To spend time with you. To be with you. You were my best friend. I miss my best friend."

"Why me?"

Beep.

Shocked, I look at the phone. Call ended. Did Parker hang up on me? What the hell? I set the phone down, propped against a small bookend on my desk, then pick it back up. On a whim, I open the video app, appalled that I ever was crazy enough to want to make a revenge sex tape. I was never going to actually do it, you know.

And technically, Parker made that video of my butthole. Not me.

But as fear rushes through me, the implications of being hung up on making me panic, I realize I'm my own worst enemy.

No, *really*. I'm as surprised as you are to see it.

And thank *God* I never made that tape. It would be the end of us.

The end of the renewed beginning of us.

The doorbell rings. I look at the clock. It's 5:43 p.m. Must be a delivery from the world's biggest store. Mom buys everything from them, and sometimes the delivery guys show up here by accident, instead of the main house. One time, we got a single tampon in an envelope, delivered with a smile on the package.

Leaving my phone on the desk, I walk down the hall to the source of the doorbell, which dings again.

I open the door, expecting a dude in a blue uniform.

Instead, I get a white knight.

"Parker? What are you doing here–"

The kiss is hot and gentle, sweet and sinful, every wild swing of the pendulum in one rolling tongue. His hands are on my back, one cupping my ass, one flat between my shoulder blades, pulling me closer to him. I pitch forward, his arm muscles tight, his mouth lush and wanting.

Kissing him back never tasted so good.

Kissing him back never felt so perfect.

"I don't do this to any woman but you," he whispers in my mouth as the hand on my ass squeezes with a possession that makes me moan. "I don't do this to any woman but *you*," he repeats as the hand at my shoulders comes around and caresses my breast, thumb turning the nipple into a pearl. He kisses me, hard and fast, all gentleness gone, his body nothing but hard muscle and dirty intent.

I break the kiss, panting hard, distracted but determined.

"By the way, I'm sorry about that slap. And for throwing sour cream on you. You're the only person in the world I've ever done anything like that to."

"I've read your arrest reports, Persephone. I know that's not true."

"Fine. You throw *one* BPA-filled fleshlight at a cop at *one* protest and suddenly it's assault."

"It was, technically."

I let our a five-year-long sigh. "But other than that police officer, you're the only person I've ever felt so angry about. And it's not right. I'm sorry. I need to be able to make a sincerely apology here, Parker. You don't have to accept it, but I am offering it."

"It's okay. I forgive you for the punch, the slap, and the sour cream. Pretty sure Mallory will never forgive you for ruining the ratio, though."

"I didn't ask for forgiveness for the punch at the wedding rehearsal rehearsal dinner. That one you totally deserved, *Skip*."

His kiss says he accepts my apology.

The ass squeeze says he's throwing in the punch whether I like it or not.

"Is this our date?" I ask as he walks me backwards a few steps into the cottage, mouth on mine again. The kiss feels like the moment death takes you, agony and ecstasy twinned in a euphoric, charged state. I'm still alive, so this is only a guess, but I'm pretty damn sure I'm right. My chest squeezes, my blood turns to fire, and Parker presses hard against my thigh, so close and yet so far.

"I need you inside me," I confess.

"Why?"

"Why?"

"Yes. Tell me. Tell me why you need me."

"Because I can't believe I've been able to walk and live and breathe without having you in me, Parker. All these years. All this time." My fingertips dance on the bones that protect my heart. "Every heartbeat hurt without you there to hear it."

The sun is still strong enough to make everything outside so bright, so startling, the edges of every object so distinct. The light is softer inside the cottage. He closes the door with his foot and kisses me even harder, with so much force that I have to give it back, pushing and pushing to make him know how much it hurt.

If I can make him feel it, too, then maybe we shared *something* from those five horrible years. Even shared pain is better than nothing.

My hands run under his shirt, greedy for his skin, fingernails scratching lightly, the arch of his back, the rise of his head as he reacts so satisfying. Breaking our embrace, he reaches for the hem of my shirt, moving his palms up under the cloth to cup both breasts with a breathtaking move that makes me strip out of my shirt, standing before him half naked, impatient to feel his skin against mine.

Joining me, the swift movement of his hands at his buttoned shirt is a marvel, the quick flick of his wrists, the expert-level snap as he undresses giving me a chance to pause, to watch, to reach back and unhook my bra. Hot skin meets mine as my soft nipples rub against his hard muscled chest. I rest the tip of my nose against his shoulder, a long, slow breath giving me his scent, his heat, confirming he's really here.

Eager hands drop to my waistband, his fingers making me shiver as he undresses me, my own hands at his belt matching his for excitement. Soon we're standing before each other, me in my thong panties, Parker with boxer briefs on, and he picks me up in his arms and carries me down the hall.

"Which one?" he whispers, looking at the doors.

I point. He pushes it open with my hip and I'm on my duvet, set down carefully, Parker's whole long, strong body over mine. Ah, the feel of so much of him against so much of me... The kiss is wet and long, my ribs absorbing his weight, my tongue dancing with his as he curls over me, hands in my hair. The long, thick shaft of his erection rubs along my inner thigh as I part my legs.

"These," he says, hooking one finger inside my undies, "have to go. Now."

"Then so do these," I counter, grabbing his, too.

We strip down to nothing, the sudden spring of him relieved from the cage of his underwear, the cool air hitting my clit before his naked thigh slides between mine, soft warmth surrounding me. Finally, after far too long, too many years, we're together again in bed, together in all the ways that matter. My mind chatters as if it has thousands of thoughts to tell him and they're all coming out through my hands, my mouth, my breasts, my clit, my heart.

Our bodies have five years of catching up to do.

"I owe you," I whisper, moving away so I can kiss his collarbone, his nipple, biting gently so he does that hissing sound, inhaling so sharply, it's like his back teeth vibrate. I do it again with his other nipple, one hand flat against his lower abs, the tip of him touching the back of my hand.

"Owe. Me. What?" he grinds out, clearly working hard for control.

"An orgasm."

"Why?"

"Because you gave me two. We're two and oh, Parker. And you aren't a man who likes to lose."

"Who said I lose with those orgasms? They're mine on the scoreboard."

"Is that all I am to you? A score?"

"You're everything to me, Persephone. You're the world, heaven and hell, the solar system. You're the sun and the moon, the elements and the stars. I don't know how I made it through these last five years without you."

I bite him. Hard.

He laughs. "And I don't know how I'm going to make love to you with a missing nipple."

"Mine are copyrighted, so don't even think about trying to take one."

His laughter stops abruptly as my mouth travels down the valley of his breastbone, his navel, stopping as I wrap my hand around his shaft, lightly grazing my teeth against the tip of him.

"I think you'll manage to make love to me, nipple or no nipple. You're very good at extemporaneous activities, Parker. But making it all up as you go along is a really useful professional skill for you."

And with that, I go down on him. All the way, sucking him in until my lips form a complete circle at the base and he groans.

"I've missed your mouth," he confesses. "Not like this. How you talk. How you tell me off. How you cut to the chase and just say what needs to be said without any bullshit."

I run my tongue up his shaft, hand right behind it.

"And that," he gasps, a statue of Adonis cut under my palm, the sharp curve of his muscle at the hip like touching a large gemstone. "When you do that with your mouth, I want to marry you and pound you on an altar and tell off the gods,

Persephone. Because I turn into someone I'm not with you. I turn into everyone and everything and Jesus, what the hell are you doing with those teeth?"

"You want me to stop?" I say around a mouthful of him.

"No!"

But all it takes is one more long, wet glide up before Parker grabs my hips and pulls my legs up toward his head. Confusion makes me stop my mouth for a few seconds before I realize, as his fingers stroke my wet folds, that he's going for reciprocity.

I grin.

I pull him out of my mouth and blow lightly on him, making his body tense.

"I thought this was about me giving *you* an orgasm."

"Who said I couldn't manage both?" he whispers back before his tongue does unspeakable things to my inner thighs, making me shiver. Gently, he nudges my knees until my hair drapes over his thick thighs, winding around his erection. One of his hands lovingly brushes it back, pulling it over my far shoulder, then sliding over my ribs to my ass, taking a healthy squeeze as he tongues my clit, blood rushing to make me swell.

"Parker," I moan, my thighs around his ears, his face buried so deep in me, it's like he's trying to capture me from the inside. I can't think straight, moving in small motions against him, trying to find this distant place where my body feels nothing but pleasure. I sit up and he moves me off him, my back against the bed, his hands on my breasts as they reach up. One look between my legs and I see how tightly his forearms stretch to me, how his messy hair rests against my pale leg, and I have one job and one job only.

To accept what he so readily gives.

"I want," he says, moving away from my clit, lips against my thigh, "to be in you. To come in you. To come with you, Persephone. If I can't have that, I'll take your mouth or your hand or whispered words of frenzy. You're naked in bed with me and I've spent five years waiting for this moment. Your mouth is amazing, and you taste like so many dreams of mine, but for the love of everything that is good in this world, all I want right now is to be in you. That's the only place where I feel like everything makes sense."

I'm frozen.

There's a silence that goes so deep that you can't hear it. It's the absence of sound. It's what the world does to you when it doesn't know what else it can do, and as I wait, seconds pass, the peace sinking deeper and deeper. Our eyes lock and we settle in, time an irrelevant annoyance that doesn't deserve to be here, marking and measuring what should be infinite.

"Come here and make sense, then," I insist, tugging on his shoulders, pulling harder than I should, until I am kissing him hard, so rough, so needy, because Parker's words have a weight to them, a burden, a feeling that presses like a thick stone around my heart.

And the only way to lift it is together.

He's between my legs, my hand sliding down until I guide him in, his pause enough to make me whisper, "I'm on the pill."

"It wouldn't matter," he says.

I jolt.

"Because if I'm ever going to have children with some-one, Persephone, it's with you."

"But... not *now*," I say, nipping his arm as he waits, paused between in and not in, stuck in an interminable purga-tory that is a physical representation of how I've felt for years.

"No. Not now. And just so you know, and to be perfectly clear, I'm... well..." He clears his throat, endearingly nervous suddenly.

"You're–what?"

"I'm clean. No STDs."

"Oh." I swallow, hard. "Same here."

"I haven't–it's been five years since–"

Oh.

Oh!

I move my hips, the ache of having him at the brink of entering me worth what we have to say. "Parker," I murmur, brushing his hair from his forehead. "Five years? You seriously haven't had sex for five *years*?" I reach for his hand.

"Meet my girlfriend," he says, squeezing.

I bark out a laugh. "No way."

"Would I lie to you?"

The words hang between us, bridging five years of sorrow, of thwarted passion, of my own stupidity, of his undeterred attempts. If I believe he wasn't lying all those years, then what?

Then I wasted five years.

Sounds like he did, too.

"No. No, Parker. I know you're not lying." I swallow, hard. "And me, too."

"You too... what?"

"No one else, Parker. I haven't slept with anyone since you–since, uh, the picture incident."

A long *whooosh* of air comes out of him, our chests rising and falling rapidly, the twin revelations changing the chemistry in the room, as if we've swapped elements but kept the same formula, and everything sour is now sweet and everything acidic is now a base, and we don't know exactly what this is, but it's not what we thought we were dealing with.

That's for sure.

"Five years?" we gasp in unison.

"Parker," I say, reaching for him. "Get the hell in here."

He's on top of me before I finish the sentence with, "I can't wait another second."

And then, he doesn't.

Oh, God, how good he feels. Being full like this, my thighs against his ribs, his chest crushing my breasts between us, my calves brushing up against his ass–it's a kind of body meld you can't describe. The way he kisses me is so assured, like we have forever, and as he rocks into me, the sensation sparking a deep orgasm, the friction from his angle against my clit the perfect complement, we make love.

Slowly, then faster.

It's all a blur of kisses and whispers, of strokes and touches, a choreography that takes different elements and turns them into a sweaty dance of art.

"Persephone?"

"Mmm?"

"I love you."

"Mmm," I moan, unable to say the words back as I blaze into a bonfire, burning off the pieces of me that don't fit anymore, feeling the contours of his strong arms holding him up over me, resting my fingertips on the crook of his elbow as he moves my leg just so, the angle of him sliding in and out of me so right.

So *us*.

Tensing, he gives the signal he used to send years ago before he came, the slight increase in tempo and the hard thrusts making me soak him in, my own hips urging him on until we're coming together, the only sound our heavy breath and the hushed movement of flesh against flesh, bone against bone, blood pushing in tandem to deliver pleasure.

He collapses on top of me. I feather his back with my fingertips, feeling his slow muscular release as he gives me his all.

"Those witches weren't kidding," I whisper after a few moments, unable to stop myself.

"Witches?" He props his head up on one hand, elbow making the bed sink slightly. "Did you just say 'witches'?"

"Yes."

"As in Salem? You're into that now?"

"Not quite. Technically, they're dowsers."

He rolls over on his back and rests his palm on his belly, his other arm reaching for me to snuggle. "I don't know if my brain can absorb this topic right now. What do dowsers have to do with the best sex I've had in five years?"

"Uh–the only sex."

He wiggles his hand. "Don't offend my FWB."

"Your *hand* can't be a friend with benefits!"

"Shhhh." He pretends to talk to it. "She didn't mean that," he whispers to his splayed palm.

"You are so weird, Parker. Congressmen don't act like this."

"Don't what? Masturbate?"

"Can we get back to talking about the dowsers?"

"You can talk about whatever you want," he says, grinning like an idiot. "You're a dowser now?"

"No. Fiona is. And when your best friend is obsessed with something, you go along for the ride, like it or not."

"Which is how you got me to skinny dip in the ocean, that night at Hampton Beach. And Walden Pond. And Castle Island. What did we do that time when I came up here for two weeks? Thirteen different bodies of water?"

"Fourteen if we count my parents' pool."

"And how many of them did we have sex in?"

"Twelve. Castle Island involved that unfortunate encounter with a sea lion. And Walden Pond had some Tesla-owning douchebag guy dressed like Mr. Darcy swimming in the lake the day we tried."

"Right."

"What does any of that have to do with witches?" I ask him.

"That's my question!"

"You're comparing my skinny dipping obsession to Fiona's dowsing weirdness?"

"I'm comparing the friendships. You said people go along with their best friend's fascinations." He kisses my forehead. "I'm remembering when *you* were *my* bestie." He frowns. "Did you actually visit a coven?"

"Only once. Fiona said I was banned afterward. Something about my messed-up energy."

"Then how do you know what a bunch of modern witches had to say?"

"Fiona."

"Ah." Tenderly, he brushes some of the hair away from my forehead. "I'm so glad you have her. And Mallory."

"What do you mean?"

"You weren't alone."

"Alone?"

"After you dumped me."

"I sure as hell *was* alone!"

"You had them. And that makes me feel better about the last five years."

"You–you were worried about me being alone?"

"Sometimes. Weren't you worried about me?"

Do I tell the truth? That no, I wasn't, because it never occurred to me that Parker might be hurting after he betrayed me?

After I *thought* he betrayed me?

Not once in five years did I ever consider the idea that *he* would feel loneliness, or, well, *anything*. I assumed he was a cold bastard who had hidden his true self from me. That I was a sucker. A pawn. A throwaway toy you use up and spit out and replace with a newer toy.

That his bizarre pursuit of me was just more of the taunting game.

He takes my hand, kisses the center of my palm, then places it over his heart.

"I've missed you. I didn't know that an ache could feel like granite. Like a rock in my chest, pressing down on my heart. It had to beat with extra effort to love you. But it did, Persephone. It did."

"You missed me."

"Terribly."

I punch him.

"And screw you for making the last damned time we made love be right before two dogs started humping above my head before I could even get my panties on. There's something really crass about that, Parker." I shudder.

It's clear he's in mid-thought, mid-emotion, the second law of motion (the one Mallory told me about a long time ago but I forget exactly, something about how hard it is to stop once you get started) in full force before my words can sink in. Our brains can only process information at a certain speed.

Sometimes the heart moves orders of magnitude faster. The second law of emotion.

"How," he asks slowly, "was it *my* fault my mother's dogs decided to get carnal seconds after we did?"

"You're ruining the moment."

"We're having a moment?"

"We are."

"I would have brought flowers, had I known. Or a good bottle of rosé."

"That's not how moments work. And they sure don't work when you keep bringing up your mom."

"You, Persephone, were the one who brought up the dogs. My mother's dogs. Therefore, the dogs and my mother are your emotional responsibility."

"My what?"

"You have to take ownership of introducing the dogs as a topic of conversation."

"Do not!"

"Do, too."

"I am the aggrieved party here, Parker. I get to choose what I take responsibility for."

"You can take full responsibility for my orgasm."

"You're a guy. Taking responsibility for giving you an orgasm is like saying a spell then flipping a light switch and claiming it's my own magic."

"When I'm inside you and coming, it *is* magic, Persephone."

"It's biology."

"It's both. More magic, though."

He's telling the truth. All of it. Every bit of it, all authentic and real. As he leans toward me, his face dives between my breasts, gentle lips pressing against my breastbone. Eyes darting up, he captures my gaze and says, "Don't go anywhere."

"Where would I go? I'm naked."

"Didn't stop you for that second protest in El Paso."

"We were making the point that naked sex dolls are not representative of women's real bodies."

"I'll take your very real body over a sex doll any day."

"Does that mean you've actually slept with a sex doll?"

"Of course not."

"Whew."

"Why? Because it's too perverted?"

"No. Because of the chemical load."

His laughter trickles back into the room as he leaves, ass on display, his body disappearing into the bathroom.

Flopping back against the pillows, I let out a long sigh.

Beep.

I sit straight up, searching for the source of the sound. My phone rests on the window sill, sandwiched between a candle and a sage stick so thick, it looks like the world's biggest doobie.

And it just beeped.

I climb out of bed, snatch it up, and hit the Home button.

Why did it beep?

I realize the recording app is open.

Oh, my God.

Did I just accidentally film us having sex?

Did I just get my real sex tape after all?

15

The phone feels like I'm holding a rabid bat in my hands.

I drop it and bend over to retrieve it, cradling it in my hands. The Photos button beckons, begging me to double check. Maybe I didn't record. Maybe it beeped for some other reason.

Maybe I'm denying reality.

Some force inside me, an autonomic response that I can't control, propels me forward, making me click through. Hmm. No new video. But my memory is full.

Why is the memory on my phone full?

Hell, the memory in my brain is full, too. Full of five years of anger, frustration, disappointment, regret...

I push Play, then Stop, as the vision of our lovemaking plays in my head.

I close my eyes.

For a full minute, I rewind every second of our foreplay, feeling the brush of cotton sheets against exposed skin as if I'm reliving it. Arousal makes me wet again, my nipples tingling with mirror neurons that watch me imagining sex and therefore think my body is actually having sex, sending me spinning. I'm enraptured by the thought of our naked, hot, open-mouthed sex, of Parker's head moving slowly between my legs, how he kissed my inner thigh in a way that was so complete and yet felt so tantalizing. Remembering the hush of his warm breath against the folds, leading up to his tongue on my clit, evokes all the same bodily reactions as if he were right here, touching me right now.

I grab the phone and push Play.

I get nothing.

I frown. I swipe. I find nearest video and push Play.

"Oh, God," my voice says in the audio before I realize that's my butthole video.

Parker's butthole video, technically.

"What's this?" he asks, suddenly... right here.

Right now.

Right next to me.

"NOTHING!" I shriek, flinging the phone onto the pile of our clothes.

But it doesn't turn the video off.

"Parker," my voice gasps from across the room, a long, slow groan of pleasure making it damn clear what this video is.

He goes still, not even blinking, staring at me. "You *recorded* us?"

"Um, well, it's complicated, and I–"

"Yes or no?"

"Technically, *you* did."

"*Me?* How did *I* record us having sex on *your* phone?"

"It's really, really complicated."

"You sound really, really unhinged, Persephone." Something in his tone sets off panic in me.

"Parker, please, let me explain."

"Where have I heard those words before? Oh. Right. Out of my own mouth, a thousand times, for the last five years. All aimed at *you*." Anger overflows in him, an emotion I've rarely seen directed at me. He's pumped and pissed and suddenly, remorse fills me, subsumes me, buries me in an avalanche.

My God. What have I done? What have I done to him all these years as I nursed my broken heart?

"Why?" he demands, getting in my face, seething. "Why would you even want to record us?"

"I–" My lips stick together as I open my mouth to try to explain myself, but all I taste is Parker. Licking my lips to make it easier to talk just reinforces how stupid I've been. We just made mad, passionate, sweet, hot, filthy love. His face was just between my legs, he was just inside me, his heat is still encased within me. Intimate heat that seconds ago cocooned and enveloped me now burns, searing my skin, making me feel roasted from the inside out.

His love burns bright in my cells.

What if his hate does, too?

Parker bends down and shoves one foot in his pants leg, both legs in quickly. As he grabs his shirt and buttons it so fast, like a zipper, he looks down, away, and says:

"If it really means that much to you to ruin my career with a sex tape, Persephone, I can't stop you."

"It's not like that!" I turn the phone toward him, the video playing.

He watches for a few seconds, face cringing. "Is that a spider?"

"No. It's my butthole."

"Now you're just being–"

"You could rip my phone out of my hand. Smash it."

"I could." The soundtrack of our encounter continues to play until mercifully, it ends. He glares at me. "You probably have cloud backup. If this is what you want, there's nothing I can do."

I just stare at him, unable to speak. Five years of pain distill to a pinpoint, the tip pressing hard into the skin over my heart.

Or maybe it's poking from the inside out.

"It's not what you think, Parker. I didn't–"

"You expect me to believe you when I just heard what I heard?" He points to my phone.

"You swear you never released that photo of us five years ago? Really?" I blurt out.

"I swear. But I can't keep saying it over and over if you'll never believe me. There's a point where even *I* have to move on." A low, sickening chuckle comes out of him, his tongue rolling in a tight jaw that feels so final.

Cold dread makes my bones feel like frozen swords, sharp and dangerous.

"Five years, Parker? Really? You–you really carried a torch for me for *five goddamned years*? And didn't sleep with anyone else?"

"If that hasn't sunk in yet, then clearly you aren't really listening to me." His eyes skitter to the phone. "Do what you want. Do what you believe. Show the world who you are, Persephone."

I don't tell him what, *exactly*, I'd be showing if I released that "spider" video.

"You showed way too much of me to the world five years ago!"

"What if it wasn't me?" he spits, furious, gloves off. "Have you ever, just *once*, entertained that thought?"

"Of course I have! Every waking moment of my life!"

"Then give in to it. Surrender to the *truth*."

"The last time I surrendered, it was to you, Parker. You. And look what happened."

"I can't make you believe me. But I can tell you that you can *trust* me. I didn't do it. I don't know what more to say. "

My pulse takes over my existence until I am nothing but a throbbing heartbeat, time unmeasured by anything but the next beat, and the next, and the one after that. All I can count on is that beat, even as I watch Parker storm out of my cottage.

Out of my life.

This is the first time *he* has left *me*.

For five years, I've held him at bay.

I knew I'd weaken if I let him into my life, and I was right.

The sound of his car tires on the driveway make it clear he's leaving, the sickening crunch of gravel like my body being put through a bone crusher.

I thought that making a sex tape and getting revenge for what he did to me would make me feel balanced. Even. Whole.

I was wrong.

Oh, so wrong.

What else was I wrong about?

❧ 16 ❧

There is no greater comfort than texting your besties and having them appear on your doorstep holding ice cream, chocolate, and fifty pounds of righteous indignation.

"What an asshole!" Fiona begins as they invade. I threw on jeans and made my bed, but I'm pretty sure my cottage reeks of sex and five years of stale stubbornness.

Victory has a scent, too, but if this is victory, it smells an awful lot like the Pyrrhic kind.

"Who's an asshole? Me or Parker?"

"Parker, of course!"

"I haven't even told you what happened."

"Doesn't matter. We're on your side, no matter what."

"I made a sex tape of me and Parker."

"Another one?"

"No. The butthole one. But Parker found out and–"

"I changed my mind. You're the asshole."

"Fiona!" Mallory gasps. "That's not supportive!"

"She made a sex tape with a guy who's a member of Congress. Without his permission. And he found out."

"Who would ever give permission to make a sex tape?"

Mallory blushes.

"You did not!"

"We figured it was private! Will deleted it right away!"

"Great," Fiona says. "Now I'm the only one without a sex tape. I feel really left out."

"No one's stopping you from making a sex tape."

"The lack of a sex partner is kind of a problem. Who wants to watch a sex tape of me with a vibrator?"

"Um, half the audience of YouPorn and PornHub, Fi," I inform her.

Mallory makes that shocked face that reminds me of a sex doll.

"Raul has a point about you and porn, Perky," Fiona sighs. "Your in-depth knowledge of fetishes and sex toy trends scares me."

"I heard AlwaysDoll is coming out with a male doll. You can pick your length and girth, and his mouth has a gyro-scopic tongue," I offer.

"She's a preschool teacher. She doesn't need a sex tape!"

"Gyroscopic tongue?" Fi asks, leaning in. "Tell me more."

"We're here because of Perky's moral crisis," Mallory interjects, "not to talk about *our* sex lives. This is all about hers!"

"My sex life is going just fine," I say with a contented sigh. "Or, well–it *was*. I lost count at orgasm number twelve. But then Parker left me, and–"

"You count them? Orgasms? During sex?" Fi asks.

"Not on purpose. It just worked out that way."

"You sound like Mallory."

"What does *that* mean?" Mallory objects.

"I'll bet you have color-coded spreadsheets ranking the quality of every sex encounter you've ever had with Will," Fiona jokes.

Mal's eyes get *really* wide.

"And now you'll cross-check them against your home-made sex tapes to optimize performance."

Mallory really *does* look like an AlwaysDoll when her jaw drops.

Fiona snorts. She opens my cupboard and rummages around till she finds a bar of handmade chocolate from a farm in Sudbury, which she unwraps. A deep giggle bubbles out of her. "As if people actually do that."

"Right!" Mal's voice is high and nervous. "You'd have to be pretty weird to have a color-coded spreadsheet with filters to track your sex life!"

Fi frowns. "Who said anything about filters?"

Flashing major side eye Mal's way, I slide my phone across the table. "Either of you want to watch?" I don't tell them the truth. That I reconsidered. That I didn't record. That my phone did something to make me think I'd recorded, but I didn't. Almost as if some energy force stepped in and saved me from myself.

The idea of energy brings a sudden image of Jolene, barefoot on bare ground, arms up to the sky on a stormy day, making my body tingle.

"Watch you having sex?" Fiona gasps.

"*EWWW!*" they say in unison.

"Come on. You're not curious?"

"YES!"

"NO!"

"Are you really going to release it? I can't imagine letting anyone see my O face," Mal muses, taking the thick chocolate bar from Fi and breaking off a chunk.

"You had a picture go viral that showed your body being spit roasted by a naked porn star and Will, with anal beads between your legs. Your O face was on display to the entire world," I point out, not so gently.

"But that wasn't my *real* O face. No one wants their *real* O face being shown to anyone. Not even to the sex partner they're with!"

"Huh?"

"Don't you turn away when you come?" she asks, curious. The closed-off wall of Mallory suddenly cracks open.

"No!" Fiona and I exclaim.

"Really?" Mallory's face twists into something like a

raccoon trying to lick its own nostril. "You want people seeing your face like that?" All her neck muscles tense suddenly, the corded tendons popping out. She turns bright red.

"You have Poop Face," Fiona says flatly. "And I should know. I work with three- and four-year-olds, and some of those parents lie when they claim their kids are potty trained."

"SEE?" Mallory exclaims. "People judge your O face. Who needs *more* judgment in their life?" She points to my phone and her face turns deadly serious. "And if you release that tape, everyone is going to judge you."

"In more ways than one," Fiona adds.

"What is this feeling?" I ask, alarmed. Poking at a rib over my heart, I feel tears starting. "Whenever I imagine getting back at Parker with a sex tape now, it hurts."

"That is called a conscience," Mallory says slowly, as if explaining to a child.

"Or it could be just acid reflux," Fiona contributes, picking at her cuticle.

"How good was the sex?" Mallory interrupts, the diversion simultaneously welcome and... *not*. Because it makes my body shiver with the memory of Parker's touch. He left only half an hour ago. The residue of him is still all over me.

"Sex-amnesia good."

"*That* good?"

"What is sex amnesia?"

"Where you come so hard, you forget your own name."

"That would involve brain damage."

"I KNOW! Isn't that so cool?"

"You would trade cognitive ability for literally mind-blowing orgasms?"

"Who the hell *wouldn't*?"

I grab my phone and press Play. "Here. See for yourself."

Mallory peers at us between splayed fingers, her palms over her nose. She looks mortified. "Is it safe?"

"Safe?"

"To look." As she lowers her hands, sunlight glitters on

the big-ass diamond Will gave her when he proposed at the Dance and Dairy festival two months ago. Was that really only two months? Feels like two years.

"Look at what?" I grind out, suddenly consumed by jealousy that makes no sense.

"Anything! Anywhere! All I saw was your butthole on the screen. AGAIN!"

"You don't have to watch my secret politician sex tape," I mutter, turning the screen away.

"You make it hard *not* to!"

"Because it's so good? I know, right? People are going to be drawn to this. The sex is so perfect, it's like it was choreographed."

I look up from my phone to find Fiona and Mallory staring at me like I have two heads.

"What?"

"You have a really high opinion of your sexual abilities."

I hit Play again, and point to my screen. "Can't argue with *that.*"

My butthole spider appears.

And then I laugh. I laugh until finally, I cry.

Gently, without a word, Fiona reaches over and hits Pause, then turns the phone over, screen down. She takes my hands in hers, big eyes framed by her pink glasses. Compassion pours from her like she's been put on Earth solely for this conversation.

"You can't do this. You can't keep doing this to yourself."

"I thought I was doing it to Parker!"

"I'm not even talking about the butthole tape at this point, Perk, though releasing that would be the worst form of self-immolation by internet I could possibly imagine. I'm talking about the last five years. You've closed yourself off because the person who understands you best in the world did something really awful to you, and you've never been able to let go."

"And?"

"And now it's time to let him back in."

"He left! He stormed out of here and... he left." Tears fill my eyes, my nose, my throat, my blood.

"You finally did it," Fiona says softly.

"Did what?"

"You drove him away."

Mallory makes a sound of pain, a tiny whimper in the back of her throat. It undoes me, emotions unwinding like they're racing toward a conclusion before I even know what it is.

I grab my phone in a blind rage and delete the video. Searing pain rips through all my organs just as someone knocks on my front door.

I freeze.

Oh, shit, Mallory mouths to Fiona. We turn, all three of us, and stare at my door.

We all know damn well who that is.

"I'm not ready!" I tell them. "Stall."

"Stall?"

On tiptoes, I leap out my side door. "Stall."

Racing barefoot to the garage, my phone in hand, I find Dad's neat workbench. The ball-peen hammer is there. I pick it up and it feels solid in my hand, the wooden handle polished to something close to bone by years of Dad's sweat and oils. Before they won the lottery, Dad worked as a carpenter for a living. He got bigger and better tools, but always kept his old ones.

This is one from Before.

Right now, I need to be in touch with as much of who I am as I possibly can.

Still holding the hammer, I run back to my cottage. I come to a halt when I see the tail lights of Fiona's car driving away. Parker's rental is in the driveway.

I have to face him alone.

Turning, I walk the rest of the way to my side door.

I stop.

I drop the phone.

I crouch.

And I start smashing.

Oh, the glorious feeling of Dad's ball-peen hammer clutched in my angry grip, my shoulder socket angled back, muscles tight but strong as I pound away the past. Five years of everything pours out of me in strike after strike, blow after blow, my screen shattering, the metal phone bending and twisting like my heart, splintered and damaged until it can't be put back together.

"Persephone?" Parker appears behind me, his voice filled with understandable confusion. I ignore him, stepping over the mess of my destroyed phone, running inside and grabbing my laptop. I open my front door and fling it, cocking my arm back like a shotputter, the goal a parabola of victory.

The satisfying crunch it makes as one corner connects with the gravel driveway opens something in me. Maybe it's my heart. Maybe it's my memory.

Or maybe it's the piece of me that held me back from believing Parker.

What does foolish pride sound like when it smashes?

Because that's all I hear in my ears.

And it sounds an awful lot like a hammer demolishing a laptop. In a blink, I'm crouched over it, shoulder rolling with blow after blow, the dents and bits of hard plastic my feeble attempt to rewind time.

"What the hell are you doing?" Parker shouts at me over the *bang bang bang* of my smashing, the rhythm settling into a speedy version of my heartbeat.

"I'm proving I have a conscience!"

"Proving… to whom?"

"DOES IT MATTER?"

My shoulder hurts, the abrupt clench of his hand around my biceps wrenching the bones and tendons in the socket.

"Stop, Persephone. Please."

"I deleted it, Parker. I smashed my phone. I'm destroying my computer. If it's in the cloud, I promise I'll delete it. I'll have Fiona's brother delete it. I promise. I promise. I–" The rest of my words are muffled by his chest. One of his shirt buttons scratches my lip, the strange sensation enough to make me nuzzle him, his scent an intoxicating balm. Strong arms cage me in, his hand on my hair, soothing me. We sink to the ground, his thighs holding me on his lap, our bodies twisted but not awkward.

He's saving me from myself.

"*Shhhhhh*," he whispers. "It's okay. I'm here. I'm not going anywhere. I left in anger. Went to a park and took a walk. I got a coffee. I realized you would never actually post that. Especially," he says, pinching the bridge of his nose, "since I'm not quite sure what that *is* on the video. And even if you did post it, you'd have every right. But I knew you wouldn't."

Looking up, I peek around his arm and see my destroyed laptop, the fruit logo on top cracked, the silver cover twisted like a clam that's been forced open. A pattern of vertical lines glows persistently on the shattered screen, refusing to go black.

"How? How did you know?"

"Because you don't view the world that way. You don't fix a wrong by doing another wrong."

"But that's how we met! I broke the law to protest unjust labor laws!"

"That's different. You were using a higher moral principle to guide you." He lets out a contemplative huff. "Maybe you're right. You're doing the same thing now."

"I am?"

"I knew you wouldn't release that weird sex tape of us because you always turn toward the highest moral principle when faced with conflict, Persephone. You did it five years ago. You did it today."

"I didn't mean to make that sex tape," I sniffle. "I got the app and tested it out, but you said the right combination of words to voice activate the recording, and–"

He stiffens. "You installed a voice app for recording video?"

"Yes," I confess.

"To set me up?"

"Yes." I expect him to let me go. Instead, he tightens his hold.

"To get back at me?"

"It's stupid, it's awful, but yes. And then today, I stopped myself. I pushed the Off button before we started. I guess I pushed something that made it beep, though. Then you walked in while I was looking at the old video. You caught me. I couldn't explain it. And then you left."

"I felt like it was hopeless."

"You spent five years thinking it wasn't, and finally you gave up?"

"I think my head exploded a little."

"It's remarkable that it took that long."

"Come with me, Persephone."

"Where? To Texas? DC?"

"I was thinking more along the lines of my rental here in town."

"Rental?"

"I have an Airbnb. A house on Maplecure."

"Not Will's parents' old house?"

"No. A little closer to town."

"You rented an entire house?"

"I wanted privacy." Closing the distance between us, his eyes are so complex. Multi-faceted. He should hate me for what I almost did to him.

"Why are you here, Parker?"

"I've asked myself that a thousand times. I should have let you go. Once I realized you didn't believe me, it turned into a compulsion. An obsession. I tried everything to get you to see reason. To hear the truth. To see me."

Oh, I see him all right.

"It felt like a critical organ inside you was missing. If I could just get you to hear me, you'd change your mind. If I could provide you with the exact right combination of words, I could fix this. I never sent that picture. I knew that, but you didn't. And nothing I said made a difference."

I make a sound. I think I can feel the missing organ he's talking about assert itself, as if it's growing in my chest right now, nurtured into being by this conversation.

"You've told me, repeatedly, that you wanted to trust me but couldn't. That something holds you back. I wanted so badly to let go of you, but I couldn't. Something stopped me from giving up. It's the same for both of us–there's a piece inside that is an obstacle to getting over what was done. And it was done to us both. You seem to think the only person hurt by that photo being released was you."

"I did, and I wanted to hurt you right back." My eyes jump to all the broken electronics around us, bearing witness to whatever we're doing right now.

"Do you remember, Persephone? Do you remember that day? The day you let me take that damn picture?"

"Of course I remember it, Parker. It's the day…" My voice fades out. "It's the day you broke my heart." I frown. "Or, at least, it's the day that picture was taken. And a few days later, it was sent to – "

"That was the day you broke mine," he says, matching my emotion syllable for syllable, breath for breath. "When I tried to explain for the first time. And then every other time I tried to explain. Thousands of tries. Thousands of times, thousands of bruises on my heart until I just walked around with a big ache in my chest and learned to breathe through the pain."

I close my eyes and will myself to keep breathing. We're sharing pain. That's what's been missing for the last five years. Someone to share my emotions with. Someone to share the bad with.

You can sit with another person and hold their emotional truth in the air between you. You can honor who they are and what they experience. You can smile when they smile and laugh when they laugh. With Mallory and Fiona, I can cry when they cry and know that they'll be there, too, in empathy, step by step, sob by sob.

With Parker, though, it was always different.

With Parker, there was something *more*.

He was an emotion inside me. If human beings have twenty-seven different emotional states, then Parker was my twenty-eighth.

He wasn't just a mosaic of those existing emotions, either. This wasn't a guy who took a little piece of joy and a bit of desire and a sliver of sadness and a sprinkle of sympathy and blended it all together, mixing in horny and naughty and nice.

Oh, no.

This was a man who created a completely new *feeling* that lived inside my heart.

The pain of having that emotion ripped out of me by his betrayal is one that I've had to bear alone for five years.

Until now.

Tears are streaming down my face, and Parker is reaching up with his fingertips to brush them away. The liquid clings to his skin, a thin layer of the past, drying quickly but sticking to him, the salty residue transferring a bit of me onto him.

That's what happens when you love the way we loved. When he became an emotion no one else could feel. I see it in his eyes, too. I've been living inside him, taking up a space that no one else can ever fill.

And now we are feeling the emptiness together.

"Persephone," he says, as if my name could reconnect those twinned emotions, "Persephone, I love you. And I'm sorry. I'm sorry this happened. I'm sorry that we lost five years." He thumps the space over his heart, the bones of his chest a cell that protects him from ripping it out.

I know the feeling because I've felt it, too. How many nights did I sit in bed, racing through every possible logical explanation for what he did to me five years ago and finding none, settling on conspiracy theories and crackpot ideas that all boiled down to the illogical conclusion that he did it because he didn't love me?

And now here he is, telling me that he does. Over and over.

Until I believe it.

"Parker," I say, the words forming in my head as if I've never spoken before, as if language were an abstract concept that I'm experiencing for the first time. "Parker, you have nothing to be sorry about. I'm the one who should be apologizing. I didn't believe you. I can't believe I didn't believe you. I. Can't. Believe. I. Didn't. Believe. You."

Each word comes out like a brick being laid on a wall, a thunk against wet mortar, heavy and dull. Except the walls that I built around my relationship with Parker five years ago were designed to keep him out.

This is a wall that holds him *in*.

He grabs my hands and squeezes hard, so hard, as if telling that emotion inside me that he's finally here, that it can crawl out from its hiding place, that it's safe in the sunlight again.

"We were betrayed," he says fiercely. "Both of us, together. We just didn't know it. I tried to tell you."

"I know you did. I *know*!" I cry.

His fingers press against my lips. "That's not what I mean," he says, shaking his head, eyes closing. His throat spasms with a hard swallow, his breath coming in short bursts.

I push gently on his shoulder, then slide my hand down over his heart. It gallops as if it's racing into the past to try to find us, to save us, to rescue us.

And yet it can't.

"Please come to my house," he implores, eyes rich and deep with an invitation I already know I'm accepting. "I want to bring you into my world. I want to get us out of yours. I want to go somewhere neutral."

"Neutral?"

"I ran into your father when I got here. He wasn't happy to see me."

"Great. The cops are probably on their way."

"No. Your friends stopped him from doing that."

"They did?"

He nods. "I can handle the cops. I can even handle your

father. What I can't handle is sitting here surrounded by broken pieces of your phone and computer that represent the last five years of pain. Not while I'm talking about spending the rest of my life with you."

I sniffle and look around.

"You're right. Let's get out of here."

We stand, Parker first, his hand outstretched, eyes serious. "That's it? Just yes?"

"Yes."

"To everything I said?"

"You mean the whole 'rest of my life with you' part?"

He nods.

"Yes, Parker," I say simply. "I'm done letting the wrong piece of myself believe in a piece of you that just doesn't exist."

The house Parker rented looks more like a mansion than a place to stay on a business trip, but with four staffers here with him, he explains as he kills the engine of his rental car and takes my hand, it makes sense.

"Are they all here?" I ask, suddenly realizing how much I want him alone. How much I want to be naked with him, alone.

How much I want to get loud with him.

Alone.

"No. I'm flying back tomorrow with my mom, but she doesn't like staying here with me."

"Why not? I would think she'd be in heaven surrounded by her congressman son's congressional staff."

"We have a place in Back Bay."

"Of course you do."

One shoulder goes up. "Tanager money."

"And Campbell money. Your father was no slouch there."

"If anyone knows about money, it's you, Persephone."

"Oh, no. Your mother made it very clear years ago that your family's money is better than my family's money. I didn't understand it then, and I only understand it slightly better now. To us, money is money. To your mother, money represents status."

"Power is more like it. Old money comes with power."

"New money does, too. The power to stop working. The power to solve a lot of problems for family and friends." I look at him, hard. "But not the power to stop being stupid."

He snorts. "Plenty of stupid comes from old money, too."

I change the topic and stare at the front door. "So, empty house?"

"Omaia is in Boston visiting an old college buddy. She'll come back in the morning after I leave."

The way he moves toward me would be predatory in another man, long limbs moving with pent-up energy and full-throttle need. Instead of touching me, though, he reaches across my lap, opening the door with a thrust of power that makes my heart take off.

At a sprint for his bed.

We've set the expectations. Negotiations are already settled. This isn't about whether we'll make love again.

It's about *where*. Can we make it through the front door? Would sex on the freshly cut grass be a violation of decorum in this part of town?

"Race you!" I shout as I rush to the door, the sound of his footsteps behind me urgently catching up. His arms around my waist are no surprise, just as my fingers brush against the carved oak door.

Scruff from his chin tickles my neck as he kisses me. His touch takes everything from me as he gives everything in him right back.

"I know a way that we both win," he rumbles in my ear, making me wet and wanting. The fact that we just had sex a few hours ago back at my place doesn't matter at all.

The fact that we're about to spend the night together does.

"Always finding a way to cross the aisle and make everyone happy, Congressman," I whisper as I arch my back and press against him, the hard outline of his erection instantly obvious. His groan confirms it.

"Happy endings are my favorite."

"You should write romance novels, Parker."

"Pretty sure I'm living in one." We both go still, his heart slamming against my shoulder blade, my own trying to dive into the house so he can be on me, in me.

With me.

He turns his key in the lock and swings the door open.

"This house is absolutely stunning."

"So are you." My thighs still ache from the sex a few hours ago, so the urgency isn't as strong, but oh, the rush of need sure is. Parker's hair is like a soft, sensual fabric that I crave, his tongue like every sweet taste I want to savor. He pulls me to the couch and we tumble onto the cushions, hands at each other's waists, my fingers struggling with his belt buckle.

"Stop," he says, eyes shining in the soft light of dusk. "I want to see you."

"What?"

"Undress."

"I am!" He's just unfastened my jeans.

"No, Persephone." Rolling to one side, he upsets the balance of weight on the couch, tilting me forward. "Stand up. Undress for me."

"You want me to strip? Like a striptease?"

A sexy grin makes his mouth turn up. "That's not exactly what I meant, but it's an excellent idea."

"I'm ready to be naked and let you inside me in a few seconds and instead you want to watch me?"

"Yes."

"Who turns down sex to watch someone undress? You are the strangest man I know."

"I'm the only one you'll ever know again. Biblically."

"There's no Bible verse for this."

"And I never said I'm turning down sex. Trust me," he says, reaching for his own waistband and unbuckling slowly, sliding the leather belt out of the loops with a taunting movement. He unbuttons, then unzips himself, pulling his pants off in one quick movement, peeling off his shirt.

The man looks like a damn professional model in an

underwear ad, like a blonde David Gandy decided to become a congressman and lounge on a living room sofa in his boxer briefs.

"Off," I order.

Eyebrows up, his fingers move to his boxer briefs. "You mean these?"

I nod, giving him the sauciest look I can as my clit quivers, begging to be touched.

Parker is naked in half a second, his hand wrapped around his shaft.

"What's your next order?" he asks, stroking just once, eyes going half-lidded, jaw tightening.

Ho ho!

"Watch me with your hand just like that. No moving. Not even a little. If you move your hand, no sex."

Tendons on his wrist go tight. "What?"

"You heard me. You have to watch me while you hold yourself and don't come."

"That's not fair!" But his voice is low. Interested.

Intrigued.

My shirt feels so restrictive, the caress of soft fabric against my ribs as I remove it like a lover's kiss. Having his eyes on me while I slowly disrobe makes my thighs shake, my cheeks turn red, my body on display and loving the attention. Time changes, as if the world is on our side, rooting for us after five years with no team to support.

I fling the shirt toward an ottoman, but it catches on Parker's erection.

Reflexively, he starts to move it.

"Ah, ah, ah!" I say as I walk over and reach for it, intentionally stroking his tip as I remove the shirt. He licks his lips, mouth loose, smile gone.

Eyes burning.

"Take off your bra," he demands.

"Stroke yourself once," I counter, not obeying him immediately.

He does, teeth grinding, hitched breath making it clear

this is torture. While he touches himself, I reach between my legs and, our eyes locked, slip one finger into my own wet vulva, avoiding my too-sensitive clit but oh–this feels so, so good. Not just my touch.

His *gaze*.

"You're killing me, Persephone," he hisses, eyes dropping to my hand with a hungry expression so achingly raw that I want to jump on the sofa and bury his face between my thighs.

Not yet.

But soon.

Suddenly he's moving, grabbing my hand and pulling me back to the front hall.

"Parker, where are we going?"

"You'll see."

He charges up the wide staircase and turns left, through double wooden doors and into an enormous bedroom. A king-size bed with beige linen hangings dominates the room. From the corner of my eye, I can see his open suitcase on a bench, some clothes strewn around, but I can't really focus on my surroundings.

Dropping my hand, he faces me.

"Now," he commands.

Without replying, I reach back and unclasp my bra, bending forward to cup my breasts in both hands. The exquisite delicacy of my nipples turns my own breath into a wind tunnel, the long, sharp inhale choked off by a quick swallow as I work to calibrate my own need, tantalizing myself without going too far. Moving closer to him, I smell my own scent, the tanginess making me want to mingle it with his again.

Again.

How can I want him in me again? So soon? So much? But I do. I drop to my knees in front of him.

My breasts form the perfect valley as I reach for his hand, the one holding his shaft, and replace it by centering him between, pressing them together.

"I'm not giving you a pearl necklace tonight," Parker chokes out, holding himself back. Ab muscles go rock hard, his obvious invocation of self-control requiring all his concentration. "I'm coming inside you."

"Of course you are," I say as I stand up, moving so my ass brushes against him, turning back to look at his face. "You said you wanted a tease."

"A striptease!"

"Well, then," I whisper, wiggling my hips. "Strip me the rest of the way. While I tease you."

I am flat on my back and pantiless in under two seconds, wrists pinned to the bed. The heat from his palms makes my skin flush, the rest of me ice cold by comparison. Nipples tightening, they go damn near crazy as he drags his naked body up mine, until he's grinning down at me, my squirming hips making it clear I'm more than ready.

"Do you remember," he hums in my ear, the vibration of his lips against my lobe excruciatingly arousing, "when I used to edge you?"

My eyes fly open wide. "No!"

"You don't remember?" Opening his mouth, he drags his teeth along the shell of my ear.

"I do! I do remember. But... Parker." His name is a whimper.

Victory is his. I've handed him all the power and he knows it. Of course he does. He's a politician. It's his life's work to understand power dynamics, right?

I'm the amateur here.

About to be played by a virtuoso.

"If we hadn't just made love, this wouldn't work," he says in a single breath, the words floating on the heat between us. "Neither of us would last."

"You don't have to do this," I say, but I can't even convince myself that I'm not immensely turned on by what he's saying. By the way his hand wanders down my belly to settle between my legs. How it feels to arch into his fingertips as they make me full, swollen and desperate, so quickly.

And then he's gone.

One hand moves up, his tongue against the tip of his index finger, licking. I imagine it on my clit, where it was just seconds ago, and I move my legs so I get some slight satisfaction, but the friction's not enough.

"Stroke me," he says, moving to his side so I have access. Always muscular, always perfectly proportioned, the last five years have given Parker's body an even harder edge, manhood treating him well. Daily trips to a gym with a trainer don't hurt, either.

In the semi-darkness, I see the aura of his skin, his blond body hair curly and even. Heavenly doesn't begin to describe how it feels to rub against him, the soft down always a source of attraction for me. His beard, in those rare times he ever let it grow out for a few days, had more red in it than his blond hair would indicate, giving him a fierce, Viking-like look that I loved.

Right now, as I touch him, my palm hitting the bottom edge of his mushroom cap, my tongue tracing him in circles, I feel his will to hold back.

"We're both really, really good at delayed gratification, aren't we?" I murmur as I deep throat him, stopping long enough to hum.

A hitched breath is my only answer.

I slide up, tonguing the soft nerve cluster that makes him shiver. "We are," he answers.

"Which means we've mastered it."

One eyebrow goes up as I look at him. "Your point?"

"Is this really a challenge? We know how to edge."

"You'd like to propose something more... exhilarating?"

"How about a new goal?"

"I'm intrigued."

"How many orgasms can you have in twenty-four hours?"

"How is that new? We did it five years ago. Our record was nine."

"*Your* record was nine. Mine was in the thirties."

"Your capacity for orgasm is one of my favorite traits in you."

"It's not like I have any choice in the matter. It just happens."

His hand slides between my legs. "It does?"

"Well," I say, voice going thin, "it tends to happen when you do *that*."

"Maybe you're right," he teases, fingers halting. "Maybe edging is too pedestrian."

"Let's go for volume."

"How loud can I make you scream? I like that wager."

"Wager? Who said anything about betting?"

"If I can make you lose your voice you agree to marry me."

My mouth opens and closes. I can't make a sound.

He grins. "See? I won already. And I didn't even have sex with you to do it."

"Uh–uh–uh–"

His kiss stops the strange sounds coming out of me, his body over mine, his mouth against my ear. "When I propose formally, it'll be the proper way, Persephone, but for now–I know what I want. I know who I want. And I love and want you."

"I love you, too, Parker," I gasp.

"Darn," he says in a twang. "I guess I didn't win. Your voice came back."

"How about you try again?" I say, opening my legs and pulling him into me. "Bet you could make me scream until we break a window."

"As long as you promise you won't break my heart."

"Never, Parker. Never again."

One finger strokes the hollow at my throat. "Good." He kisses the spot. "Because you're stuck with me."

"Pretty sure after all this sex and edging, I'm stuck *to* you."

He pulls out, slowly, achingly, then glides in, deep. "Let's work on that, then."

And so we do.

SUNLIGHT HATES POST-COITAL BLISS.

"I have to get back to Texas," Parker says as he yawns, the movement stretching his sentence out, the word Texas going deep and sonorous, as if he's bored by the very idea of the Lone Star State. His phone buzzes softly, and I realize it's been making some sort of interrupting noise for a bit. Reluctantly, he reaches for it, then rolls his eyes at the screen.

"It's my mother. We're flying back to Texas together and she's insisting I'm going to make her late."

"Your private jet waits for you, though, right?"

"Private? Hah. No."

"Congressmen don't get private jets?"

"We fly commercial like everyone else. It'll be a few decades before I get to use Air Force One." He winks at me.

I toss a pillow at him. He tackles me. His erection presses, hard and urgent, against my upper thigh. The kiss that follows makes it very clear that his mother is right: He's going to be late for that plane.

"Shower sex," he murmurs in my ear, then licks my collarbone.

"What?"

"Shower sex. We can kill two birds with one stone. Get clean and dirty at the same time."

"You have a way with words."

"I have to, as a servant of the people."

"When we're naked together, you serve only me."

"Yes, ma'am."

"Before you leave for Texas, I want to give your penis a hug with my vagina."

"Isn't that the same as sex?"

"My way of saying it is so much more intimate."

"You sound like a porny Care Bear."

"I'm Love-a-Lot Bear."

"Thanks for ruining *that* childhood memory. Whenever I see you naked, I'll be struck with images of Care Bears, and then I'll go soft."

"Your mom let you watch Care Bears? Were they all dressed in suits and carrying briefcases? Because I have a hard time imagining Jennifer letting you watch anything other than policy briefings as a kid."

"You're bringing up my mother in bed?" He looks under the sheet. "Might as well retire my cock."

I take a peek. "Hmmm. Your penis definitely needs a nice, warm, wet hug."

As he slides his hand between my legs, one finger slips between already-wet folds and enters me, the sudden sensation making me stretch, long and slow. I feel my blood moving to warm the surface of my skin, swelling the place where a larger, hotter, wetter—

DING DONG!

The doorbell startles us both, our mouths banging together as we kiss, teeth knocking against teeth with a painful rattle.

"Ow!"

"Ouch!"

DING DONG! DING DONG!

"Someone's impatient!" I gape, pressing my fingers against my front teeth, willing the nervy pain away. Shrugging into a shirt and sweatpants, he half-jogs down the stairs. I follow him to the top of the stairs, curious. Smoothing his hair back, he bends down, looks through the peephole, and goes dead still with an abrupt horror I can feel.

"Who is it?" I call out.

"My mother."

"Crap!"

He shrugs. "You decent?"

"Never enough for her."

"I meant, are you dressed yet?"

"Oh! No. Hold on." I run down to grab my clothes from the living room and put them on. The tag of my shirt scratches the base of my throat. Pulling my arms back out of the sleeves, I spin the shirt around, tugging so hard that I almost garrote myself. Without a bra, my girls are pert and nipples poking like they're trying to escape.

"Ready," I call out, zipping my jeans.

He opens the door.

Jennifer Tanager Campbell always looks like she's just been freshly made up on a television set, ready to take her seat on a panel of guests to be interviewed. The strong scent of expensive makeup and moisturizer overpowers her perfume. She's foundation in human form.

And she's scary as hell.

The second her eyes alight on me, I realize I'm really, really in the wrong place. I expect condescension. I expect irritation. I expect a lot of negative attitudes from Parker's mom, but then she says the unexpected:

"I came here to speak with Parker, but I suppose it's fitting to tell this to you, too."

"Me?"

She hesitates for a beat.

"It's about that photo."

I inhale forever, my body unable to stop.

Parker's eyes narrow. "Which photo?"

"You know the one." Her mouth purses with distaste.

"What *about* it?" Parker growls. That's the closest word to describe the sound that comes out of him.

Jennifer flinches.

"It was you," I whisper, my voice dropping at the end with an accusation.

"Yes. I–I had never used a smartphone before! They were so new!"

A confirmation.

"This was five years ago, not 1987. Your excuse is invalid," I snap.

Parker's face is completely blank. No tight jaw. No flushed face. Not the seething, narrow-eyed anger I would expect.

His expression is downright deadly in a lawyer.

Doubly so in an assistant district attorney.

But in a guy who is all that *and* a member of the U.S. House of Representatives, that singular look aimed at his mother right now—it's lethal.

It's sodium pentathol for Jennifer, his unblinking eyes a truth serum that works because of his astonishing lack of emotion. Being stared down by your own son as you admit to leaking a naked picture of his then-girlfriend to the dregs of the internet in a move that could have killed his political career—this has to be her low point, right?

"I–I...," she stammers, face aflame, all the anger Parker should be radiating coming off her in a sudden burst. "I thought it would ruin *her*! Not you!"

Huh. She just sank even lower.

One blink. Parker gives her exactly one, open and shut.

Open and shut *case*.

"Who did you send the picture to, Mom?"

"What?"

"Who? Who, *exactly*, did you send that picture to?"

"I don't remember."

"It got onto a gossip website. If you were so inept with technology, I doubt you knew how to FTP it. And the forensic computer scientist I hired after Persephone broke my heart never could figure out who you sent it to. I hired an ex-hacker– " he makes a scoffing sound. "More like I coerced him. I had some dirt on him, so I used it. Got him to find out who posted the photo. They traced it back to a small gossip site in Macedonia. Someone had used a security vulnerability to hack their way in from the dark web and inject the file. It was *clearly* professional. Impossible to trace. That means you had help. It didn't magically appear on the internet. And there's no record of an email you forwarded it to, or a phone number you sent the picture to."

"You *knew* she did it?" I gasp, horrified. Jennifer's face has no muscles in it, her skin just a pearly, make-up-covered canvas.

"Until this moment? No. But I knew *I* didn't."

"But you knew someone sent it somewhere?"

"When I had my phone analyzed, someone had downloaded and then deleted a Russian dark web app. That's as far as we got. And then it magically appeared on FapMagic."

"Right. They were the first to host it," I say, recalling Fiona's brother's report.

His head tilts as he looks at me with that same blank expression. "*You* knew?"

"My parents hired forensic data specialists, too."

"Of course they did," Jennifer says, a resigned tone to her voice giving my justice-seeking heart a victory.

"And thank God they did, Mom," Parker rebukes her. "It's because of Bart and Sofia that the picture was contained. If Persephone's parents hadn't acted swiftly, if they hadn't assembled the best damned legal team possible, if she hadn't copyrighted her own damn nude picture that *I* took with her phone and that she forwarded to me and then sued for copyright infringement to contain it, my political career would be over. And I would deserve it."

"What?" Jennifer gasps. "Of course you wouldn't! Saoirse never meant–" Her palms fly to cover her mouth, horrified eyes pinning Parker in place, her confession setting all my radar to screaming red alert.

"What the hell did *Saoirse* have to do with any of this?" he barks, getting right in Jennifer's face, imposingly regal and terrifyingly exacting in his words. She's not weaseling her way out of this one.

And she knows it.

For a split second, I admire her. Why? Because she's being honest. Forthright.

But she could have done this five years ago and saved us so, so much pain.

Admiration turns to fury.

Ah. There we go. I'm back to my comfort zone.

"She... helped me."

Boom.

Finally.

After five years, ladies and gentlemen, we get to the truth. The skanky seahorse did it.

"Helped you?" Parker's hands fly up to his head, fingertips digging into his scalp as if he's trying to rake the rage out of his head. "HELPED you? *She* uploaded that photo from my phone to the secure FTP site? And how in the HELL did you two get your hands on my phone?"

"I, um, well, Parker," she stammers. "I don't know what FTP is, but we didn't send anyone flowers."

"That's FTD," I point out helpfully.

"Answer my other question!"

Jennifer's lips form a thin line of refusal.

For a long moment, no one says a word. Then, "Leave." His arm goes up, finger pointing as he uses his other hand to snap the door open. "Get out, Mom."

"But Parker! I..." To my surprise, she turns to me with a begging expression, as if she expects me to intervene, to help her.

I simply shake my head.

"I never meant to hurt you!" she rasps through tears, looking at Parker, who won't even glance at her. She finally looks at me. "Or you," she adds feebly.

"You are so full of shit, Mom."

"Parker!"

"Get. Out. Now."

"Wait," I blurt out. "Why did you come here and tell Parker now, after all this time?"

She drops her eyes, two tears splashing directly on the floor. "After Parker made his announcement about that revenge-porn bill, I worried that this could come back to haunt him. I wanted you to be on top of it."

"You finally told the truth when my career was on the line. Not when my heart was broken," he hisses.

"I—"

"Leave, Jennifer. Now."

To my surprise, she responds to my words. As she steps

outside, she calls back, "I never meant to–"

Parker clicks the door shut, hard.

We look at each other in silence for a moment. I walk to the foot of the stairs and sit down, all of my strength suddenly gone.

"It was your mother and Saoirse. You knew all along it wasn't you, though," I say finally, my voice filled with a kind of marvel rather than accusation.

"Of course I knew. I had reports from a forensic data specialist that confirmed I was interviewing a defendant in a maximum security prison when that file was texted to the anonymous website." His shoulders slump.

"And you never told me."

"Oh, I told you."

"No, you didn't, Parker."

"I told you so many times, Persephone! Over and over again! I sent emails. I sent screenshots. I left voicemails. I texted you!"

Here comes the anger.

Here comes the anger I *deserve*.

"You know what? You're right." My eyes seek his. "You're *right*. You did. I'm sorry. I'm *so* sorry. I'm sorry I didn't listen to you. I'm sorry I didn't believe you. I'm sorry that whatever stupid story I was telling myself became more important than the truth."

My throat is shaking. I didn't know it could do that, but it's quaking in front of him. The words are pouring up and out, words I've wanted to say for five years, but I couldn't give myself permission to believe that he really felt this way about me.

Is it too late?

"You know," I say, rubbing my hands up and down my knees as if they are stones that need to be polished, the move-ment soothing because of the tsunami of emotion inside me, spinning round and round, crashing against the inside of my chest. "You know, Parker, even if I had read the reports, I don't think it would have mattered."

"I know."

"You do?"

"After about a year, I realized that. You were dug in."

"A year? It took you a *year* to give up?"

"No."

"When did you give up, then?"

"Never! I never gave up. That's the only reason we're here right now. Because I never gave up. Why do you think I crashed Will and Mallory's wedding rehearsal rehearsal dinner?"

"You said that it was an accident."

"It was. Until it wasn't. Those ten minutes or so in the beginning, when I pieced it all together and realized you were there... God, Persephone, it was as if Fate herself stepped in, reached down through my mouth into my chest, and cracked my heart like an egg. When I saw you from across the room and realized who Will's Mallory was, it felt like divine intervention. I wasn't expecting it. In fact, I'd been so busy with the events of the last year that I'd been living on autopilot."

"You were pretty busy with Saoirse, too."

"No. Saoirse came back angling for me with that too-smooth, too-perfect way she has of turning people like me into goalposts. And you know, for a split second, I decided to say yes to her. I don't know why, but I said yes."

I clear my throat.

"Not sex," he clarifies with a disgusted huff. "Look what one or two dates got me. You saw that picture of us. She happened to be there the night that guy choked, and then the heart attack... you got the wrong impression. You decided my motives weren't pure, and you seduced me for revenge, Persephone. But you know what?"

"What?" I whisper.

"You seduced me five years ago. Five years, nine months, and six days ago. What we had in bed yesterday, or on that videotape you made? That wasn't a seduction. That was a *reclamation*. That's what we can do right now. Reclaim."

"Yes."

He eyes me where I sit, then pulls me up, kissing me. I melt into him, the bizarre visit from his mother still ringing in my ears, my surprising lack of anger more destabilizing than her admission of guilt. For five years I've been so livid, but how can I be mad when Parker Campbell is kissing me like *this*?

And touching me *there*?

He pulls one of my legs up, my calf against his now-bare ass as I realize his pants are off again, he's tugging on mine, and... here we go.

"You want sex *now*?" The tip of him is against my inner thigh, nudging, seeking, finding.

He enters me. "Sorry to be so ambiguous."

I laugh, tightening around him. "Again? I can't believe it."

"You're judging me for wanting sex?"

"No. Judging myself. I'm ashamed that this is the way I recover from big shocks. That having a quickie with you is the thing I crave most in the world."

"It's a reset button." His thumb moves down to my clit. "Like this one."

"That gets turned On when you touch it. Never Off." Words fail me as he drives into me, the mention of a quickie a promise to our future selves. I'm more *me* with him than I am without, feeling this emotion that doesn't exist anywhere but in his orbit.

As my orgasm rides up, up, up from within me, it connects with that feeling, stroking Parker as he curls his hips, his thumb performing magic in a rhythm that we ride until I'm biting his shoulder. He's breathing hard against my ear as we come hard–so hard–against the wall, Parker holding me up, my body driven into so deeply, it's like he's touching the past.

And rewriting it.

Heat pulses deep inside, as if I've captured his heartbeat and am holding it for safe keeping.

Which is the best way to describe love that I can imagine.

❧ 18 ❧

E pilogue. Or stinger. You decide.

COFFEE TASTES BETTER WHEN I'M HOLDING HANDS WITH Parker.

It's a biochemical feat. You know those chemical companies in New Jersey, with the labs that develop ways to make products taste the same so they become addictive? So you experience the exact same rush of the familiar that lights up the neurons of your brain, to coax you into buying more, more, more of the same product?

That's Parker for me.

He has three hours before his plane leaves. Our plane, I should say. He canceled the flight with his mother and stayed for another night, a night we spent talking nonstop.

Ok–fine. We stopped a few times.

More than a few, if you know what I mean.

Now I'm headed to Texas with him. There is no timeline. Raul says I can take as long as I want, but I need to be back for the barista competition in Boston in two months.

Meanwhile, Jennifer has apologized up and down. She

even FaceTimed with the two of us this morning, pleading with Parker to forgive her.

He did.

Because Parker's superpower is finding connection with people.

But he hasn't forgiven Saoirse. Guess who's in for a shock when she learns Parker's buddy, Congressman Ouemann, has an in-law who works at a certain major media outlet–the very same outlet Saoirse's been gunning for–and who now has her on his permanent NFW list?

I'll let you guess what the F stands for.

DC is all about buddies helping each other out.

My parents are understandably nervous, but they're trusting me. Mom says the energy read is positive. I visited Jolene this morning, drank some basil tea, gave her a huge tip, and told her she was right.

"I know," was all she said, with a grin.

Meanwhile, Parker is making plans to submit lots and lots of bipartisan bills with Congressman Ouemann here in Massachusetts, so there's that. We'll be back. We have to.

Malzilla Marries Boston is coming in 2020 and we need to see the advance screening, so I anticipate racking up the frequent flyer miles between Texas and Massachusetts as Mallory figures out new ways to torture the wedding party.

Logistics are just ways around obstacles that aren't really important. What matters is that Parker and I are together. Period.

Forever.

As I sit at a table at Beanerino and sip this outstanding cup of fresh Sumatran, Parker rubs his chin absentmindedly and watches a campaign ad on television.

"Ugh. This is what happens when you live so close to New Hampshire. It's never-ending election season now," I complain.

"I like elections."

"Good. I'd imagine you have to as a member of Congress."

"No. Plenty of people hate it. But not me." A gleam in his eyes as he watches the presidential hopeful on screen makes my throat close.

"You seriously want to be president, don't you?" I finally say, each word like a brick I'm pushing out of my mouth.

"Eventually. It's a longshot, but–"

I bark laugh, because who answers *yes* to that question?

Parker. Parker does, that's who.

"You are totally perfect for the presidency, Parker. But if that's your goal, you need to dump me." I clear my throat.

"Dump you?"

"I am a liability."

"You are anything *but* a liability."

"A first lady with naked pictures of her all over the internet?"

"Wouldn't be the first time."

I frown. He's not wrong.

"My boobs would be resurrected and blasted everywhere."

"Zombie boobs!" He laughs, then stares at my rack and leans forward, lips brushing against my hair. "Jesus tits, though..."

"If you want to be president, you can't be caught in public saying things like 'Jesus tits.'"

"Then shut me up before I get myself in more trouble." He touches my holy breast and gives me a kissy face. I kiss him to stop the stupid. It's like throwing yourself on a land mine to save a group of little kids.

Only instead of dying, I get laid.

I break the kiss. "Plus, my name. You know. Persephone was Hades' wife. She ruled the underworld with him."

"Again, not that different from modern American politics."

I can't help but laugh. "You really are jaded for being one of the youngest members of Congress. Aren't you supposed to be full of idealism and bright-eyed naiveté?"

"I was an assistant DA for a few years, Perky. That got drummed out of me fast."

The television changes from some cooking show to a Breaking News banner, a woman standing on a lawn in front of a very familiar building.

"An incoming report from Anderhill, Massachusetts, shows a knife attack at a preschool on Stately Road."

I scream at the screen, all the blood draining from my face, pooling in my feet, which turn to ice. "That's Fiona's school!"

Raul comes out of the storeroom to find out what's going on, stopping short when he sees the news footage.

"...The Grounded Child, one of the most popular preschools on the North Shore, where more than twenty children were directly in harm's way. Parents are flooding into the school parking lot behind a police perimeter..."

Parker stands, protective instincts kicking in. "How far is it from here?"

"About a mile." I can't stop looking at the screen.

He takes my hand. "Let's go."

"...the attacker was subdued and is now in custody," the newscaster is saying. *"According to parents who witnessed the attack on the live-streaming feed available for monitoring their children, the school's head teacher, Fiona Gaskill, single-handedly dropkicked the attacker, moved the knife out of his reach, then–uh..."* She presses her finger against her earpiece. *"...Ms. Gaskill stepped on his neck and restrained him until police arrived."*

Raul gasps, and Parker lets out a low whistle of approval.

"We have an eyewitness, one of the assistant teachers, Michelle Riotta, who confirms that Ms. Gaskill personally disarmed the assailant. Video of the incident is coming in right now, from one of the parents who captured it with her cellphone. The Grounded Child features closed-circuit webcams that parents can watch on a remote system that..."

"We have to go to her!" I shout. Parker is already sprinting for the door.

And then the screen shows Fiona–my bestie–with the sole of her foot on the guy's neck, her face tipped to the sky, wavy hair like seaweed flowing with the tide. Her long skirt ripples like the ocean, the outline of thick, strong thigh muscles under the gauzy fabric an Amazonian delight.

Then, fist thrust high in the air in victory, like a goddess, she opens her mouth–

And *roars*.

A NOTE FOR READERS

THANK YOU for reading Perky!

As always, world of mouth makes ALL the difference in the world when it comes to a book's success.

If you liked Perky, spread the word! Even in our tech-heavy world, world of mouth is still the best way for a book to get out and grow in readership.

And in case you're wondering: YES, *Feisty* is next. <3

ACKNOWLEDGMENTS

A huge thank you to Blair Babylon for her help with the Game of Thrones reference. :)

Many thanks, as always, to my husband "Clark" for his technical assistance (and support).

Elisa Reed made this book so much better with her painstaking editing, while Hang Le's cover is just plain old amazing.

There is an old saying (okay, maybe it's just an internet meme…) that writers are machines that take coffee and turn it into words. That's me, except I've cut back from 8 cups a day to 4 during the writing of this book.

Pretty sure my next book will involve an identity crisis. :P

ABOUT THE AUTHOR

New York Times and USA Today bestselling author Julia Kent writes romantic comedy with an edge. Since 2013, she has sold more than 2 million books, with 4 New York Times bestsellers and more than 19 appearances on the USA Today bestseller list. Her books have been translated into French and German, with more titles releasing in the future.

From billionaires to BBWs to new adult rock stars, Julia finds a sensual, goofy joy in every contemporary romance she writes. Unlike Shannon from *Shopping for a Billionaire*, she did not meet her husband after dropping her phone in a men's room toilet (and he isn't a billionaire in a rom com).

She lives in New England with her husband and children in a household where everyone but Julia lacks the gene to change empty toilet paper rolls.

Join her newsletter at http://www.jkentauthor.com

ALSO BY JULIA KENT

Shopping for a Billionaire: The Collection (Parts 1-5 in one bundle, 500 pages!)

- Shopping for a Billionaire 1
- Shopping for a Billionaire 2
- Shopping for a Billionaire 3
- Shopping for a Billionaire 4
- Christmas Shopping for a Billionaire

Shopping for a Billionaire's Fiancée

Shopping for a CEO

Shopping for a Billionaire's Wife

Shopping for a CEO's Fiancée

Shopping for an Heir

Shopping for a Billionaire's Honeymoon

Shopping for a CEO's Wife

Shopping for a Billionaire's Baby

Shopping for a CEO's Honeymoon

Shopping for a Baby's First Christmas

Little Miss Perfect

Fluffy

Perky

Feisty (coming soon)

Her Billionaires

It's Complicated

Completely Complicated

It's Always Complicated

Random Acts of Crazy
Random Acts of Trust
Random Acts of Fantasy
Random Acts of Hope
Randomly Ever After: Sam and Amy
Random Acts of Love
Random on Tour: Los Angeles
Merry Random Christmas
Random on Tour: Las Vegas

Maliciously Obedient
Suspiciously Obedient
Deliciously Obedient

Our Options Have Changed (with Elisa Reed)
Thank You For Holding (with Elisa Reed)

Made in the USA
Columbia, SC
10 August 2019